# GRYLL GRANGE

# THOMAS LOVE PEACOCK

## GRYLL GRANGE

ALAN SUTTON
1984

Alan Sutton Publishing Limited
Brunswick Road
Gloucester

First published 1860/1

Copyright © in this edition 1984
Alan Sutton Publishing Limited


British Library Cataloguing in Publication Data

Peacock, Thomas Love
   Gryll Grange.—(Pocket classics)
   I. Title
   823'.7[F]      PR5162.G7

   ISBN 0-86299-095-5

*Cover picture: detail from* Landscape with Rainbow
*by Joseph Wright. Derby Art Gallery*

Typesetting and origination
by Alan Sutton Publishing Limited
Photoset Bembo 9/10
Printed in Great Britain
by The Guernsey Press Company Limited
Guernsey, Channel Islands.

# BIOGRAPHICAL NOTE

THOMAS LOVE PEACOCK (1785–1866) was born on 18 October 1785, at Weymouth, the only son of a glass merchant. His boyhood was spent chiefly at Chertsey, and from his seventh to his thirteenth year he was educated at a private school in Englefield Green. He proved an apt and industrious student, took instinctively to literature and broke out into verse-writing.

In 1808 he was employed on a man-of-war, being assistant secretary to Admiral Popham, but found his duties on this 'floating inferno' did not conduce to literary study, so gave up the appointment within the year. Soon after this he found employment at the East India House, but never took kindly to any business occupation. During a tramp in North Wales he fell in love with a pretty Welsh girl, and when his finances were in a more settled condition, wooed and won her. She was the 'Caernarvonshire nymph' whom he mentions in a letter to a friend as having 'pleased him by talking of Scipio and Hannibal and the Emperor Otho.' Evidently the interest felt in this young lady was not so entirely academic as he wished to make out. Certainly Jane Gryffyd was much more than a Cymric edition of Cornelia Blimber. The marriage, in 1820, proved a long and happy one despite the delicate health of Mrs. Peacock.

Previous to his marriage, Peacock had published a volume of verse, and three of his satires and romantic novels: *Headlong Hall* (1816), *Melincourt* (1817), and *Nightmare Abbey* (1818). In the year of his marriage he published his *Four Ages of Poetry*. *Maid Marian* (1822) was his most romantic and least satirical fiction, being followed by his Arthurian fantasy *The Misfortune of Elphin* (1829), *Crotchet Castle* (1831), and then after a long interval, *Gryll Grange* in 1860, written when he was an old man.

After he had married, Peacock lived in the country near Shepperton. He was not a sociable man, though kindly in his own household, but he was much attached to a few friends such as Hobhouse (Lord Broughton), and the poet Shelley; and though quick-tempered and something of a crank, he was essentially lovable. He was passionately fond of wild scenery, a fact obvious to readers of his fiction, where he never loses an opportunity of satirising landscape gardening. His acquaintance with Shelley started in 1812, and in 1813 we find Peacock, Shelley, and Harriet living together at Edinburgh. Peacock introduced Shelley to Greek literature and read Greek with him during the next five years. He tried to wean the poet, moreover, from his vegetarian fare and monotonous round of lemonade, tea, and bread and butter, and so dieted him for a while with well-peppered chops. Thus, in his own words, he 'gave him one week of thorough enjoyment.' His friendship with Shelley may have predisposed him to regard with disfavour the so-called Lake Poets. Though his enthusiasm was focussed upon literature he was an able business man, often helped Shelley in his financial affairs, and looked after the interests of Harriet on Shelley's behalf, when the two had separated. He died in January 1866.

Apart from literature, music was his only other relaxation, and for some years he attended the opera and wrote criticisms for the *Globe* and *Examiner*. He had no lack of Landor's independence and self-sufficiency, as well as his fiery nature.

Peacock's associations with the literary history of the earlier years of the nineteenth century were many and interesting. He was the friend and adviser of Shelley, knew most of the Benthamite Radicals, and had written for many of the important reviews and magazines, including Bentley's (which he helped to start) and Fraser's. Byron admired his work, especially *Melincourt*, and his literary eclogue exhibits traces of Peacock's influence.

Robert Buchanan admitted frankly to his influence. Thackeray and Frederick Locker admired his verse and have recorded their admiration. But with a few exceptions he was practically disregarded when at the height of his powers, and never received the critical meed of praise that was his due. The reason for this may be found in the character of the satirist's work. Writing in the full flush of the romantic revival, Peacock is far too eclectic in his tastes to catch the ear of the lover of romanticism.

Nor did he fit in any better with the literary tendencies of the succeeding age; neither with the democratic ideals of the early Victorian era, nor the scientific tendencies of the mid-Victorian, had he anything especially in common. He declines to be placed. No label fits him. The friend of Shelley, he mocks at romanticism. A lover of the classics, he is far too idiosyncratic a writer to observe the classical conventions; a writer of fiction, he flouts all those points over which the novelist usually expends his art; there is the roughest characterisation, next to no plot, scarcely any action and no passion. As a witty controversialist he is no more likely to attract those who care for didactic writing; for he plays with rather than advocates opinions, and makes merry at everyone's expense. Life for Peacock was a pleasant holiday where everything was fit food for laughter. Yet to the few who are attracted by the cynic's attitude, once again Peacock proves disconcerting. He is for ever railing at men and women, but there is no bitterness in his mockery. Yet there is not, as there was with men like Hood, warm democratic feeling at the back of his jesting. He is kindly enough, but an intellectual aristocrat to the core. 'I am more afraid of deference to public clamour,' he said, 'than I am of anything under heaven.'

Here then one may think to fix Peacock – among the Tory thinkers of his day; and his abuse of the present, his praise of the past, would tend to suggest that view. Yet once again he eludes. With a strong Conservative bias in his nature there existed a contradictory strain of Liberalism. Most of his friends were Radicals, and his own seal bore the Horatian tag, 'I neither follow in the rear, nor pursue those who go before me.' He loved the past, not with the Tory love of tradition, but for certain harmonious elements which he found lacking in the present.

In short, this paradoxical personality, with its many contradictions, must be taken as an independent force in letters and not bound over to any school. The one thing about him that is clear, straightforward and indisputable, is that he was an artist in irony, who loved to depict human frailties from sheer high

viii BIOGRAPHICAL NOTE

spirits. And so he made of farcical extravagance a fine art. He is serious about nothing save his work as an artist. As Friar Tuck said, 'The worst thing is good enough to be laughed at, though it be good for nothing else; and the best thing, though it be good for something else, is good for nothing better.'

It is this point that divides Peacock from the contemporary satirists of his day. Dickens, Thackeray, Disraeli, were moralists as well as satirists; humour with them subserved a serious purpose. Peacock is as guiltless of preaching as was Jane Austen. He did not laugh at the world to improve its morals, but merely to improve his own digestion. It pleased him to do so, and he would laugh at his best friends or himself with the same zest as he laughed at those whom he disliked.

His style is admirable: lucid, harmonious, apposite. In his care for achieving his effects, in his fastidious sensibility for the precise phrase and proper emphasis, he reminds one rather of the great eighteenth-century humorists than of his contemporaries. We think of Congreve rather than Hood; of Sterne rather than Thackeray. Romantic, satirical, tender, sardonic, reactionary, liberal; a cynic to outward appearance, a sensitive and affectionate man beneath the cold exterior. One must not be misled by his ironic detachment, and devotion to the comic spirit; it was an artist's pose to conceal from the world a proud and over delicately responsive nature. He jested wildly often as Lamb did, to conceal some inner ache. And he pays the penalty as a writer for thus concealing his finer qualities as a man. But all who care for ironic humour, flecked with flashes of poetic feeling, will hold Peacock in affectionate remembrance.

*Opinion governs all mankind,*
*Like the blind leading of the blind:—*
*And like the world, men's jobbernoles*
*Turn round upon their ears the poles,*
*And what they're confidently told*
*By no sense else can be controll'd.*

BUTLER

In the following pages the New Forest is always mentioned as if it were still unenclosed. This is the only state in which the Author has been acquainted with it. Since its enclosure he has never seen it, and purposes never to do so.

The mottoes are sometimes specially apposite to the chapters to which they are prefixed; but more frequently to the general scope, or, to borrow a musical term, the *motivo* of the *operetta*.

# CHAPTER 1

## MISNOMERS

Ego sic semper et ubique vixi, ut ultimam quamque lucem,
tamquam non redituram, consumerem.

PETRONIUS ARBITER.

Always and everywhere I have so lived, that I might
consume the passing light as if it were not to return.

'Palestine soup!' said the Reverend Doctor Opimian, dining
with his friend Squire Gryll; 'a curiously complicated misnomer. We have an excellent old vegetable, the artichoke, of
which we eat the head; we have another of subsequent
introduction, of which we eat the root, and which we also call
artichoke, because it resembles the first in flavour, although,
*me judice,* a very inferior affair. This last is a species of the
helianthus, or sunflower genus of the *Syngenesia frustranea* class
of plants. It is therefore a girasol, or turn-to-the-sun. From
this girasol we have made Jerusalem, and from the Jerusalem
artichoke we make Palestine soup.'

*Mr. Gryll*
A very good thing, doctor.

*The Rev.Dr. Opimian*
A very good thing; but a palpable misnomer.

*Mr. Gryll*
I am afraid we live in a world of misnomers and of a worse
kind than this. In my little experience I have found that a gang
of swindling bankers is a respectable old firm; that men who
sell their votes to the highest bidder, and want only 'the
protection of the ballot' to see the promise of them to both

1

parties, are a free and independent constituency; that a man who successively betrays everybody that trusts him, and abandons every principle he ever professed, is a great statesman, and a Conservative, forsooth, *a nil conservando;* that schemes for breeding pestilence are sanitary improvements; that the test of intellectual capacity is in swallow, and not in digestion; that the art of teaching everything, except what will be of use to the recipient, is national education; and that a change for the worse is reform. Look across the Atlantic. A Sympathiser would seem to imply a certain degree of benevolent feeling. Nothing of the kind. It signifies a ready-made accomplice in any species of political villainy. A Know-Nothing would seem to imply a liberal self-diffidence – on the scriptural principle that the beginning of knowledge is to know that thou art ignorant. No such thing. It implies furious political dogmatism, enforced by bludgeons and revolvers. A Locofoco is the only intelligible term; a fellow that would set any place on fire to roast his own eggs. A Filibuster is a pirate under national colours; but I suppose the word in its origin implies something virtuous: perhaps a friend of humanity.

*The Rev. Dr. Opimian*
More likely a friend of roaring – φιλοβωστρής – in the sense in which roaring is used by our old dramatists; for which see Middleton's *Roaring Girl,* and the commentators thereon.

*Mr. Gryll*
While we are on the subject of misnomers, what say you to the wisdom of Parliament?

*The Rev. Dr. Opimian*
Why, sir, I do not call that a misnomer. The term wisdom is used in a parliamentary sense. The wisdom of Parliament is a wisdom *sui generis.* It is not like any other wisdom. It is not the wisdom of Socrates, nor the wisdom of Solomon. It is the wisdom of Parliament. It is not easily analysed or defined; but it is very easily understood. It has achieved wonderful things by itself, and still more when Science has come to its aid. Between them they have poisoned the Thames, and killed the fish in the river. A little further development of the same

wisdom and science will complete the poisoning of the air, and kill the dwellers on the banks. It is pleasant that the precious effluvium has been brought so efficiently under the Wisdom's own wise nose. Thereat the nose, like Trinculo's, has been in great indignation. The Wisdom has ordered the Science to do something. The Wisdom does not know what, nor the Science either. But the Wisdom had empowered the Science to spend some millions of money; and this, no doubt, the Science will do. When the money has been spent, it will be found that the something has been worse than nothing. The Science will want more money, to do some other something, and the Wisdom will grant it. *Redit labor actus in orbem.** But you have got on moral and political ground. My remark was merely on a perversion of words, of which we have an inexhaustible catalogue.

*Mr. Gryll*
Whatever ground we take, doctor, there is one point common to most of these cases: the word presents an idea which does not belong to the subject, critically considered. Palestine soup is not more remote from the true Jerusalem than many an honourable friend from public honesty and honour. However, doctor, what say you to a glass of old Madeira, which I really believe is what it is called?

*The Rev. Dr. Opimian*
*In vino veritas.* I accept with pleasure.

*Miss Gryll*
You and my uncle, doctor, get up a discussion on everything that presents itself; dealing with your theme like a series of variations in music. You have run half round the world *à propos* of the soup. What say you to the fish?

*The Rev. Dr. Opimian*
Premising that this is a remarkably fine slice of salmon, there is much to be said about fish: but not in the way of misnomers. Their names are single and simple. Perch, sole,

* The labour returns, compelled into a circle.

cod, eel, carp, char, skate, tench, trout, brill, bream, pike, and
many others, plain monosyllables: salmon, dory, turbot,
gudgeon, lobster, whitebait, grayling, haddock, mullet, herring, oyster, sturgeon, flounder, turtle, plain dissyllables: only
two trisyllables worth naming, anchovy and mackerel; unless
any one should be disposed to stand up for halibut, which for
my part, I have excommunicated.

*Mr. Gryll*
I agree with you on that point; but I think you have named one
or two that might as well keep it company.

*The Rev. Dr. Opimian*
I do not think I have named a single unpresentable fish.

*Mr. Gryll*
Bream, doctor: there is not much to be said for bream.

*The Rev. Dr. Opimian*
On the contrary, sir, I think there is much to be said for him.
In the first place, there is the authority of the monastic
brotherhoods, who are universally admitted to have been
connoisseurs in fish, and in the mode of preparing it; and you
will find bream pie set down as a prominent item of luxurious
living in the indictments prepared against them at the dissolution of the monasteries. The work of destruction was rather
too rapid, and I fear the receipt is lost. But he can still be
served up as an excellent stew, provided always that he is
full-grown, and has swum all his life in clear running water. I
call everything fish that seas, lakes, and rivers furnish to
cookery; though, scientifically, a turtle is a reptile, and a
lobster an insect. Fish, Miss Gryll – I could discourse to you
on fish by the hour; but for the present I will forbear: as Lord
Curryfin is coming down to Thornback Bay to lecture the
fishermen on fish and fisheries, and to astonish them all with
the science of their art. You will, no doubt, be curious to hear
him. There will be some reserved seats.

*Miss Gryll*
I shall be very curious to hear him, indeed. I have never heard

a lecturing lord. The fancy of lords and gentlemen to lecture everybody on everything, everywhere, seems to me something very comical; but perhaps it is something very serious, gracious in the lecture, and instructive to the audience. I shall be glad to be cured of my unbecoming propensity to laugh whenever I hear of a lecturing lord.

*The Rev. Dr. Opimian*
I hope, Miss Gryll, you will not laugh at Lord Curryfin: for you may be assured nothing will be farther from his lordship's intention than to say anything in the slightest degree droll.

*Mr. Gryll*
Doctor Johnson was astonished at the mania for lectures, even in his day, when there were no lecturing lords, He thought little was to be learned from lectures, unless where, as in chemistry the subject required illustration by experiment. Now, if your lord is going to exhibit experiments in the art of cooking fish, with specimen in sufficient number for all his audience to taste, I have no doubt his lecture will be well attended, and a repetition earnestly desired.

*The Rev. Dr. Opimian*
I am afraid the lecture will not have the aid of such pleasant adventitious attractions. It will be a pure scientific exposition, carefully classified, under the several divisions and subdivisions of Ichthyology, Entomology, Herpetology, and Conchology. But I agree with Doctor Johnson, that little is to be learned from lectures. For the most part those who do not already understand the subject will not understand the lecture, and those who do will learn nothing from it. The latter will hear many things they would like to contradict, which the *bienséance* of the lecture room does not allow. I do not comprehend how people can find amusement in lectures. I should much prefer a *tenson* of the twelfth century, when two or three masters of the *Gai Saber* discussed questions of love and chivalry.

*Miss Gryll*

I am afraid, doctor, our age is too prosy for that sort of thing.
We have neither wit enough, nor poetry enough, to furnish
the disputants. I can conceive a state of society in which such
*tensons* would form a pleasant winter evening amusement: but
that state of society is not ours.

*The Rev. Dr. Opimian*

Well, Miss Gryll, I should like, some winter evening, to
challenge you to a *tenson,* and your uncle should be umpire. I
think you have wit enough by nature, and I have poetry
enough by memory, to supply a fair portion of the requisite
materials, without assuming an absolute mastery of the *Gai
Saber.*

*Miss Gryll*

I shall accept the challenge, doctor. The wit on one side will, I
am afraid, be very shortcoming; but the poetry on the other
will no doubt be abundant.

*Mr. Gryll*

Suppose, doctor, you were to get up a *tenson* a little more
relative to our own wise days. Spirit-rapping, for example, is
a fine field. *Nec pueri credunt . . . Sed tu vera puta.** You might
go beyond the limits of a *tenson.* There is ample scope for an
Aristophanic comedy. In the contest between the Just and the
Unjust in the *Clouds,* and in other scenes of Aristophanes, you
have ancient specimens of something very like *tensons,* except
that love has not much share in them. Let us for a moment
suppose this same spirit-rapping to be true – dramatically so,
at least. Let us fit up a stage for the purpose: make the invoked
spirits visible as well as audible: and calling before us some of
the illustrious of former days, ask them what they think of us
and our doings? Of our astounding progress of intellect? Our
march of mind? Our higher tone of morality? Our vast
diffusion of education? Our art of choosing the most unfit
man by competitive examination?

---

* Not even boys believe it: but suppose it to be true.

*The Rev. Dr. Opimian*
You had better not bring on many of them at once, nor ask many similar questions, or the chorus of ghostly laughter will be overwhelming. I imagine the answer would be something like Hamlet's: 'You yourselves, sires, shall be as wise as we were, if, like crabs, you could go backward.' It is thought something wonderful that uneducated persons should believe in witchcraft in the nineteenth century: as if educated persons did not believe in grosser follies: such as this same spirit-rapping, unknown tongues, clairvoyance, table-turning, and all sorts of fanatical impositions, having for the present their climax in Mormonism. Herein all times are alike. There is nothing too monstrous for human credulity. I like the notion of the Aristophanic comedy. But it would require a numerous company, especially as the chorus is indispensable. The *tenson* may be carried on by two.

*Mr. Gryll*
I do not see why we should not have both.

*Miss Gryll*
Oh pray, doctor! let us have the comedy. We hope to have a houseful at Christmas, and I think we may get it up well, chorus and all. I should so like to hear what my great ancestor, Gryllus, thinks of us: and Homer, and Dante, and Shakespeare, and Richard the First, and Oliver Cromwell.

*The Rev. Dr. Opimian*
A very good *dramatis personae*. With these, and the help of one or two Athenians and Romans, we may arrive at a tolerable judgment on our own immeasurable superiority to everything that has gone before us.

Before we proceed further, we will give some account of our interlocutors.

# CHAPTER II

## THE SQUIRE AND HIS NIECE

FORTUNA . SPONDET . MULTA . MULTIS . PRAESTAT .
NEMINI . VIVE . IN . DIES . ET . HORAS . NAM . PROPRIUM
EST . NIHIL.*

*Marmor vetus apud Feam, ad Hor. Epist. i. II, 23.*

Fortune makes many promises to many,
Keeps them to none. Live to the days and hours,
For nothing is your own.

Gregory Gryll, Esq., of Gryll Grange in Hampshire, on the borders of the New Forest, in the midst of a park which was a little forest in itself, reaching nearly to the sea, and well stocked with deer, having a large outer tract, where a numerous light-rented and well-conditioned tenantry fattened innumerable pigs, considered himself well located for what he professed to be, *Epicuri de grege porcus,** and held, though he found it difficult to trace the pedigree, that he was lineally descended from the ancient and illustrious Gryllus, who maintained against Ulysses the superior happiness of the life of other animals to that of the life of man.*

---

* This inscription appears to consist of comic senarii, slightly dislocated for the inscriptional purpose.

    Spondet
    Fortuna multa multis, praestat nemini.
    Vive in dies et horas: nam proprium est nihil.

* *A pig from the herd of Epicurus.* The old philosophers accepted good-humouredly the disparaging terms attached to them by their enemies or rivals. The Epicureans acquiesced in the pig, the Cynics in the dog, and Cleanthes was content to be called the Ass of Zeno, as being alone capable of bearing the burthen of the Stoic philosophy.

* PLUTARCH. *Bruta animalia ratione uti.* Gryllus in this dialogue seems to have the best of the argument. Spenser, however, did not think so, when he introduced his Gryll, in the Paradise of Acrasia, reviling Sir Guyon's Palmer for having restored him to the human form.

It might be seen that, to a man who traced his ancestry from the palace of Circe, the first care would be the continuance of his ancient race; but a wife presented to him the forethought of a perturbation of his equanimity, which he never could bring himself to encounter. He liked to dine well, and withal to dine quietly, and to have quiet friends at his table, with whom he could discuss questions which might afford ample room for pleasant conversation, and none for acrimonious dispute. He feared that a wife would interfere with his dinner, his company, and his after-dinner bottle of port. For the perpetuation of his name, he relied on an orphan niece, whom he had brought up from a child, who superintended his household, and sate at the head of his table. She was to be his heiress, and her husband was to take his name. He left the choice to her, but reserved to himself a veto, if he should think the aspirant unworthy of the honourable appellation.

---

Streightway he with his virtuous staff them strooke,
And streight of beasts they comely men became:
Yet being men they did unmanly looke,
And stared ghastly, some for inward shame,
And some for wrath to see their captive dame:
But one above the rest in speciall,
That had an hog been late, hight Grylle by name,
Repyned greatly, and did him miscall,
That had from hoggish forme him brought to naturall.
    Said Guyon: 'See the mind of beastly man,
That hath so soon forgot the excellence
Of his creation when he life began,
That now he chooseth, with vile difference,
To be a beast, and lacke intelligence.'

*Faery Queen,* book ii. canto 12.

In Plutarch's dialogue, Ulysses, after his own companions have been restored to the human form, solicits Circe to restore in the same manner any other Greeks who may be under her enchantments. Circe consents, provided they desire it. Gryllus, endowed with speech for the purpose, answers for all, that they had rather remain as they are; and supports the decision by showing the greater comfort of their condition as it is, to what it would probably be if they were again sent forth to share the common lot of mankind. We have unfortunately only the beginning of the dialogue, of which the greater portion has perished.

The young lady had too much taste, feeling, and sense to be likely to make a choice which her uncle would not approve; but time, as it rolled on, foreshadowed a result which the squire had not anticipated. Miss Gryll did not seem likely to make any choice at all. The atmosphere of quiet enjoyment in which she had grown up seemed to have steeped her feelings in its own tranquillity; and still more, the affection which she felt for her uncle, and the conviction that, though he had always premeditated her marriage, her departure from his house would be the severest blow that fate could inflict on him, led her to postpone what she knew must be an evil day to him, and might peradventure not be a good one to her.

'Oh, the ancient name of Gryll!' sighed the squire to himself. 'What if it should pass away in the nineteenth century, after having lived from the time of Circe!'

Often, indeed, when he looked at her at the head of his table, the star of his little circle, joyous herself, and the source of joy in others, he thought the actual state of things admitted no change for the better, and the perpetuity of the old name became a secondary consideration; but though the purpose was dimmed in the evening, it usually brightened in the morning. In the meantime, the young lady had many suitors, who were permitted to plead their cause, though they made little apparent progress.

Several young gentlemen of fair promise, seemingly on the point of being accepted, had been, each in his turn, suddenly and summarily dismissed. Why, was the young lady's secret. If it were known, it would be easy, she said, in these days of artificial manners, to counterfeit the presence of the qualities she liked, and, still more easy, the absence of the qualities she disliked. There was sufficient diversity in the characters of the rejected to place conjecture at fault, and Mr. Gryll began to despair.

The uncle and niece had come to a clear understanding on this subject. He might present to her attention any one whom he might deem worthy to be her suitor, and she might reject the suitor without assigning a reason for so doing. In this way several had appeared and passed away, like bubbles on a stream.

Was the young lady over-fastidious, or were none among

the presented worthy, or had that which was to touch her heart not yet appeared?

Mr. Gryll was the godfather of his niece, and to please him, she had been called Morgana. He had had some thoughts of calling her Circe, but acquiesced in the name of a sister enchantress, who had worked out her own idea of a beautiful garden, and exercised similar power over the minds and forms of men.

## CHAPTER III

## THE DUKE'S FOLLY

τέγγε πνεύμονας οἴνῳ· τὸ γὰρ ἄστρον περιτέλλεται·
ἃ δ᾽ ὥρα χαλεπά, πάντα δὲ διψᾷ ὑπὸ καύματος.
                                          ALCAEUS.

Moisten your lungs with wine. The dog-star's sway
Returns, and all things thirst beneath his ray.

FALERNUM . OPIMIANUM . ANNORUM . CENTUM

Heu! Heu! inquit Trimalchio, ergo diutius vivit vinum quam homuncio! Quare τέγ γε πνεύμονας faciamus. Vita vinum est.
                                          PETRONIUS ARBITER.

FALERNIAN OPIMIAN WINE AN HUNDRED YEARS OLD

Alas! Alas! exclaimed Trimalchio. This wine lives longer than man! Wherefore let us sing, 'moisten your lungs.' Wine is life.

Wordsworth's question, in his *Poet's Epitaph,*

Art thou a man of purple cheer,
A rosy man, right plump to see?

might have been answered in the affirmative by the Reverend Doctor Opimian. The worthy divine dwelt in an agreeably situated vicarage, on the outskirts of the New Forest. A good living, a comfortable patrimony, a moderate dowry with his wife, placed him sufficiently above the cares of the world to enable him to gratify all his tastes without minute calculations of cost. His tastes, in fact were four: a good library, a good dinner, a pleasant garden, and rural walks. He was an athlete in pedestrianism. He took no pleasure in riding, either on horseback or in a carriage; but he kept a brougham for the service of Mrs. Opimian, and for his own occasional use in dining out.

Mrs. Opimian was domestic. The care of the doctor had supplied her with the best books on cookery, to which his own inventive genius and the kindness of friends had added a large, and always increasing manuscript volume. The lady studied them carefully, and by diligent superintendence left the doctor nothing to desire in the service of his table. His cellar was well stocked with a selection of the best vintages, under his own especial charge. In all its arrangements his house was a model of order and comfort; and the whole establishment partook of the genial physiognomy of the master. From the master and mistress to the cook, and from the cook to the tom-cat, there was about the inhabitants of the vicarage a sleek and purring rotundity of face and figure that denoted community of feelings, habits, and diet; each in its kind, of course, for the doctor had his port, the cook her ale, and the cat his milk, in sufficiently liberal allowance. In the morning, while Mrs. Opimian found ample occupation in the details of her household duties and the care of her little family, the doctor, unless he had predestined the whole day to an excursion, studied in his library. In the afternoon he walked; in the evening he dined; and after dinner read to his wife and family, or heard his children read to him. This was his home life, Now and then he dined out; more frequently than at any other place with his friend and neighbour, Mr. Gryll, who entirely sympathised with him in his taste for a good dinner.

Beyond the limits of his ordinary but within those of his occasional range was a solitary round tower on an eminence backed with wood, which had probably in old days been a landmark for hunters; but having in modern days no very obvious use, was designated, as many such buildings are, by the name of The Folly. The country people called it 'The Duke's Folly,' though who the Duke in question was nobody could tell. Tradition had dropped his name.

One fine Midsummer day, with a southerly breeze and a cloudless sky, the doctor, having taken an early breakfast, in the progress of which he had considerably reduced the altitude of a round of beef, set out with a good stick in his hand and a Newfoundland dog at his heels for one of his longest walks, such as he could only take in the longest days.

Arriving at the Folly, which he had not visited for a long time, he was surprised to find it enclosed, and having at the back the novelty of a covered passage, built of the same grey stone as the tower itself. This passage passed away into the wood at the back, whence was ascending a wreath of smoke which immediately recalled to him the dwelling of Circe.* Indeed, the change before him had much the air of enchantment; and the Circean similitude was not a little enhanced by the antique masonry,* and the expanse of sea which was

* καὶ τότ᾽ ἐγὼν ἐμὸν ἔγχος ἑλὼν καὶ φάσγανον ὀξὺ
   καρπαλίμως παρὰ νηὸς ἀνήϊον ἐς περιωπήν,
   εἴ πως ἔργα ἴδοιμι βροτῶν ἐνοπήν τε πυθοίμην.
   ἔστην δὲ σκοπιὴν ἐς παιπαλόεσσαν ἀνελθών,
   καί μοι ἐείσατο καπνὸς ἀπὸ χθονὸς εὐρυοδείης
   Κίρκης ἐν μεγάροισι διὰ δρυμὰ πυκνὰ καὶ ὕλην.
   μερμήριξα δ᾽ ἔπειτα κατὰ φρένα καὶ κατὰ θυμὸν
   ἐλθεῖν ἠδὲ πυθέσθαι, ἐπεὶ ἴδον αἴθοπα καπνόν.

Od. κ 145–152.

I climbed a cliff with spear and sword in hand,
Whose ridge o'erlooked a shady length of land:
To learn if aught of mortal works appear,
Or cheerful voice of mortal strike the ear.
From the high point I marked, in distant view,
A stream of curling smoke ascending blue,
And spiry tops, the tufted trees above,
Of Circe's palace bosomed in the grove.
Thither to haste, the region to explore,
Was first my thought . . .

* εὗρον δ᾽ ἐν βήσσῃσι τετυγμένα δώματα Κίρκης
   ξεστοῖσιν λάεσσι, περισκέπτῳ ἐνὶ χώρῳ.

Ib. 210, 211.

The palace in a woody vale they found,
High-raised of stone, a shaded space around.

POPE

visible from the eminence. He leaned over the gate, repeated aloud the lines of the *Odyssey,* and fell into a brown study, from which he was aroused by the approach of a young gentleman from within the enclosure.

'I beg your pardon, sir,' said the doctor, 'but my curiosity is excited by what I see here; and if you do not think it impertinent, and would inform me how these changes have come about, I should be greatly obliged.'

'Most willingly, sir,' said the other; 'but if you will walk in, and see what has been done, the obligation will be mine.'

The doctor readily accepted the proposal. The stranger led the way, across an open space in the wood, to a circular hall, from each side of which a wide passage led, on the left hand to the tower, and on the right to the new building, which was so masked by the wood as not to be visible except from within the glade. It was a square structure of plain stone, much in the same style as that of the tower.

The young gentleman took the left-hand passage, and introduced the doctor to the lower floor of the tower.

'I have divided the tower,' he observed, 'into three rooms: one on each floor. This is the dining-room; above it is my bedroom; above it again is my library. The prospect is good from all the floors, but from the library it is most extensive, as you look over the woods far away into the open sea.'

'A noble dining-room,' said the doctor. 'The height is well proportioned to the diameter. That circular table well becomes the form of the room, and gives promise of a fine prospect in its way.'

'I hope you will favour me by forming a practical judgment on the point,' said his new acquaintance, as he led the way to the upper floor, the doctor marvelling at the extreme courtesy with which he was treated. 'This building,' thought he, 'might belong to the age of chivalry, and my host might be Sir Calidore himself.' But the library brought him back to other days.

The walls were covered with books the upper portion accessible by a gallery, running entirely round the apartment. The books of the lower circle were all classical; those of the upper, English, Italian, and French, with a few volumes in Spanish.

The young gentleman took down a Homer, and pointed out to the doctor the passage which, as he leaned over the gate, he had repeated from the *Odyssey*. This accounted to the doctor for the deference shown to him. He saw at once into the Greek sympathy.

'You have a great collection of books,' said the doctor.

'I believe,' said the young gentleman, 'I have all the best books in the languages I cultivate. Horne Tooke says: "Greek, Latin, Italian, and French are unfortunately the usual bounds of an English scholar's acquisition." I think any scholar fortunate whose acquisition extends so far. These languages and our own comprise, I believe, with a few rare exceptions, all the best books in the world. I may add Spanish for the sake of Cervantes, Lope de Vega, and Calderon.* It was a *dictum* of Porson, that 'Life is too short to learn German': meaning, I apprehend, not that it is too difficult to be acquired within the ordinary space of life, but that there is nothing in it to compensate for the portion of life bestowed on its acquirement, however little that may be.'*

The doctor was somewhat puzzled what to say. He had some French and more Italian, being fond of romances of chivalry; and in Greek and Latin he thought himself a match for any man; but he was more occupied with speculations on

* Mr. Buchanan says that Peacock learned Spanish at an advanced period of life, which ought to have been mentioned in our introductory memoir. Scarcely a Spanish book, however, appears in the catalogue of his library. – G.

* Mr. Hayward's French hotel-keeper in Germany had a different, but not less cogent, reason for not learning German. 'Whenever a dish attracts attention by the art displayed in its conception or preparation, apart from the material, the artist will commonly be discovered to be French. Many years ago we had the curiosity to inquire at the Hôtel de France, at Dresden, to whom our party were indebted for the enjoyment they had derived from a *suprême de volaille*, and were informed the cook and the master of the hotel were one and the same person: A Frenchman, *ci-devant chef* of a Russian minister. He had been eighteen years in Germany but knew not a word of any language but his own. "*A quoi bon, messieurs,*" was his reply to our expression of astonishment; "à quoi bon apprendre la langue d'un peuple qui ne possède pas une cuisine?"'

*Art of Dining*, pp. 69–70.

the position and character of his new acquaintance than on the
literary opinions he was enunciating. He marvelled to find a
young man, rich enough to do what he here saw done, doing
anything of the kind, and fitting up a library in a solitary
tower, instead of passing his time in clubs and *réunions*, and
other pursuits and pleasures of general society. But he thought
is necessary to say something to the point, and rejoined:

'Porson was a great man, and his *dictum* would have
weighed with me if I had had a velleity towards German; but I
never had any. But I rather wonder you should have placed
your library on the upper instead of the middle floor. The
prospect, as you have observed, is fine from all the floors; but
here you have the sea and the sky to the greatest advantage;
and I would assign my best look-out to the hours of dressing
and undressing; the first thing in the morning, the last at
night, and the half-hour before dinner. You can give greater
attention to the views before you when you are following
operations, important certainly, but mechanical from repetition, and uninteresting in themselves, than when you are
engaged in some absorbing study, which probably shuts out
all perception of the external world.'

'What you say is very true, sir,' said the other; 'but you
know the lines of Milton –

> Or let my lamp, at midnight hour,
> Be seen in some high lonely tower,
> Where I may oft outwatch the Bear,
> With thrice great Hermes.

'These lines have haunted me from very early days, and
principally influenced me in purchasing this tower, and plac-
ing my library on the top of it. And I have another association
with such a mode of life.'

A French clock in the library struck two, and the young
gentleman proposed to his visitor to walk into the house.
They accordingly descended the stairs, and crossed the entrance hall to a large drawing room, simply but handsomely
furnished; having some good pictures on the walls, an organ at
one end of the room, a piano and harp at the other, and an
elegantly disposed luncheon in the middle.

'At this time of the year,' said the young gentleman, 'I lunch at two, and dine at eight. this gives me two long divisions of the morning for any in-door and out-door purposes. I hope you will partake with me. You will not find a precedent in Homer for declining the invitation.'

'Really,' said the doctor, 'that argument is cogent and conclusive. I accept with pleasure: and indeed my long walk has given me an appetite.'

'Now you must know,' said the young gentleman, 'I have none but female domestics. You will see my two waiting-maids.'

He rang the bell, and the specified attendants appeared: two young girls about sixteen and seventeen; both pretty, and simply, but very becomingly, dressed.

Of the provision set before him the doctor preferred some cold chicken and tongue. Madeira and sherry were on the table, and the young attendants offered him hock and claret. The doctor took a capacious glass from each of the fair cup-bearers, and pronounced both wines excellent, and deliciously cool. He declined more, not to overheat himself in walking, and not to infringe on his anticipations of dinner. The dog, who had behaved throughout with exemplary propriety, was not forgotten. The doctor rose to depart.

'I think,' said his host, 'I may now ask you the Homeric question – Τίς πόθεν εἰς ἀνδρῶν;'*

'Most justly,' said the doctor. 'My name is Theophilus Opimian. I am a Doctor of Divinity, and the incumbent of Ashbrook-cum-Ferndale.'

'I am simply,' said the other, 'Algernon Falconer. I have inherited some money, but no land. Therefore, having the opportunity, I made this purchase to fit it up in my own fashion, and live in it in my own way.'

The doctor preparing to depart, Mr. Falconer proposed to accompany him part of the way, and calling out another Newfoundland dog, who immediately struck up a friendship with his companion, he walked away with the doctor, the two dogs gambolling before them.

---

* Who, and whence, are you?

# CHAPTER IV

## THE FOREST – A SOLILOQUY ON HAIR

Mille hominum species, et rerum discolor usus:
Velle suum cuique est, nec voto vivitur uno.
                                                    PERSIUS.

In mind and taste men differ as in frame:
Each has his special will, and few the same.

*The Rev. Dr. Opimian*
It strikes me as singular that, with such a house, you should
have only female domestics.

*Mr. Falconer*
It is not less singular perhaps that they are seven sisters, all the
children of two old servants of my father and mother. The
eldest is about my own age, twenty-six, so that they have all
grown up with me in time and place. They live in great
harmony together, and divide among them the charge of all
the household duties. Those whom you saw are the two
youngest.

*The Rev. Dr. Opimian*
If the others acquit themselves as well, you have a very
efficient staff; but seven young women as the establishment of
one young bachelor, for such I presume you to be (Mr.
Falconer *assented*), is something new and strange. The world is
not over charitable.

*Mr. Falconer*
The world will never suppose a good motive where it can
suppose a bad one. I would not willingly offend any of its
prejudices. I would not affect eccentricity. At the same time, I
do not feel disposed to be put out of my way because it is not
the way of the world – *Le Chemin du Monde,* as a Frenchman

entitled Congreve's comedy* – but I assure you these seven young women live here as they might do in the temple of Vesta. It was a singular combination of circumstances that induced and enabled me to form such an establishment; but I would not give it up, nor alter it, nor diminish it, nor increase it, for any earthly consideration.

*The Rev. Dr. Opimian*
You hinted that, besides Milton's verses, you had another association of ideas with living in the top of a tower.

*Mr. Falconer*
I have read of somebody who lived so, and admitted to his *sanctum* only one young person, a niece or a daughter, I forget which, but on very rare occasions would descend to speak to some visitor who had previously propitiated the young lady to obtain him an interview. At last the young lady introduced one who proposed for her, and gained the consent of the recluse (I am not sure of his name, but I always call him Lord Noirmont) to carry her off. I think this was associated with some affliction that was cured, or some mystery that was solved, and that the hermit returned into the everyday world. I do not know where I read it, but I have always liked the idea of living like Lord Noirmont, when I shall have become a sufficiently disappointed man.

*The Rev. Dr. Opimian*
You look as little like a disappointed man as any I have seen; but as you have neither daughter nor niece, you would have seven links instead of one between the top of your tower and the external world.

*Mr. Falconer*
We are all born to disappointment. It is as well to be prospective. Our happiness is not in what is, but in what is to be. We may be disappointed in our everyday realities, and if

* Congreve, le meilleur auteur comique d'Angleterre: ses pièces les plus estimées sont *Le Fourbe, Le Vieux Garçon, Amour pour Amour, L'Epouse du Matin, Le Chemin du Monde. Manuel Bibliographique.* Par G. Peignot. Paris, 1800.

not, we may make an ideality of the unattainable, and quarrel with Nature for not giving what she has not to give. It is unreasonable to be so disappointed, but it is disappointment not the less.

### The Rev. Dr. Opimian

It is something like the disappointment of the men of Gotham, when they could not fish up the moon from the sea.

### Mr. Falconer

It is very like it, and there are more of us in the predicament of the men of Gotham than are ready to acknowledge the similitude.

### The Rev. Dr. Opimian

I am afraid I am too matter-of-fact to sympathise very clearly with this form of æstheticism; but here is a charming bit of forest scenery. Look at that old oak with the deer under it; the long and deep range of fern running up from it to that beech-grove on the upland, the lights and shadows on the projections and recesses of the wood, and the blaze of foxglove in its foreground. It is a place in which a poet might look for a glimpse of a Hamadryad.

### Mr. Falconer

Very beautiful for the actual present – too beautiful for the probable future. Some day or other the forest will be disforested; the deer will be either banished or destroyed; the wood will be either shut up or cut down. Here is another basis for disappointment. The more we admire it now, the more we shall regret it then. The admiration of sylvan and pastoral scenery is at the mercy of an Enclosure Act, and, instead of the glimpse of a Hamadryad, you will some time see a large board warning you off the premises under penalty of rigour of law.

### The Rev. Dr. Opimian

But, my dear young friend, you have yourself enclosed a favourite old resort of mine and of many others. I did not see such a board as you speak of; but there is an effective fence which answers the purpose.

*Mr. Falconer*

True; but when the lot of crown land was put up for sale, it was sure to be purchased and shut up by somebody. At any rate, I have not interfered with the external picturesque; and I have been much more influenced by an intense desire of shutting up myself than of shutting up the place, merely because it is my property.

About half-way from their respective homes the two new friends separated, the doctor having promised to walk over again soon to dine and pass the night.

The doctor soliloquised as he walked.

Strange metamorphosis of the old tower. A good dining room. A good library. A bedroom between them: he did not show it me. Good wine: excellent. Pretty waiting-maids, exceedingly pretty. Two of seven Vestals, who maintain the domestic fire on the hearth of the young Numa. By the way, they had something of the Vestal costume: white dresses with purple borders. But they had nothing on their heads but their own hair, very gracefully arranged. The Vestals had head-dresses, which hid their hair, if they had any. They were shaved on admission. Perhaps the hair was allowed to grow again. Perhaps not. I must look into the point. If not, it was a wise precaution. 'Hair, the only grace of form,'* says the *Arbiter elegantiarum,* who compares a bald head to a fungus.* A head without hair, says Ovid, is as a field without grass, and a shrub without leaves.* Venus herself, if she had appeared with

---

* Quod solum formæ decus est, cecidere capilli. PETRONIUS, c. 109.

* . . . lævior . . . rotundo
  Horti tubere, quod creavit unda – *Ibid.*

'A head, to speak in the gardener's style, is a bulbous excrescence, growing up between the shoulders.' G.A. STEEVENS, *Lecture on Heads.*

* Turpe pecus mutilum; turpe est sine gramine campus;
  Et sine fronde frutex; et sine crine caput.
                                        OVID, *Artis Amatoriæ,* iii. 249.

a bald head, would not have tempted Apuleius:* and I am of his mind. A husband, in Menander,* in a fit of jealous madness, shaves his wife's head; and when he sees what he has made of her, rolls at her feet in a paroxysm of remorse. He was at any rate safe from jealousy till it grew again. And here is a subtlety of Euripides, which none of his commentators have seen into. Ægisthus has married Electra to a young farmer, who cultivates his own land. He respects the Princess from magnanimity, and restores her a pure virgin to her brother Orestes. 'Not probable,' say some critics. But I say highly probable: for she comes on with her head shaved. There is the talisman, and the consummate artifice of the great poet. It is ostensibly a symbol of grief; but not the less a most efficient ally of the aforesaid magnanimity. 'In mourning,' says Aristotle, 'sympathising with the dead, we deform ourselves by cutting off our hair.' And truly, it is sympathy in approximation. A woman's head shaved is a step towards a death's head. As a symbol of grief it was not necessary to the case of Electra; for in the sister tragedies of Æschylus and Sophocles her grief is equally great, and she appears with flowing hair; but in them she is an unmarried maid, and there is no dramatic necessity for so conspicuous an antidote to her other charms. Neither is it according to custom; for in recent

---

* At vero, quod nefas dicere, neque sit ullum hujus rei tam dirum exemplum: si cujuslibet eximiæ pulcherrimæque fœminæ caput capillo exspoliaveris, et faciem nativa specie nudaveris, licet illa cœlo dejecta, mari edita, fluctibus educata, licet, inquam, Venus ipsa fuerit, licet omni Gratiarum choro stipata, et toto Cupidinum populo comitata, et balteo suo cincta, cinnama fragrans, et balsama rorans, calva processerit, placere non poterit nec Vulcano suo. APULEIUS, *Metamorph*.ii. 25.

But, indeed, what it is profanation to speak, not let there be hereof any so dire example, if you despoil of its hair the head of any most transcendent and perfectly beautiful woman, and present her face thus denuded of its native loveliness, though it were even she, the descended from heaven, the born of the sea, the educated in the waves, though, I say, it were Venus herself, attended by the Graces, surrounded by the Loves, cinctured with her girdle, fragrant with spices, and dewy with balsams, yet, if she appeared with a bald head, she could not please even her own Vulcan.

* περικειρομένη.

grief the whole hair was sacrificed, but in the memory of an old sorrow only one or two curls were cut off.* Therefore, it was the dramatic necessity of a counter-charm that influenced Euripides. Helen knew better than to shave her head in a case where custom required it. Euripides makes Electra reproach Helen for thus preserving her beauty;* which further illustrates his purpose in shaving the head of Electra where custom did not require it. And Terence showed his taste in not shaving the head of his heroine in the *Phormio,* though the severity of Athenian custom would have required it. Her beauty shone through her dishevelled hair, but with no hair at all she would not have touched the heart of Antipho. ἀλλὰ τίη μοι ταῦτα φίλος διελέξατο θυμός; But wherefore does my mind discourse these things to me, suspending dismal images on lovely realities? for the luxuriant hair of these young girls is of no ordinary beauty. Their tresses have not been deposited under the shadow of the sacred lotus, as Pliny tells us those of the Vestals were. Well, this young gentleman's establishment may be perfectly moral, strictly correct, but in one sense it is morality thrown away: the world will give him no credit for it. I am sure Mrs. Opimian will not. If he were married it would be different. But I think, if he were to marry now, there would be a fiercer fire than Vesta's among his Lares. The temple would be too hot for the seven virgins. I suppose, as he is so resolute against change, he does not mean to marry. Then he talks about anticipated disappointment in some unrealistic ideality, leading him to live like Lord Noirmont, whom I never heard of before. He is far enough off from that while he lunches and walks as he does, and no doubt dines in accordance. He will not break his heart for any moon in the water if his cooks are as good as his waiting-maids, and the wine which he gave me is a fair specimen of his cellar. He is learned too. Greek seems to be the strongest chord in his sympathies. If it had not been for the singular accident of his overhearing me repeat half a dozen lines of Homer, I should not have been asked to walk in. I might have leaned over the gate till sunset,

---

* Sophocles, *Electra,* V.449.
* Euripides, *Orestes,* V.128

and have had no more notice taken of me than if I had been a crow.'

At dinner the doctor narrated his morning adventure to Mrs. Opimian, and found her, as he had anticipated, most virtuously uncharitable with respect to the seven sisters. She did not depart from her usual serenity, but said, with equal calmness and decision, that she had no belief in the virtue of young men.

'My dear,' said the doctor, 'it has been observed, though I forget by whom, that there is in every man's life a page which is usually doubled down. Perhaps there is such a page in the life of our young friend; but if there be, the volume which contains it is not in the same house with the seven sisters.'

The doctor could not retire to rest without verifying his question touching the hair of the Vestals; and stepping into his study, was taking out an old folio, to consult *Lipsius de Vestalibus,* when a passage flashed across his memory which seemed decisive on the point 'How could I overlook it?' he thought –

> 'Ignibus Iliacis aderam: cum lapsa capillis
>    Decidit ante sacros lanea vitta focos:*

says Rhea Sylvia in the *Fasti.*'

He took down the *Fasti,* and turning over the leaves, lighted on another line:–

> Attonitæ flebant demisso crine ministræ.*

With the note of an old commentator: 'This will enlighten those who doubt if the Vestals wore their hair.' 'I infer,' said the doctor, 'that I have doubted in good company; but it is clear that the Vestals did wear their hair of second growth. But if it was wrapped up in wool, it might as well not have been there.' The *vitta* was at once the symbol and the talisman of chastity. Shall I recommend my young friend to wrap up the

---

* The woollen wreath, by Vesta's inmost shrine,
    Fell from my hair before the fire divine.
* With hair dishevelled wept the vestal train.

heads of his Vestals in a *vitta*? It would be safer for all parties. But I cannot imagine a piece of advice for which the giver would receive less thanks. And I had rather see them as they are. So I shall let well alone.'

## CHAPTER V

## THE SEVEN SISTERS

εὔφοαινε σαυτόν· πίνε· τὸν καθ᾽ ἡμέραν
βίον λογίζου σόν, τὰ ἄλλα τῆς Τύχης.
                        EURIPIDES, *Alcestis*.

Rejoice thy spirit: drink: the passing day
Esteem thine own, and all beyond as Fortune's.

The doctor was not long without remembering his promise to revisit his new acquaintance, and, purposing to remain till the next morning, he set out later in the day. The weather was intensely hot: he walked slowly, and paused more frequently than usual, to rest under the shade of trees. He was shown into the drawing-room, where he was shortly joined by Mr. Falconer, and very cordially welcomed.

The two friends dined together in the lower room of the tower. The dinner and wine were greatly to the doctor's mind. In due time they adjourned to the drawing-room, and the two young handmaids who had waited at dinner attended with coffee and tea. The doctor then said – 'You are well provided with musical instruments. Do you play?'

*Mr. Falconer*
No. I have profited by the observation of Doctor Johnson: 'Sir, once on a time I took to fiddling; but I found that to fiddle well I must fiddle all my life, and I thought I could do something better.'

*The Rev. Dr. Opimian*
Then, I presume, these are pieces of ornamental furniture, for the use of occasional visitors?

*Mr. Falconer*
Not exactly. My maids play on them, and sing to them.

*The Rev. Dr. Opimian*
Your maids!

*Mr. Falconer*
Even so. They have been thoroughly well educated, and are all accomplished musicians.

*The Rev. Dr. Opimian*
And at what time do they usually play on them?

*Mr. Falconer*
Every evening about this time, when I am alone.

*The Rev. Dr. Opimian*
And why not when you have company?

*Mr. Falconer*
*La Morgue aristocratique*, which pervades all society, would not tolerate such a proceeding on the part of young women of whom some had superintended the preparation of the dinner, and others attended on it. It would not have been incongruous in the Homeric age.

*The Rev. Dr. Opimian*
Then I hope you will allow it to be not incongruous this evening, Homer being the original *vinculum* between you and me.

*Mr. Falconer*
Would you like to hear them?

*The Rev. Dr. Opimian*
Indeed I should.

The two younger sisters having answered the summons, and the doctor's wish having been communicated, the seven appeared together, all in the same dress of white and purple.

'The seven Pleiads!' thought the doctor. 'What a constellation of beauty!' He stood up and bowed to them, which they gracefully acknowledged.

They then played on, and sang to, the harp and piano. The doctor was enchanted.

After a while, they passed over to the organ, and performed some sacred music of Mozart and Beethoven. They then paused and looked round, as if for instructions.

'We usually end,' said Mr. Falconer, 'with a hymn to St. Catharine, but perhaps it may not be to your taste; although Saint Catharine is a saint of the English Church Calendar.'

'I like all sacred music,' said the doctor. 'And I am not disposed to object to a saint of the English Church Calendar.'

'She is also,' said Mr. Falconer, 'a most perfect emblem of purity, and in that sense alone there can be no fitter image to be presented to the minds of young women.'

'Very true,' said the doctor. 'And very strange withal,' he thought to himself.

The sisters sang their hymn, made their obeisance, and departed.


*The Rev. Dr. Opimian*
The hands of these young women do not show signs of menial work.


*Mr. Falconer*
They are the regulating spirits of the household. They have a staff of their own for the coarser and harder work.


*The Rev. Dr. Opimian*
Their household duties, then, are such as Homeric damsels discharged in the homes of their fathers, with δμωαί for the lower drudgery?


*Mr. Falconer*
Something like it.

*The Rev. Dr. Opimian*
Young ladies, in short, in manners and accomplishments,
though not in social position; only more useful in a house than
young ladies generally are.

*Mr. Falconer*
Something like that, too. If you know the tree by its fruit, the
manner in which this house is kept may reconcile you to the
singularity of the experiment.

*The Rev. Dr. Opimian*
I am perfectly reconciled to it. The experiment is eminently
successful.

The doctor always finished his day with a tumbler of brandy
and water: soda water in summer, and hot water in winter.
After his usual draught he retired to his chamber, where he
slept like a top, and dreamed of Electra and Nausicaa, Vestals,
Pleiads, and Saint Catharine, and woke with the last words he
had heard sung on the preceding night still ringing in his ears:—

> Dei virgo Catharina,
> Lege constans in divina,
> Cœli gemma preciosa,
> Margarita fulgida,
> Sponsa Christi gloriosa,
> Paradisi viola!*

* Virgin bride, supremely bright,
  Gem and flower of heavenly light,
  Pearl of the empyreal skies,
  Violet of Paradise!

## CHAPTER VI

## THE RUSTIC LOVER

Despairing beside a clear stream
A shepherd forsaken was laid.

The next morning, after a comfortable breakfast, the doctor
set out on his walk home. His young friend accompanied him
part of the way, and did not part with him till he had obtained
a promise of another and longer visit.

The doctor, as usual, soliloquised as he walked. 'No doubt
these are Vestals. The purity of the establishment is past
question. This young gentleman has every requisite which her
dearest friends would desire in a husband for Miss Gryll. And
she is in every way suited to him. But these seven damsels
interpose themselves, like the sevenfold shield of Ajax. There
is something very attractive in these damsels:

facies non omnibus una,
Nec diversa tamen: qualem decet esse sororum.*

If I had such an establishment, I should be loath to break it up.
It is original, in these days of monotony. It is satisfactory, in
these days of uncongenial relations between master and servant. it is effective, in the admirable arrangements of the
household. It is graceful, in the personal beauty and tasteful
apparel of the maidens. It is agreeable, in their manners, in
their accomplishments, in their musical skill. It is like an
enchanted palace. Mr. Gryll, who talks so much of Circe,
would find himself at home; he might fancy himself waited on
by her handmaids, the daughters of fountains, groves and
rivers. Miss Gryll might fancy herself in the dwelling of her

* Though various features did the sisters grace,
  A sister's likeness was in every face.
                                    ADDISON, *Ovid. Met.* 1. ii.

namesake. Morgana. But I fear she would be for dealing with it as Orlando did with Morgana, breaking the talisman and dissolving the enchantment. This would be a pity; but it would also be a pity that these two young persons should not come together. But why should I trouble myself with matchmaking? It is always a thankless office. If it turns out well, your good service is forgotten. If it turns out ill, you are abused by both parties.'

The doctor's soliloquy was cut short by a sound of lamentation, which, as he went on, came to him in louder and louder bursts. He was attracted to the spot whence the sounds proceeded, and had some difficulty in discovering a doleful swain, who was ensconced in a mass of fern, taller than himself if he had been upright; and but that, by rolling over and over in the turbulence of his grief, he had flattened a large space down to the edge of the forest brook near which he reclined, he would have remained invisible in his lair. The tears in his eyes, and the passionate utterances of his voice, contrasted strangely with a round russetin face, which seemed fortified by beef and ale against all possible furrows of care; but against love, even beef and ale, mighty talismans as they are, are feeble barriers. Cupid's arrows had pierced through the *æs triplex* of treble X, and the stricken deer lay mourning by the stream.

The doctor approaching kindly inquired, 'What is the matter?' but was answered only by a redoubled burst of sorrow, and an emphatic rejection of all sympathy.

'You can't do me any good.'

'You do not know that,' said the doctor. 'No man knows what good another can do him till he communicates his trouble.'

For some time the doctor could obtain no other answer than the repetition of 'You can't do me any good.' But at length the patience and kind face of the inquirer had their effect on the sad shepherd, and he brought out with a desperate effort and a more clamorous explosion of grief –

'She won't have me!'

'Who won't have you?'

'Well, if you must know,' said the swain, 'you must. It's one of the young ladies up at the Folly.'

'Young ladies?' said the doctor.

'Servants they call themselves,' said the other; 'but they are more like ladies, and hold their heads high enough, when one of them won't have me. Father's is one of the best farms for miles round, and it's all his own. He's a true old yeoman, father is. And there's nobody but him and me. And if I had a nice wife, that would be a good housekeeper for him, and play and sing to him of an evening – for she can do anything, she can – read, write, and keep accounts, and play and sing – I've heard her – and make a plum-pudding – I've seen her – we should be as happy as three crickets – four, perhaps, at the year's end: and she won't have me!'

'You have put the question?' said the doctor.

'Plump,' said the other. 'And she looked at first as if she was going to laugh. She didn't, though. Then she looked serious, and said she was sorry for me. She said she saw I was in earnest. She knew I was a good son, and deserved a good wife; but she couldn't have me. Miss, said I, do you like anybody better? No, she said very heartily.'

'That is one comfort,' said the doctor.

'What comfort,' said the other, 'when she won't have me?'

'She may alter her mind,' said the doctor, 'if she does not prefer any one else. Besides she only says she can't.'

'Can't,' said the other, 'is civil for won't. That's all.'

'Does she say why she can't?' said the doctor.

'Yes,' said the other. 'She says she and her sisters won't part with each other and their young master.'

'Now,' said the doctor, 'you have not told me which of the seven sisters is the one in question.'

'It's the third,' said the other. 'What they call the second cook. There's a housekeeper and two cooks, and two house-maids and two waiting-maids. But they only manage for the young master. There are others that wait on them.

'And what is her name?' said the doctor.

'Dorothy,' said the other; 'her name is Dorothy. Their names follow, like A B C, only that A comes last. Betsey, Catherine, Dorothy, Eleanor, Fanny, Grace, Anna. But they told me it was not the alphabet they were christened from; it was the key of A minor, if you know what that means.

'I think I do,' said the doctor, laughing. 'They were

christened from the Greek diatonic scale, and make up two conjunct tetrachords, if you know what that means.'

'I can't say I do,' said the other, looking bewildered.

'And so,' said the doctor, 'the young gentleman, whose name is Algernon, is the Proslambanomenos, or keynote, and makes up the octave. His parents must have designed it as a foretelling that he and his seven foster-sisters were to live in harmony all their lives. But how did you become acquainted?'

'Why,' said the other, 'I take a great many things to the house from our farm, and it's generally she that takes them in.'

'I know the house well,' said the doctor, 'and the master, and the maids. Perhaps he may marry, and they may follow the example. Live in hope. Tell me your name.'

'Hedgerow,' said the other; 'Harry Hedgerow. And if you know her, ain't she a beauty?'

'Why, yes,' said the doctor; 'They are all good-looking.'

'And she won't have me,' cried the other, but with a more subdued expression. The doctor had consoled him, and given him a ray of hope. And they went on their several ways.

The doctor resumed his soliloquy.

'Here is the semblance of something towards a solution of the difficulty. If one of the damsels should marry, it would break the combination. One will not by herself. But what if seven apple-faced Hedgerows should propose simultaneously, seven notes in the key of A minor, an octave below? Stranger things have happened. I have read of six brothers who had the civility to break their necks in succession, that the seventh, who was the hero of the story, might inherit an estate. But, again and again, why should I trouble myself with match-making? I had better leave things to take their own course.'

Still in his interior *speculum* the doctor could not help seeing a dim reflection of himself pronouncing the nuptial benediction on his two young friends.

# CHAPTER VII

## THE VICAR AND HIS WIFE – FAMILIES OF LOVE – THE NEWSPAPER

Indulge Genio: carpamus dulcia: nostrum est
Quod vivis: cinis, et manes, et fabula fies.
Vive memor lethi: fugit hora: hoc quod loquor, inde est.
                                                    PERSIUS.

Indulge thy Genius, while the hour's thine own:
Even while we speak, some part of it has flown.
Snatch the swift-passing good: 'twill end ere long
In dust and shadow, and an old wife's song.

'Agapetus and Agapêtê,'* said the Reverend Doctor Opimian, the next morning at breakfast, 'in the best sense of the words: that, I am satisfied, is the relation between this young gentleman and his handmaids.'

*Mrs. Opimian*
Perhaps, doctor, you will have the goodness to make your view of this relation a little more intelligible to me.

*The Rev. Dr. Opimian*
Assuredly, my dear. The word signifies 'beloved,' in its purest sense. And in this sense it was used by Saint Paul in reference to some of his female co-religionists and fellow-labourers in the vineyard, in whose houses he occasionally dwelt. And in this sense it was applied to virgins and holy men, who dwelt under the same roof in spiritual love.

*Mrs. Opimian*
Very likely, indeed. You are a holy man, doctor, but I think, if you were a bachelor, and I were a maid, I should not trust myself to be your aga – aga –

---

* ἀγαπητὸς καὶ ἀγαπηταί.

*The Rev. Dr. Opimian*
Agapêtê. But I never pretended to this sort of spiritualism. I followed the advice of Saint Paul, who says it is better to marry.

*Mrs. Opimian*
You need not finish the quotation.

*The Rev. Dr. Opimian*
Agapêtê is often translated 'adoptive sister.' A very possible relation, I think, where there are vows of celibacy, and inward spiritual grace.

*Mrs. Opimian*
Very possible, indeed: and equally possible where there are none.

*The Rev. Dr. Opimian*
But more possible where there are seven adoptive sisters than where there is only one.

*Mrs. Opimian*
Perhaps.

*The Rev. Dr. Opimian*
The manners, my dear, of these damsels towards their young master are infallible indications of the relations between them. Their respectful deference to him is a symptom in which I cannot be mistaken.

*Mrs. Opimian*
I hope you are not.

*The Rev. Dr. Opimian*
I am sure I am not. I would stake all my credit for observation and experience on the purity of the seven Vestals. I am not strictly accurate in calling them so: for in Rome the number of Vestals was only six. But there were seven Pleiads, till one disappeared. We may fancy she became a seventh Vestal. Or as the planets used to be seven, and are now more than fifty,

we may pass a seventh Vestal in the name of modern progress.

*Mrs. Opimian*
There used to be seven deadly sins. How many has modern
progress added to them?

*The Rev. Dr. Opimian*
None, I hope, my dear. But this will be due, not to its own
tendencies, but to the comprehensiveness of the old defini-
tions.

*Mrs. Opimian*
I think I have heard something like your Greek word before.

*The Rev. Dr. Opimian*
Agapêmonê, my dear. You may have heard the word
Agapêmonê.

*Mrs. Opimian*
That is it. And what may it signify?

*The Rev. Dr. Opimian*
It signifies Abode of Love: spiritual love of course.

*Mrs. Opimian*
Spiritual love, which rides in carriages and four, fares sump-
tuously, like Dives, and protects itself with a high wall from
profane observation.

*The Rev. Dr. Opimian*
Well, my dear, and there may be no harm in all that.

*Mrs. Opimian*
Doctor, you are determined not to see harm in anything.

*The Rev. Dr. Opimian*
I am afraid I see more harm in many things than I like to see.
But one reason for not seeing harm in this Agapêmonê matter
is, that I hear so little about it. The world is ready enough to
promulgate scandal; but that which is quietly right may rest in
peace.

*Mrs. Opimian*
Surely, doctor, you do not think this Agapêmonê right?

*The Rev. Dr. Opimian*
I only say I do not know whether it is right or wrong. It is
nothing new. Three centuries ago there was a Family of Love,
on which Middleton wrote a comedy. Queen Elizabeth
persecuted this family; Middleton made it ridiculous; but it
outlived them both, and there may have been no harm in it
after all.

*Mrs. Opimian*
Perhaps, doctor, the world is too good to see any novelty
except in something wrong.

*The Rev. Dr. Opimian*
Perhaps it is only wrong that arrests attention, because right is
common, and wrong is rare. Of the many thousand persons
who walk daily through a street you only hear of one who has
been robbed or knocked down. If ever Hamlet's news – 'that
the world has grown honest' – should prove true, there would
be an end of our newspaper. For, let us see, what is the
epitome of a newpaper? In the first place, specimens of all the
deadly sins, and infinite varieties of violence and fraud; a great
quantity of talk, called by courtesy legislative wisdom, of
which the result is 'an incoherent and undigested mass of law,
shot down, as from a rubbish-cart, on the heads of the
people';* lawyers barking at each other in that peculiar style of
hylactic delivery which is called forensic eloquence, and of
which the first and most distinguished practitioner was Cerberus;* bear-garden meetings of mismanaged companies, in
which directors and shareholders abuse each other in choice
terms, not all to be found even in Rabelais; burstings of bank
bubbles, which, like a touch of harlequin's wand, strip off
their masks and dominoes from 'highly respectable' gentlemen, and leave them in their true figures of cheats and

* Jeremy Bentham.
* Cerberus forensis erat causidicus. PETRONIUS ARBITER.

pickpockets; societies of all sorts, for teaching everybody everything, meddling with everybody's business, and mending everybody's morals; mountebank advertisements promising the beauty of Helen in a bottle of cosmetic, and the age of Old Parr in a box of pills; folly all alive in things called réunions; announcements that some exceedingly stupid fellow has been 'entertaining' a select company; matters, however multiform, multifarious, and multitudinous, all brought into family likeness by the varnish of false pretension with which they are all overlaid.

*Mrs. Opimian*
I did not like to interrupt you, doctor; but it struck me, while you were speaking, that in reading the newspaper you do not hear the bark of the lawyers.

*The Rev. Doctor Opimian*
True; but no one who has once heard the wow-wow can fail to reproduce it in imagination.

*Mrs. Opimian*
You have omitted accidents, which occupy a large space in the newspaper. If the world grew ever so honest, there would still be accidents.

*The Rev. Dr. Opimian*
But honesty would materially diminish the number. High-pressure steam-boilers would not scatter death and destruction around them if the dishonesty of avarice did not tempt their employment, where the more costly low pressure would ensure absolute safety. Honestly built houses would not come suddenly down and crush their occupants. Ships, faithfully built and efficiently manned, would not so readily strike on a lee shore, nor go instantly to pieces on the first touch of the ground. Honestly made sweetmeats would not poison children; honestly compounded drugs would not poison patients. In short, the larger portion of what we call accidents are crimes.

*Mrs. Opimian*
I have often heard you say, of railways and steam-vessels, that
the primary cause of their disasters is the insane passion of the
public for speed. That is not crime, but folly.

*The Rev. Dr. Opimian*
It is crime in those who ought to know better than to act in
furtherance of the folly. But when the world has grown
honest, it will no doubt grow wise. When we have got rid of
crime, we may consider how to get rid of folly. So that
question is adjourned to the Greek kalends.

*Mrs. Opimian*
There are always in a newspaper some things of a creditable
character.

*The Rev. Dr. Opimian*
When we are at war, naval and military heroism abundantly;
but in time of peace these virtues sleep. They are laid up like
ships in ordinary. No doubt, of the recorded facts of civil life
some are good, and more are indifferent, neither good nor
bad; but good and indifferent together are scarcely more than a
twelfth part of the whole. Still, the matters thus presented are
all exceptional cases. A hermit reading nothing but a newspaper might find little else than food for misanthropy; but living
among friends, and in the bosom of our family, we see the
dark side of life in the occasional picture, the bright is its
everyday aspect. The occasional is the matter of curiosity, of
incident, of adventure, of things that really happen to few, and
may possibly happen to any. The interest attendant on any
action or event is in just proportion to its rarity; and, happily,
quiet virtues are all around us, and obtrusive virtues seldom
cross our path. On the whole, I agree in opinion with
Theseus,* that there is more good than evil in the world.

*Mrs. Opimian*
I think, doctor, you would not maintain any opinion if you
had not an authority two thousand years old for it.

* Eurip. *Suppl.* 207: Herm.

*The Rev. Dr. Opimian*
Well, my dear, I think most opinions worth mentioning have
an authority of about that age.

## CHAPTER VIII

## PANTOPRAGMATICS

ψῦξον τόν οἶνον, Δῶρι.——
——ἔγχεον σὺ δὴ πιεῖν·
εὐζωρότερόν γε νὴ Δί', ὦ παῖ, δός· τὸ γὰρ
ὕδαρες ἅπαν τοῦτ' ἐστὶ τῇ ψυχῇ κακόν.

Cool the wine, Doris. Pour it in the cup,
Simple, unmixed with water. Such dilution
Serves only to wash out the spirit of man.

The doctor, under the attraction of his new acquaintance, had
allowed more time than usual to elapse between his visits to
Gryll Grange, and when he resumed them he was not long
without communicating the metamorphosis of the old Tower,
and the singularities of its inhabitants. They dined well as
usual, and drank their wine cool.

*Miss Gryll*
There are many things in what you have told us that excite my
curiosity; but first, what do you suppose is the young
gentleman's religion?

*The Rev. Dr. Opimian*
From the great liking he seems to have taken to me, I should
think he was of the Church of England if I did not rather
explain it by our Greek sympathy. At the same time, he kept
very carefully in view that Saint Catharine is a saint of the
English Church Calendar. I imagine there is less of true piety
than of an abstract notion of ideal beauty, even in his devotion
to her. But it is so far satisfactory that he wished to prove his

religion, such as it is, to be within the pale of the Church of
England.

*Miss Gryll*
I like the idea of his closing the day with a hymn, sung in
concert by his seven Vestals.

*The Rev. Dr. Opimian*
I am glad you think charitably of the damsels. It is not every
lady that would. But I am satisfied they deserve it.

*Mr. Gryll*
I should like to know the young gentleman. I wish you could
manage to bring him here. Should not you like to see him,
Morgana?

*Miss Gryll*
Yes, uncle.

*Mr. Gryll*
Try what you can do, doctor. We shall have before long some
poetical and philosophical visitors. That may tempt him to
join us.

*The Rev. Dr. Opimian*
It may; but I am not confident. He seems to me to be
indisposed to general society, and to care for nothing but
woods, rivers, and the sea; Greek poetry, Saint Catharine, and
the seven Vestals. However, I will try what can be done.

*Mr. Gryll*
But, doctor, I think he would scarcely have provided such a
spacious dining-room, and so much domestic accommoda-
tion, if he had intended to shut himself up from society
altogether. I expect that some day when you go there you will
find a large party. Try if he will co-operate in the Aristophanic
comedy.

*The Rev. Dr. Opimian*
A good idea. That may be something to his mind.

*Miss Gryll*
Talking of comedy, doctor, what has become of Lord Curryfin, and his lecture on fish?

*The Rev. Dr. Opimian*
Why, Lord Michin Malicho,* Lord Facing-both-ways, and
two or three other arch-quacks, have taken to merryandrewis-
ing in a new arena, which they call the Science of Pantopragmatics, and they have bitten Lord Curryfin into tumbling
with them; but the mania will subside when the weather
grows cool; and no doubt we shall still have him at Thornback
Bay, teaching the fishermen how to know a herring from a
halibut.

*Miss Gryll*
But pray, doctor, what is this new science?

*The Rev. Dr. Opimian*
Why that, Miss Gryll, I cannot well make out. I have asked
several professors of the science, and have got nothing in
return but some fine varieties of rigmarole, of which I can
make neither head nor tail. It seems to be a real art of talking
about an imaginary art of teaching every man his own
business. Nothing practical comes of it, and, indeed, so much
the better. It will be at least harmless as long as it is like
Hamlet's reading, 'words, words, words.' Like most other
science, it resolves itself into lecturing, lecturing, lecturing,
about all sorts of matters, relevant and irrelevant: one enormous bore prating about jurisprudence, another about statis-
tics, another about education, and so forth; the *crambe repetita*
of the same rubbish, which has already been served up 'twiës
hot and twiës cold,'* at as many other associations nicknamed
scientific.

---

* 'Marry, this is *miching mallecho*: it means mischief.' *Hamlet*
* And many a Jacke of Dover hast thou sold,
  That hath been twiës hot and twiës cold.
                          CHAUCER, *The Coke's Prologue.*

*Miss Gryll*

Then, doctor, I should think Lord Curryfin's lecture would be a great relief to the unfortunate audience.

*The Rev. Dr. Opimian*

No doubt more amusing and equally profitable. Not a fish more would be caught for it, and this will typify the result of all such scientific talk. I had rather hear a practical cook lecture on bubble and squeak: no bad emblem of the whole affair.

*Mr. Gryll*

It has been said a man of genius can discourse on anything. Bubble and squeak seems a limited subject; but in the days of the French Revolution there was an amusing poem with the title;* and there might be an amusing lecture; especially if it were like the poem, discursive and emblematical. But men so dismally far gone in the affectation of earnestness would scarcely relish it.


CHAPTER IX

SAINT CATHARINE


> . . . gli occhi su levai,
> E vidi lei che si facea corona,
> Riflettendo da sè gli eterni rai.
> DANTE, *Paradiso,* xxxi. 70–72.

> I lifted up my gaze,
> And looked on her who made herself a crown,
> Reflecting from herself the eternal rays.

It was not long before the doctor again walked over to the Tower, to propose to his young friend to co-operate in the Aristophanic comedy.


* 'Bubble and Squeak: a Gallimaufry of British Beef with the Chopped Cabbage of Gallic Philosophy,' by HUDDESFORD.

He found him well disposed to do so, and they passed a portion of the afternoon in arranging their programme.

They dined, and passed the evening much as before. The next morning, as they were ascending to the library to resume their pleasant labour, the doctor said to himself, 'I have passed along galleries wherein were many chambers, and the doors in the day were more commonly open than shut, yet this chamber door of my young friend is always shut. There must be a mystery in it.' And the doctor, not generally given to morbid curiosity, found himself very curious about this very simple matter.

At last he mustered up courage to say, 'I have seen your library, dining-room, and drawing-room; but you have so much taste in internal arrangements, I should like to see the rest of the house.'

*Mr. Falconer*
There is not much more to see. You have occupied one of the best bedrooms. the rest do not materially differ.

*The Rev. Dr. Opimian*
To say the truth, I should like to see your own.

*Mr. Falconer*
I am quite willing. But I have thought, perhaps erroneously, it is decorated in a manner you might not altogether aprove.

*The Rev. Dr. Opimian*
Nothing indecorous, I hope.

*Mr. Falconer*
Quite the contrary. You may, perhaps, think it too much devoted to my peculiar views of the purity of ideal beauty, as developed in Saint Catharine.

*The Rev. Dr. Opimian*
You have not much to apprehend on that score.

*Mr. Falconer*
You see, there is an altar, with an image of Saint Catharine,

and the panels of the room are painted with subjects from her life, mostly copied from Italian masters. The pictures of St. Catharine and her legend very early impressed her on my mind as the type of ideal beauty — of all that can charm, irradiate, refine, exalt, in the best of the better sex.

*The Rev. Dr. Opimian*
You are enthusiastic; but indeed, though she is retained as a saint in the Reformed Church, I am not very familiar with her history. And to me some of these pictures require explanation.

*Mr. Falconer*
I will tell you her legend as briefly as I may. And we will pass from picture to picture as the subjects arise.


## THE LEGEND OF SAINT CATHARINE

Catharine was a Princess of Alexandria in the third century. She embraced the Christian religion by divine inspiration. She was pre-eminent in beauty, learning, and discourse. She converted her father and mother, and all with whom she came into communication. The Emperor Maxentius brought together the fifty wisest men of the empire to convert her from the error of her way, and she converted them all to the new faith. Maxentius burned her proselytes, and threatened her with a similar death. She remained firm. He had her publicly scourged, and cast her into prison to perish by famine. Going on an expedition, he left the execution of his orders to the empress and his chief general, Porphyrius. Angels healed her wounds and supplied her with food; and in a beatific vision the Saviour of the world placed a ring on her finger, and called her His bride.* The presence of the ring showed to her the truth of the visitation. The empress and Porphyrius visited the prison, and she converted them also.

---

* Maria, Vergine delle Vergini, e Misericordia delle Misericordie, vestita de i lampi del Sole, e coronata de i raggi delle Stelle, prese il sottile, il delicato, ed il sacro dito di Catarina, humile di core e mansueta di vita, ed il largo, il clemente, ed il pietoso figliuol suo lo cinse con lo anello. *Vita di Santa Catarina,* 1. ii. Vinegia, 1541.

The emperor, returning, put the empress and Porphyrius to death; and after many ineffectual expostulations with Catharine, determined on putting her to death by the wheel which bears her name. Four of these wheels, armed with iron teeth, and revolving towards each other, were to cut her to pieces. Angels broke the wheels. He then brought her to the stake, and the angels extinguished the flames. He then ordered her to be beheaded by the sword. This was permitted, and in the meantime the day had closed. The body, reserved for exposure to wild beasts, was left under guard at the place of execution. Intense darkness fell on the night, and in the morning the body had disappeared. The angels had borne it to the summit of the loftiest mountain of the Horeb range, where still a rock, bearing the form of a natural sarcophagus, meets the eye of the traveller. Here it was watched by angel-guards, and preserved in unchanging beauty, till, in the fulness of time, it was revealed to a holy man, who removed it to the shrine, under which it lies to this day, with the ring still on its hand, in the convent which was then founded, and which bears her name – the convent Saint Catharine of Mount Sinai.

*The Rev.Dr. Opimian*
Most of this is new to me. Yet I am not unfamiliar with pictures of the marriage of Saint Catharine, which was a favourite subject with the great Italian masters. But here is a picture which the legend, as you have related it, does not illustrate, What is this tomb, with flames bursting from it, and monks and others recoiling in dismay?

*Mr. Falconer*
It represents a remarkable incident at the tomb of the saint. The Empress Catharine II was a great benefactress to the Convent of Mount Sinai, and desired to possess Saint Catharine's ring. She sent a mitred abbot as an envoy to request it from the brotherhood. The monks, unwilling to displease the empress, replied that they did not dare to remove it themselves, but that they would open the tomb, and the envoy might take it. They opened the tomb accordingly, and the envoy looked on the hand and the ring. He approached to draw it off; but flames burst forth: he recoiled, and the tomb

closed. Under such a manifestation of the saint's displeasure, the fathers could not again attempt to open it.*

*The Rev. Dr. Opimian*
I should like to have seen the empress receiving the envoy's report.

*Mr. Falconer*
Her reception of it would depend on the degree of faith which she either actually felt, or might have thought it politic to assume. At any rate, the fathers had shown their devotion, and afforded her a good opportunity for exhibiting hers. She did not again seek to obtain the ring.

*The Rev. Dr. Opimian*
Now, what are these three pictures in one frame, of chapels on hills?

*Mr. Falconer*
These chapels are here represented as they may be supposed to have been in the Catholic days of England. Three sisters, named Catharine, Martha and Anne, built them to their namesake saints, on the summits of three hills, which took from these dedications the names they still bear. From the summit of each of these chapels the other two were visible. The sisters thought the chapels would long remain memorials of Catholic piety and sisterly love. The Reformation laid them in ruins. Nothing remains of the chapel of St. Anne but a few grey stones, built into an earthen wall, which, some half-century ago, enclosed a plantation. The hill is now better known by the memory of Charles Fox than by that of its ancient saint. The chapel of Saint Martha has been restored and applied to Protestant worship. The chapel of Saint Catharine remains a picturesque ruin, on the banks of the Wey, near Guildford.

*The Rev. Dr. Opimian*
And that old church?

* *Illustrations of Jerusalem and Mount Sinai* (1837), p. 27.

*Mr. Falconer*

That was the church of Saint Catharine, which was pulled down to make way for the dock by which her name is now profaned; an act of desecration which has been followed by others, and will be followed by many more, whenever it may suit the interests of commerce to commit sacrilege on consecrated ground, and dissipate the ashes of the dead; an act which, even when that of a barbarian invader, Horace thought it would be profanation even to look on.* Whatever may be in other respects the superiority of modern piety, we are far inferior to the ancients in reverence for temples and tombs.

*The Rev. Dr. Opimian*

I am afraid I cannot gainsay that observation. But what is that stained glass window?

*Mr. Falconer*

It is copied on a smaller scale, and with more of Italian artistic beauty in the principal figure, from the window in West Wickham church. She is trampling on the Emperor Maxentius. You see all her emblems: the palm, which belongs to all sainted martyrs; the crown, the wheel, the fire, the sword, which belong especially to her; and the book, with which she is always represented, as herself a miracle of learning, and its chosen universal patroness in the schools of the Middle Ages.

*The Rev. Dr. Opimian*

Unquestionably the legend is interesting. At present your faith is simply poetical. But take care, my young friend, that you do not finish by becoming the dupe of your own mystification.

*Mr. Falconer*

I have no fear of that. I think I can clearly distinguish devotion to ideal beauty from supersititous belief. I feel the necessity of some such devotion to fill up the void which the world, as it is, leaves in my mind, I wish to believe in the presence of some local spiritual influence; genius or nymph; linking us by a

* *Epod.* 16, 13.

medium of something like human feeling, but more pure and more exalted, to the all-pervading, creative, and preservative spirit of the universe; but I cannot realise it from things as they are. Everything is too deeply tinged with sordid vulgarity. There can be no intellectual power resident in a wood, where the only inscription is not *'Genio loci,'* but 'Trespassers will be prosecuted'; no Naiad in a stream that turns a cotton-mill; no Oread in a mountain dell, where a railway train deposits a cargo of vandals; no Nereids or Oceanitides along the seashore, where a coastguard is watching for smugglers. No; the intellectual life of the material world is dead. Imagination cannot replace it. But the intercession of saints still forms a link between the visible and invisible. In their symbols I can imagine their presence. Each in the recess of our own thought we may preserve their symbols from the intrusion of the world. And the saint whom I have chosen presents to my mind the most perfect ideality of physical, moral, and intellectual beauty.

*The Rev. Dr. Opimian*
I cannot object to your taste. But I hope you will not be led into investing the ideality with too much of the semblance of reality. I should be sorry to find you far gone in hagiolatry. I hope you will acquiesce in Martin, keeping equally clear of Peter and Jack.

*Mr. Falconer*
Nothing will more effectually induce me so to acquiesce than your company, dear doctor. A tolerant liberality like yours has a very persuasive influence.

From this digression the two friends proceeded to the arrangement of their Aristophanic comedy, and divided their respective shares after the manner of Beaumont and Fletcher.

# CHAPTER X

## THE THUNDERSTORM

Si bene calculum ponas, ubique naufragium est.
                                    PETRONIUS ARBITER.

If you consider well the events of life, shipwreck is everywhere.

After luncheon the doctor thought of returning home, when a rumbling of distant thunder made him pause. They reascended the Tower, to reconnoitre the elements from the library. The windows were so arranged as to afford a panoramic view.

The thunder muttered far off, but there was neither rain nor visible lightning.

'The storm is at a great distance,' said the doctor, 'and it seems to be passing away on the verge of the sky.'

But on the opposite horizon appeared a mass of dark-blue cloud, which rose rapidly, and advanced in the direct line of the Tower. Before it rolled a lighter but still lurid volume of vapour, which curled and wreathed like eddying smoke before the denser blackness of the unbroken cloud.

Simultaneously followed the flashing of lightning, the rolling of thunder and a deluge of rain like the bursting of a waterspout.

They sate some time in silence, watching the storm as it swept along, with wind, and driving rain, and whirling hail, bringing for a time almost the darkness of night, through which the forked lightning poured a scarcely interrupted blaze.

Suddenly came a long dazzling flash, that seemed to irradiate the entire circumference of the sky, followed instantaneously by one of those crashing peals of thunder which always indicate that something very near has been struck by lightning.

The doctor turned round to make a remark on the awful grandeur of the effect, when he observed that his young friend had disappeared. On his return, he said he had been looking for what had been struck.

'And what was?' said the doctor.

'Nothing in the house,' said his host.

'The Vestals,' thought the doctor; 'these were all his solicitude.

But though Mr. Falconer had looked no farther than to the safety of the seven sisters, his attention was soon drawn to a tumult below, which seemed to indicate that some serious mischief had resulted from the lightning; and the youngest of the sisters, appearing in great trepidation, informed him that one of two horses in a gentleman's carriage had been struck dead, and that a young lady in the carriage had been stunned by the passing flash, though how far she was injured by it could not be immediately known. The other horse, it appeared, had been prancing in terror, and had nearly overthrown the carriage; but he had been restrained by the vigorous arm of a young farmer, who had subsequently carried the young lady into the house, where she was now resting on a couch in the female apartments, and carefully attended by the sisters.

Mr. Falconer and the doctor descended into the hall, and were assured that the young lady was doing well, but that she would be much better for being left some time longer undisturbed. An elderly gentleman issued from the female apartments, and the doctor with some amazement recognised his friend Mr. Gryll, to whom and his niece this disaster had occurred.

The beauty of the morning had tempted them to a long drive; and they thought it would be a good opportunity to gratify at least a portion of the curiosity which the doctor's description of the Folly and its inhabitants had excited in them. They had therefore determined on taking a circuit in which they would pass under the walls of the Tower. They were almost at the extremity of their longest radius when the storm burst over them, and were just under the Tower when the lightning struck one of their horses. Harry Hedgerow was on his way with some farm produce when the accident occurred, and was the young farmer who had subdued the surviving horse and carried the young lady into the house.

Mr. Gryll was very panegyrical of this young man's be-
haviour, and the doctor, when he recognised him, shook him
heartily by the hand, and told him he felt sure that he was a lad
who would make his way: a remark which Harry received as a
good omen: for Dorothy heard it, and looked at him with a
concurrent, though silent, approbation.

The drawing-room and the chambers for visitors were
between the tower and the *gynæceum*, or female apartments,
which were as completely separated from the rest of the house
as they could have been in Athens.

After some anxious inquiries, it was reported that the young
lady was sleeping, and that one or other of the sisters would
keep constant watch by her. It was therefore arranged that Mr.
Gryll should dine and pass the night where he was. Before
dinner he had the satisfaction of hearing from medical authority that all would be well after a little time.

Harry Hedgerow had bethought him of a retired physician,
who lived with a maiden sister in a cottage at no great distance
from the tower, and who often gave gratuitous advice to his
poorer neighbours. If he prescribed anything beyond their
means, himself or his sister was always ready to supply it.
Though their own means were limited, they were the good
angels of a small circumference.

The old physician confirmed the opinion already given by
the sisters, that the young lady for the present only required
repose; but he accepted the invitation to remain till the
morning, in the event of his advice being needed.

So Miss Gryll remained with the elder sisters. Mr. Gryll and
the two doctors, spiritual and temporal, sat down to dinner
with Mr. Falconer, and were waited on, as usual, by the
younger handmaids.

# CHAPTER XI

## ELECTRICAL SCIENCE – THE DEATH
## OF PHILEMON

> οἴνου μὴ παρεόντος ἀτερπέα δεῖπνα τραπέ ης˙
> οἴνου μὴ παρεόντος, ἀθελγέες εἰσὶ χορεῖαι.
> ἀνὴρ πένθος ἔχων, ὅτε γεύσεται ἡδέος οἴνου,
> στυγνὸν ἀεξομένης ἀποσείσεται ὄγκον ἀνίης.

> Where wine is not, no mirth the banquet knows:
> Where wine is not, the dance all joyless goes.
> The man, oppressed with cares, who tastes the bowl,
> Shall shake the weight of sorrow from his soul.

> BACCHUS, on the birth of the vine, predicting its benefits:
>       in the twelfth book of the *Dionysiaca* of NONNUS.

The conversation at dinner turned on the occurrences of the
morning and the phenomena of electricity. The physician,
who had been a traveller, related many anecdotes from his
own observation: especially such as tended to show by
similarity that the injury to Miss Gryll would not be of long
duration. He had known, in similar cases, instances of apparent total paralysis; but he had always found it temporary.
Perhaps in a day or two, but at most in a very few days, it
would certainly pass away. In the meantime he recommended
absolute repose. Mr. Falconer entreated Mr. Gryll to consider
the house as his own. Matters were arranged accordingly; and
it was determined that the next morning a messenger should
be despatched to Gryll Grange for a supply of apparel. The
Rev. Dr. Opimian, who was as fond as the Squire himself of
the young lady, had been grievously discomposed by the
accident of the morning, and felt that he should not thoroughly recover his serenity till he could again see her in her proper
character, the light and life of her society. He quoted Homer,
Æschylus, Aristotle, Plutarch, Athenæus, Horace, Persius,
and Pliny, to show that all which is practically worth knowing

on the subject of electricity had been known to the ancients. The electric telegraph he held to be a nuisance, as disarranging chronology, and giving only the heads of a chapter, of which the details lost their interest before they arrived, the heads of another chapter having intervened to destroy it. Then, what an amount of misery it inflicted, when, merely saying that there had been a great battle, and that thousands had been wounded or killed, it maintained an agony of suspense in all who had friends on the field, till the ordinary channels of intelligence brought the names of the sufferers. No Sicilian tyrant had invented such an engine of cruelty. This declamation against a supposed triumph of modern science, which was listened to with some surprise by the physician, and with great respect by his other auditors, having somewhat soothed his troubled spirit, in conjunction with the physician's assurance, he propitiated his Genius by copious libations of claret, pronouncing high panegyrics on the specimen before him, and interspersing quotations in praise of wine as the one great panacea for the cares of this world.

A week passed away, and the convalescent had made good progress. Mr. Falconer had not yet seen his fair guest. Six of the sisters, one remaining with Miss Gryll, performed every evening, at the earnest request of Mr. Gryll, a great variety of music, but always ending with the hymn to their master's saint. The old physician came once or twice, and stayed the night. The Reverend Doctor Opimian went home for his Sunday duties, but took too much interest in the fair Morgana not to return as soon as he could to the Tower. Arriving one morning in the first division of the day, and ascending to the library, he found his young friend writing. He asked him if he were working on the Aristophanic comedy. Mr. Falconer said he got on best with that in the doctor's company. 'But I have been writing,' he said, 'on something connected with the Athenian drama. I have been writing a ballad on the death of Philemon, as told by Suidas and Apuleius.' The doctor expressed a wish to hear it, and Mr. Falconer read it to him.

## THE DEATH OF PHILEMON*

### I

Closed was Philemon's hundredth year:
The theatre was thronged to hear
    His last completed play:
In the mid scene, a sudden rain
Dispersed the crowd – to meet again
    On the succeeding day.

He sought his home, and slept, and dreamed,
Nine maidens through his door, it seemed,
    Passed to the public street.
He asked them, 'Why they left his home?'
They said, 'A guest will hither come
    We must not stay to meet.'

He called his boy with morning light,
Told him the vision of the night,
    And bade his play be brought.
His finished page again he scanned,
Resting his head upon his hand,
    Absorbed in studious thought.

He knew not what the dream foreshowed:
That nought divine may hold abode
    Where death's dark shade is felt:
And therefore were the Muses nine
Leaving the old poetic shrine,
    Where they so long had dwelt.

### II

The theatre was thronged once more,
More thickly than the day before,
    To hear the half-heard song.
The day wore on. Impatience came.
They called upon Philemon's name,
    With murmurs loud and long.

* Suidas, *sub voce* Φιλήμων. Apuleius, *Florid.* 16.

Some sought at length his studious cell,
And to the stage returned, to tell
　　What thousands strove to ask.
'The poet we have been to seek
Sate with his hand upon his cheek,
　　As pondering o'er his task.


'We spoke. He made us no reply.
We reverentially drew nigh,
　　And twice our errand told.
He answered not. We drew more near.
The awful mystery then was clear:
　　We found him stiff and cold.


'Struck by so fair a death, we stood
Awhile in sad admiring mood:
　　Then hastened back, to say
That he, the praised and loved of all,
Is deaf for ever to your call:
　　That on this self-same day,


'When here presented should have been
The close of his fictitious scene,
　　His life's true scene was o'er:
We seemed, in solemn silence awed,
To hear the 'Farewell and applaud,'
　　Which he may speak no more.


'Of tears the rain gave prophecy:
The nuptial dance of comedy
　　Yields to the funeral train.
Assemble where his pyre must burn:
Honour his ashes in their urn:
And on another day return
　　To hear his songs again.'


*The Rev. Dr. Opimian*
A beautiful fiction.

*Mr. Falconer*

If it be a fiction. The supernatural is confined to the dream. All the rest is probable; and I am willing to think it true, dream and all.

*The Rev. Dr. Opimian*

You are determined to connect the immaterial with the material world, as far as you can.

*Mr. Falconer*

I like the immaterial world. I like to live among thoughts and images of the past and the possible, and even of the impossible, now and then.

*The Rev. Dr. Opimian*

Certainly, there is much in the material world to displease sensitive and imaginative minds; but I do not know any one who has less cause to complain of it than you have. You are surrounded with all possible comforts and with all the elements of beauty and of intellectual enjoyment.

*Mr. Falconer*

It is not my own world that I complain of. It is the world on which I look 'from the loopholes of retreat.' I cannot sit here, like one of the Gods of Epicurus, who, as Cicero says, was satisfied with thinking, through all eternity, 'how comfortable he was.'* I look with feelings of intense pain on the mass of poverty and crime; of unhealthy, unavailing, unremunerated toil, blighting childhood in its blossom, and womanhood in its prime; of 'all the oppressions that are done under the sun.'

*The Rev. Dr. Opimian*

I feel with you on all these points; but there is much good in the world; more good than evil, I have always maintained.

They would have gone off in a discussion on this point, but the French cook warned them to luncheon.

---

* Comprehende igitur animo, et propone ante oculos, deum nihil aliud in omni æternitate, nisi, Mihi pulchre est, et, Ego beatus sum, cogitantem. CICERO, *De natura deorum,* l. i. c. 41.

In the evening the young lady was sufficiently recovered to
join the little party in the drawing-room, which consisted, as
before, of Mr. Falconer, Mr. Gryll, Doctor Anodyne, and the
Reverend Doctor Opimian. Miss Gryll was introduced to Mr.
Falconer. She was full of grateful encomium for the kind
attention of the sisters, and expressed an earnest desire to hear
their music. The wish was readily complied with. She heard
them with great pleasure, and, though not yet equal to much
exertion, she could not yet refrain from joining in with them
in their hymn to Saint Catharine.

She accompanied them when they retired.

*The Rev. Dr. Opimian*
I presume those Latin words are genuine old monastic verses:
they have all the air of it.

*Mr. Falconer*
They are so, and they are adapted to old music.

*Dr. Anodyne*
There is something in this hymn very solemn and impressive.
In an age like ours, in which music and pictures are the
predominant tastes, I do not wonder that the forms of the old
Catholic worship are received with increasing favour. There is
a sort of adhesion to the old religion, which results less from
faith than from a certain feeling of poetry; it finds its disciples;
but it is of modern growth; and has very essential differences
from what it outwardly resembles.

*The Rev. Dr. Opimian*
It is, as I have frequently had occasion to remark, and as my
young friend here will readily admit, one of the many forms
of the love of ideal beauty, which, without being in itself
religion, exerts on vivid imaginations an influence that is very
often like it.

*Mr. Falconer*
An orthodox English Churchman was the poet who sang to
the Virgin:

'Thy image falls to earth. Yet some, I ween,
Not unforgiven the suppliant knee might bend,
As to a visible Power, in which did blend
All that was mixed and reconciled in thee,
Of mother's love with maiden purity,
Of high with low, celestial with terrene.'*

*The Rev. Dr. Opimian*
Well, my young friend, the love of ideal beauty has exercised
none but a benignant influence on you, whatever degree of
orthodoxy there may be in your view of it.

The little party separated for the night.


CHAPTER XII

THE FOREST DELL – THE POWER OF LOVE – THE
LOTTERY OF MARRIAGE

τί δεῖ γὰρ ὄντα θνητόν, ἱκετεύω, ποιεῖν,
πλὴν ἡδέως ζῆν τὸν βίον καθ' ἡμέραν,
ἐὰν ἔχῃ τις ὁπόθεν . . .
εἰς αὔριον δὲ μηδὲ φροντίζειν ὅ τι
ἔσται . . . PHILETÆRUS, *Cynagis.*

I pray you, what can mortal man do better
Than live his daily life as pleasantly
As daily means avail him? Life's frail tenure
Warns not to trust to-morrow.

The next day Mr. Falconer was perfectly certain that Miss
Gryll was not yet well enough to be removed. No one was
anxious to refute the proposition; they were all so well
satisfied with the place and the company they were in, that
they felt, the young lady included, a decided unwillingness to

* Wordsworth, *Ecclesiastical Sonnets*, i. 21.

go. That day Miss Gryll came to dinner, and the next day she came to breakfast, and in the evening she joined in the music, and, in short, she was once more altogether herself; but Mr. Falconer continued to insist that the journey home would be too much for her. When this excuse failed, he still entreated his new friends to remain; and so passed several days. At length Mr. Gryll found he must resolve on departing, especially as the time had arrived when he expected some visitors. He urgently invited Mr. Falconer to visit him in return. The invitation was cordially accepted, and in the meantime considerable progress had been made in the Aristophanic comedy.

Mr. Falconer, after the departure of his visitors, went up into his library. He took down one book after another, but they did not fix his attention as they used to do; he turned over the leaves of Homer, and read some passages about Circe; then took down Bojardo, and read of Morgana and Falerina and Dragontina; then took down Tasso and read of Armida. He would not look at Ariosto's Alcina, because her change into an old woman destroyed all the charm of the previous picture. He dwelt on the enchantress who remained in unaltered beauty. But even this he did only by fits and starts, and found himself continually wandering away towards a more enchanting reality.

He descended to his bedroom, and meditated on ideal beauty in the portraits of Saint Catharine. But he could not help thinking that the ideal might be real, at least in one instance, and he wandered down into his drawing-room. There he sat absorbed in thought, till his two young handmaids appeared with his luncheon. He smiled when he saw them, and sat down to the table as if nothing had disturbed him. Then, taking his stick and his dog, he walked out into the forest.

There was within moderate distance a deep dell, in the bottom of which ran a rivulet, very small in dry weather, but in heavy rains becoming a torrent, which had worn itself a high-banked channel, winding in fantastic curves from side to side of its narrow boundaries. Above this channel old forest trees rose to a great height on both sides of the dell. The slope every here and there was broken by promontories which during centuries the fall of the softer portions of the soil had

formed; and on these promontories were natural platforms,
covered, as they were more or less accessible to the sun, with
grass and moss and fern and foxglove, and every variety of
forest vegetation. These platforms were favourite resorts of
deer, which imparted to the wild scene its own peculiar life.

This was the scene in which, but for the deeper and deeper
wear of the floods and the bolder falls of the promontories,
time had made little change. The eyes of the twelfth century
had seen it much as it appeared to those of the nineteenth. The
ghosts of departed ages might seem to pass through it in
succession, with all their changes of faith and purpose and
manners and costume. To a man who loved to dwell in the
past, there could not be a more congenial scene. One old oak
stood in the centre of one of the green platforms and a portion
of its gnarled roots presented a convenient seat. Mr. Falconer
had frequently passed a day here when alone. The deer had
become too accustomed to him to fly at his approach, and the
dog had been too well disciplined to molest them. There he
had sat for hours at a time, reading his favourite poets. There
was no great poet with some of whose scenes this scenery did
not harmonise. The deep woods that surrounded the dwelling
of Circe, the obscure sylvan valley in which Dante met Virgil,
the forest depths through which Angelica fled, the enchanted
wood in which Rinaldo met the semblance of Armida, the
forest-brook by which Jaques moralised over the wounded
deer, were all reproduced in this single spot, and fancy
peopled it at pleasure with nymphs and genii, fauns and satyrs,
knights and ladies, friars, foresters, hunters, and huntress
maids, till the whole diurnal world seemed to pass away like a
vision. There, for him, Matilda had gathered flowers on the
opposite bank;*Laura had risen from one of the little pools –
resting-places of the stream – to seat herself in the shade;*
Rosalind and Maid Marian had peeped forth from their alleys
green; all different in form, in feature, and in apparel; but now

* Dante, *Purgatorio*, c. 28.
* Or in forma di Ninfa o d' altra Diva,
   Che del più chiaro fondo di Sorga esca,
   E pongasi a seder in sulla riva.

                                         PETRARCA, *Sonetto* 240.

they were all one; each, as she rose in imagination, presented herself under the aspect of the newly known Morgana.

Finding his old imaginations thus disturbed, he arose and walked home. He dined alone, drank a bottle of Madeira as if it had been so much water, summoned the seven sisters to the drawing-room earlier and detained them later than usual, till their music and its old associations had restored him to something like tranquillity. He had always placed the *summum bonum* of life in tranquillity, and not in excitement. He felt that his path was now crossed by a disturbing force, and determined to use his utmost exertions to avoid exposing himself again to its influence.

In this mood the Reverend Doctor Opimian found him one morning in the library reading. He sprang up to meet the divine, exclaiming, 'Ah, dear doctor, I am very glad to see you. Have you any special favourite among the Odes of Pindar?'

The doctor thought this an odd question for the first salutation. He had expected that the first inquiry would have been for the fair convalescent. He divined that the evasion of this subject was the result of an inward struggle. He thought it would be best to fall in with the mood of the questioner, and said, 'Charles Fox's favourite is said to have been the second Olympic; I am not sure that there is, or can be, anything better. What say you?'

*Mr. Falconer*
It may be that something in it touches a peculiar tone of feeling; but to me there is nothing like the ninth Pythian.

*The Rev. Dr. Opimian*
I can understand your fancy for that ode. You see an image of ideal beauty in the nymph Cyrene.

*Mr. Falconer*
'Hidden are the keys of wise persuasion of sacred endearments,'* seems a strange phrase in English; but in Greek the

* κρυπταὶ κλαῖδες ἐντὶ σοφᾶς Πειθοῦς ἱερᾶν φιλοτάτων.
                                                        PINDAR?

words invest a charming sentiment with singular grace. Fit words to words as closely as we may, the difference of the mind which utters them fails to reproduce the true semblance of the thought. The difference of the effect produced, as in this instance, by exactly corresponding words, can only be traced to the essential difference of the Greek and the English mind.

*The Rev. Dr. Opimian*
And indeed, as with the words, so with the image. We are charmed by Cyrene wrestling with the lion; but we should scarcely choose an English girl so doing as the type of ideal beauty.

*Mr. Falconer*
We must draw the image of Cyrene, not from an English girl but from a Greek statue.

*The Rev. Dr. Opimian*
Unless a man is in love, and then to him all images of beauty take something of the form and features of his mistress.

*Mr. Falconer*
That is to say, a man in love sees everything through a false medium. It must be a dreadful calamity to be in love.

*The Rev. Dr. Opimian*
Surely not when all goes well with it.

*Mr. Falconer*
To me it would be the worst of all mischances.

*The Rev. Dr. Opimian*
Every man must be subject to Love once in his life. It is useless to contend with him. 'Love,' says Sophocles, 'is unconquered in battle, and keeps his watch in the soft cheeks of beauty.'*

*Mr. Falconer*
I am afraid, doctor, the Morgana to whom you have intro-

---

* Ἔρως ἀνίκατε μάχαν. κ.τ.λ. *Antigone.*

duced me is a veritable enchantress. You find me here, determined to avoid the spell.

*The Rev. Dr. Opimian*
Pardon me. You were introduced, as Jupiter was to Semele, by thunder and lightning, which was, happily, not quite as fatal.

*Mr. Falconer*
I must guard against its being as fatal in a different sense; otherwise I may be myself the *triste bidental*.* I have aimed at living, like an ancient Epicurean, a life of tranquillity. I had thought myself armed with triple brass against the folds of a three-formed Chimera. What with classical studies, and rural walks and a domestic society peculiarly my own, I led what I considered the perfection of life: 'days so like each other they could not be remembered.'*

*The Rev. Dr. Opimian*
It is vain to make schemes of life. The world will have its slaves, and so will Love.

> Say, if you can, in what you cannot change.
> For such the mind of man, as is the day
> The Sire of Gods and men brings over him.*

*Mr. Falconer*
I presume, doctor, from the complacency with which you speak of Love, you have had no cause to complain of him.

*The Rev. Dr. Opimian*
Quite the contrary. I have been an exception to the rule that 'The course of true love never did run smooth.' Nothing

---

* *Bidental* is usually a place struck by lightning: thence enclosed, and the soil forbidden to be moved. Persius uses it for a person so killed.

* Wordsworth, *The Brothers*.

* Quid placet aut odio est, quod non mutabile credas?
　　τοῖος γὰρ νόος ἐστὶν ἐπιχθονίων ἀνθρώπων,
　　οἷον ἐπ' ἦμαρ ἄγῃσι πατὴρ ἀνδρῶν τε θεῶν τε.

These two quotations form the motto of Knight's *Principles of Taste*.

could run more smooth than mine. I was in love. I proposed. I was accepted. No crossings before. No bickerings after. I drew a prize in the lottery of marriage.

*Mr. Falconer*

It strikes me, doctor, that the lady may say as much.

*The Rev. Dr. Opimian*

I have made it my study to give her cause to say so. And I have found my reward.

*Mr. Falconer*

Still, yours is an exceptional case. For, as far as my reading and limited observation have shown me, there are few happy marriages. It has been said by an old comic poet that a man who brings a wife into his house, brings into it with her either a good or an evil genius.'* And I may add from Juvenal: 'The Gods only know which it will be.'*

*The Rev. Dr. Opimian*

Well, the time advances for the rehearsals of our Aristophanic comedy, and, independently of your promise to visit the Grange, and their earnest desire to see you, you ought to be there to assist in the preliminary arrangements.

*Mr. Falconer*

Before you came, I had determined not to go; for, to tell you the truth, I am afraid of falling in love.

*The Rev. Dr. Opimian*

It is not such a fearful matter. Many have been the better for it.

---

* ὅταν γὰρ ἄλοχον εἰς δόμους ἄγῃ πόσις,
  οὐχ ὡς δοκεῖ γυναῖκα λαμβάνει μόνον,
  ὁμοῦ δὲ τῇδ' ἐπεισκομί ζεται λαβὼν
  καὶ δαίμον' ἤτοι χρηστὸν ἢ τοὐναντίον.

                THEODECTES, *apud Stobaeum.*

* Conjugium petimus partumque uxoris, at illis
  Notum, qui pueri, qualisque futura sit uxor.

                JUV. *Sat.* x. 352–3.

Many have been cured of it. It is one of those disorders which every one must have once.

*Mr. Falconer*
The later the better.

*The Rev. Dr. Opimian*
No the later the worse, if it falls into a season when it cannot be reciprocated.

*Mr. Falconer*
That is just the season for it. If I were sure that it would not be reciprocated, I think I should be content to have gone through it.

*The Rev. Dr. Opimian*
Do you think it would be reciprocated?

*Mr. Falconer*
Oh, no. I only think it possible that it might be.

*The Rev. Dr. Opimian*
Well there is a gentleman doing his best to bring about your wish.

*Mr. Falconer*
Indeed! Who?

*The Rev. Dr. Opimian*
A visitor at the Grange, who seems in great favour with both uncle and niece – Lord Curryfin.

*Mr. Falconer*
Lord Curryfin! I never heard you speak of him but as a person to be laughed at.

*The Rev. Dr. Opimian*
That was my impression of him before I knew him. Barring his absurdities, in the way of lecturing on fish, and of shining in absurd company in the science of pantopragmatics, he has

very much to recommend him: and I discover in him one quality which is invaluable. He does all he can to make himself agreeable to all about him, and he has great tact in seeing how to do it. In any intimate relation of life – with a reasonable wife, for instance – he would be the pink of a good husband.

The doctor was playing, not altogether unconsciously, the part of an innocent Iago. He only said what was true, and he said it with a good purpose; for, with all his repeated resolutions against match-making, he could not dismiss from his mind the wish to see his young friends come together; and he would not have liked to see Lord Curryfin carry off the prize through Mr. Falconer's neglect of his opportunity. Jealousy being the test of love, he thought a spice of it might be not unseasonably thrown in.

*Mr. Falconer*
Notwithstanding your example, doctor, love is to be avoided, because marriage is at best a dangerous experiment. The experience of all time demonstrates that it is seldom a happy condition. Jupiter and Juno to begin with; Venus and Vulcan. Fictions, to be sure, but they show Homer's view of the conjugal state. Agamemnon in the shades, though he congratulates Ulysses on his good fortune in having an excellent wife, advises him not to trust even her too far. Come down to realities, even to the masters of the wise: Socrates with Xantippe; Euripides with his two wives, who made him a woman-hater; Cicero, who was divorced; Marcus Aurelius. – Travel downwards: Dante, who, when he left Florence, left his wife behind him; Milton, whose first wife ran away from him; Shakespeare, who scarcely shines in the light of a happy husband. And if such be the lot of the lights of the world, what can humbler men expect?

*The Rev. Dr. Opimian*
You have given two or three heads of a catalogue which, I admit, might be largely extended. You can never read a history, you can never open a newspaper, without seeing some example of unhappy marriage. But the conspicuous are not the frequent. In the quiet path of everyday life – the

*secretum iter et fallentis semita vitæ* – I could show you many couples who are really comforts and helpmates to each other. Then, above all things, children. The great blessing of old age, the one that never fails, if all else fail, is a daughter.

*Mr. Falconer*
All daughters are not good.

*The Rev. Dr. Opimian*
Most are. Of all relations in life, it is the least disappointing: where parents do not so treat their daughters as to alienate their affections, which unhappily many do.

*Mr. Falconer*
You do not say so much for sons.

*The Rev. Dr. Opimian*
Young men are ambitious, self-willed, self-indulgent, easily corrupted by bad example, of which there is always too much. I cannot say much for those of the present day, though it is not absolutely destitute of good specimens.

*Mr. Falconer*
You know what Paterculus says of those of his own day.

*The Rev. Dr. Opimian*
'The faith of wives towards the proscribed was great; of freed-men, middling; of slaves, some; of sons, none.'* So he says; but there were some: for example, of the sons of Marcus Oppius and Quintus Cicero.* You may observe, by the way, he gives the first place to the wives.

*Mr. Falconer*
Well, that is a lottery in which every man must take his chance. But my scheme of life was perfect.

---

* Id tamen notandum est, fuisse in proscriptos uxorum fidem summam, libertorum mediam, servorum aliquam, filiorum nullam.
                                        PATERCULUS 1. ii. c. 67.
   * A compendious and comprehensive account of these and other instances of filial piety, in the proscription of the second triumvirate, will be found in *Freinshemius; Supplementa Liviania,* cxx. 77–80.

*The Rev. Dr. Opimian*
Perhaps there is something to be said against condemning
seven young women to celibacy.

*Mr. Falconer*
But if such were their choice –

*The Rev. Dr. Opimian*
No doubt there are many reasons why they should prefer the
condition they are placed in to the ordinary chances of
marriage: but, after all, to be married is the natural aspiration
of a young woman, and if favourable conditions presented
themselves –

*Mr. Falconer*
Conditions suitable to their education are scarcely compatible
with their social position.

*The Rev. Dr. Opimian*
They have been educated to be both useful and ornamental.
The ornamental need not, and in their case certainly does not,
damage the useful, which in itself would procure them
suitable matches.

Mr. Falconer shook his head, and, after a brief pause, poured
out a volume of quotation, demonstrating the general un-
happiness of marriage. The doctor responded by as many,
demonstrating the contrary. He paused to take breath. Both
laughed heartily. But the result of the discussion and the
laughter was, that Mr. Falconer was curious to see Lord
Curryfin, and would therefore go to Gryll Grange.

# CHAPTER XIII

## LORD CURRYFIN – SIBERIAN DINNERS – SOCIAL MONOTONY

Ille potens sui
laetusque deget, cui licet in diem
dixisse, Vixi: cras vel atra
    nube polum pater occupato,
vel sole puro: non tamen irritum
quodcumque retro est, efficiet; neque
    diffinget infectumque reddet,
    quod fugiens semel hora vexit.
                    HOR. *Carm.* iii. 29.

Happy the man, and happy he alone,
He who can call today his own:
He who, secure within, can say,
Tomorrow do thy worst, for I have lived today.
Be storm, or calm, or rain, or shine,
The joys I have possessed in spite of fate are mine.
Not heaven itself upon the past has power,
But what has been has been, and I have had my hour.
                    DRYDEN

A large party was assembled at the Grange. Among them
were some of the young ladies who were to form the chorus;
one elderly spinster, Miss Ilex, who passed more than half her
life in visits, and was everywhere welcome, being always
good humoured, agreeable in conversation, having much
knowledge in music; sound judgment in dress, which alone
sufficed to make her valuable to young ladies; a fair amount of
reading, old and new; and on most subjects an opinion of her
own, for which she had always something to say; Mr.
MacBorrowdale, an old friend of Mr. Gryll, a gentleman who
comprised in himself all that Scotland had ever been supposed
to possess of mental, moral, and political philosophy; 'And yet

he bore it not about'; not 'as being loth to wear it out,'* but because he held that there was a time for all things, and that dinner was the time for joviality, and not for argument; Mr. Minim, the amateur composer of the music for the comedy; Mr. Pallet, the amateur painter of the scenery; and last, not least, the newly made acquaintance, Lord Curryfin.

Lord Curryfin was a man on the younger side of thirty, with a good person, handsome features, a powerful voice, and an agreeable delivery. He had a strong memory, much power of application, and a facility of learning rapidly whatever he turned his mind to. But with all this, he valued what he learned less for the pleasure which he derived from the acquisition, than from the effect which it enabled him to produce on others. He liked to shine in conversation, and there was scarcely a subject which could be mooted in any society on which his multifarious attainments did not qualify him to say something. He was readily taken by novelty in doctrine, and followed a new lead with great pertinacity; and in this way he had been caught by the science of pantopragmatics, and firmly believed for a time that a scientific organisation for teaching everybody everything would cure all the evils of society. But being one of those 'over sharp wits whose edges are very soon turned,' he did not adhere to any opinion with sufficient earnestness to be on any occasion betrayed into intemperance in maintaining it. So far from this, if he found any unfortunate opinion in a hopeless minority of the company he happened to be in, he was often chivalrous enough to come to its aid, and see what could be said for it. When lecturing became a mania, he had taken to lecturing; and looking about for an unoccupied subject, he had lighted on the natural history of fish in which he soon became sufficiently proficient to amuse the ladies and astonish the fishermen in any seaside place of fashionable resort. Here he always

---

* We grant, although he had much wit,
  H' was very shy of using it,
  As being loth to wear it out;
  And therefore bore it not about,
  Except on holidays or so,
  As men their best apparel do.

HUDIBRAS.

arranged his lecture-room so that the gentility of his audience could sit on a platform and the natives in a gallery above, and that thus the fishy and tarry odours which the latter were most likely to bring with them might ascend into the upper air, and not mingle with the more delicate fragrances that surrounded the select company below. He took a summer tour to several watering-places, and was thoroughly satisfied with his success. The fishermen at first did not take cordially to him; but their wives attended from curiosity, and brought their husbands with them on nights not favourable to fishing; and by degrees he won on their attention, and they took pleasure in hearing him, though they learned nothing from him that was of any use in their trade. But he seemed to exalt their art in the eyes of themselves and others, and he told them some pleasant anecdotes of strange fish, and of perilous adventures of some of their own craft, which led in due time to the crowding of his gallery. The ladies went, as they always will go, to lectures, where they fancy they learn something, whether they learn anything or not; and on these occasions, not merely to hear the lecture, but to be seen by him. To them, however attractive the lecture might have been, the lecturer was more so. He was an irresistible temptation to matrons with marriageable daughters, and wherever he sojourned he was overwhelmed with invitations. It was a contest who should have him to dinner, and in the simplicity of his heart he ascribed to admiration of his science and eloquence all the courtesies and compliments with which he was everywhere received. He did not like to receive unreturned favours, and never left a place in which he had accepted many invitations without giving in return a ball and supper on a scale of great munificence; which filled up the measure of his popularity, and left on all his guests a very enduring impression of a desire to see him again.

So his time passed pleasantly, with a heart untouched by either love or care, till he fell in at a dinner party with the Reverend Doctor Opimian. The doctor spoke of Gryll Grange and the Aristophanic comedy which was to be produced at Christmas, and Lord Curryfin, with his usual desire to have a finger in every pie, expressed an earnest wish to be introduced to the squire. This was no difficult matter. The doctor had quickly brought it about, and Lord Curryfin had gone over in the doctor's company to pass a few days at the Grange. Here, in a very short time, he had made himself completely at home; and had taken on himself the office of architect, to superintend the construction of the theatre, receiving with due deference instructions on the subject from the Reverend Doctor Opimian.

Sufficient progress had been made in the comedy for the painter and musician to begin work on their respective portions; and Lord Curryfin, whose heart was in his work, passed whole mornings in indefatigable attention to the progress of the building. It was near the house, and was to be approached by a covered way. It was a miniature of the Athenian theatre, from which it differed in having a roof, but it resembled it in the arrangements of the stage and orchestra, and in the graduated series of semicircular seats for the audience.

When dinner was announced, Mr. Gryll took in Miss Ilex, Miss Gryll, of course, took the arm of Lord Curryfin. Mr. Falconer took in one of the young ladies, and placed her on the left hand of the host. The Reverend Dr. Opimian took in another, and was consequently seated between her and Miss Ilex. Mr. Falconer was thus as far removed as possible from the young lady of the house, and was consequently, though he struggled as much as possible against it, frequently *distrait* unconsciously and unwillingly observing Miss Gryll and Lord Curryfin, and making occasional observations very wide of the mark to the fair damsels on his right and left, who set him down in their minds for a very odd young man. The soup and fish were discussed in comparative silence; the entrées not much otherwise; but suddenly a jubilant expression from Mr. MacBorrowdale hailed the disclosure of a large sirloin of beef which figured before Mr. Gryll.

*Mr. MacBorrowdale*
You are a man of taste, Mr. Gryll. That is a handsomer ornament of a dinner-table than clusters of nosegays, and all sorts of uneatable decorations. I detest and abominate the idea of a Siberian dinner, where you just look on fiddle-faddles, while your dinner is behind a screen, and you are served with rations like a pauper.

*The Rev. Dr. Opimian*
I quite agree with Mr. MacBorrowdale. I like to see my dinner. And herein I rejoice to have Addison on my side; for I remember a paper, in which he objects to having roast beef placed on a sideboard. Even in his day it had been displaced to make way for some incomprehensible French dishes, among which he could find nothing to eat.* I do not know what he would have said to its being placed altogether out of sight. Still there is something to be said on the other side. There is hardly one gentleman in twenty who knows how to carve; and as to ladies, though they did know once on a time, they do not now. What can be more pitiable than the right-hand man of the lady of the house, awkward enough in himself, with the dish twisted round to him in the most awkward possible position, digging in unutterable mortification for a joint which he cannot find, and wishing the unanatomisable *volaille* behind a Russian screen with the footmen?

*Mr. MacBorrowdale*
I still like to see the *volaille*. It might be put on table with its joints divided.

*Mr. Gryll*
As that turkey-poult is, Mr. MacBorrowdale, which gives my niece no trouble; but the precaution is not necessary with such a right-hand man as Lord Curryfin, who carves to perfection.

*Mr. MacBorrowdale*
Your arrangements are perfect. At the last of these Siberian dinners at which I had the misfortune to be present, I had offered me, for two of my rations, the tail of a mullet and the drumstick of a fowl. Men who carve behind screens ought to

---

* I was now in great hunger and confusion, when I thought I smelled the agreeable savour of roast beef; but could not tell from which dish it arose, though I did not question but it lay disguised in one of them. Upon turning my head I saw a noble sirloin on the side-table, smoking in the most delicious manner. I had recourse to it more than once, and could not see without some indignation that substantial English dish banished in so ignominious a manner, to make way for French kickshaws. *Tatler*, No. 148.

pass a competitive examination before a jury of gastronomers. Men who carve at a table are drilled by degrees into something like tolerable operators by the mere shame of the public process.

*Mr. Gryll*
I will guarantee you against a Siberian dinner whenever you dine with me.

*The Rev. Dr. Opimian*
Mr. Gryll is a true conservative, in dining.

*Mr. Gryll*
A true conservative, I hope. Not what a *soi-disant* conservative is practically: a man who sails under national colours, hauls them down, and hoists the enemy's. I like old customs. I like a glass of wine with a friend. What say you, doctor? Mr. MacBorrowdale will join us?

*Mr. MacBorrowdale*
Most willingly.

*Miss Gryll*
My uncle and the doctor have got as usual into a discussion, to the great amusement of the old lady who sits between them and says nothing.

*Lord Curryfin*
Perhaps their discussion is too recondite for her.

*Miss Gryll*
No; they never talk before ladies of any subject in which ladies cannot join. And she has plenty to say for herself when she pleases. But when conversation pleases her, she likes to listen and be silent. It strikes me, by a few words that float this way, that they are discussing the Art of Dining. She ought to be a proficient in it, for she lives much in the world, and has met as many persons whom she is equally willing either to meet to-morrow, or never to meet again, as any regular *dineur en ville*. And indeed that is the price that must be paid for society.

Whatever difference of character may lie under the surface, the persons you meet in its circles are externally others yet the same: the same dress, the same manners, the same tastes and opinions, real or assumed. Strongly defined characteristic differences are so few, and artificial general resemblances so many, that in every party you may always make out the same theatrical company. It is like the flowing of a river: it is always different water, but you do not see the difference.

*Lord Curryfin*
For my part I do not like these monotonous exteriors. I like visible character. Your uncle and Mr. MacBorrowdale are characters. Then the Reverend Dr. Opimian. He is not a man made to pattern. He is simple-minded, learned, tolerant, and the quintessence of *bonhomie*. The young gentleman who arrived today, the Hermit of the Folly, is evidently a character. I flatter myself, I am a character (*laughing*).

*Miss Gryll* (laughing)
Indeed you are, or rather many characters in one. I never knew a man of such infinite variety. You seem always to present yourself in the aspect in which those you are with would best wish to see you.

There was some ambiguity in the compliment; but Lord Curryfin took it as implying that his aspect in all its variety was agreeable to the young lady. He did not then dream of a rival in the Hermit of the Folly.

## CHAPTER XIV

## MUSIC AND PAINTING – JACK OF DOVER

οὐ φίλος, ὅς κρατῆρι παρὰ πλέῳ οἰνοποτά ζων
   νείκεα καὶ πόλεμον δακρυόεντα λέγει,
ἀλλ' ὅστις, Μουσέων τε καὶ ἀγλαὰ δῶρ' 'Αφροδίτης
   συμμίσγων ἐρατῆς μνήσκεται εὐφροσύνης.
                         ANACREON.

I love not him, who o'er the wine-cup's flow
Talks but of war, and strife, and scenes of woe:
But him who can the Muses' gifts employ,
To mingle love and song with festal joy.

The dinner and dessert passed away. The ladies retired to the
drawing-room: the gentlemen discoursed over their wine.
Mr. MacBorrowdale pronounced a eulogium on the port,
which was cordially echoed by the divine in regard to the
claret.

*Mr. Falconer*
Doctor, your tastes and sympathies are very much with the
Greeks; but I doubt if you would have liked their wine.
Condiments of sea-water and turpentine must have given it an
odd flavour; and mixing water with it, in the proportion of
three to one, must have reduced the strength of merely
fermented liquor to something like the smallest ale of Christ-
ophero Sly.

*The Rev. Dr. Opimian*
I must say I should not like to put either salt water or
turpentine into this claret: they would not improve its bou-
quet; nor to dilute it with any portion of water: it has to my
mind, as it is, just the strength it ought to have, and not more.
But the Greek taste was so exquisite in all matters in which we
can bring it to the test, as to justify a strong presumption that
in matters in which we cannot test it, it was equally correct.

Salt water and turpentine do not suit our wine: it does not follow that theirs had not in it some basis of contrast, which may have made them pleasant in combination. And it was only a few of their wines that were so treated.

*Lord Curryfin*
Then it could not have been much like their drink of the present day. 'My master cannot be right in his mind,' said Lord Byron's man Fletcher, 'or he would not have left Italy, where we had everything, to go to a country of savages; there is nothing to eat in Greece but tough billy-goats, or to drink but spirits of turpentine.'*

*The Rev. Dr. Opimian*
There is an ambiguous present, which somewhat perplexes me, in an epigram of Rhianus, 'Here is a vessel of half-wine, half-turpentine, and a singularly lean specimen of kid: the sender, Hippocrates, is worthy of all praise.'* Perhaps this was a doctor's present to a patient. Alcæus, Anacreon, and Nonnus could not have sung as they did under the inspiration of spirit of turpentine. We learn from Athenæus, and Pliny, and the old comedians, that the Greeks had a vast variety of wine, enough to suit every variety of taste. I infer the unknown from the known. We know little of their music. I have no doubt it was as excellent in its kind as their sculpture.

*Mr. Minim*
I can scarcely think that, sir. They seem to have had only the minor key, and to have known no more of counter-point than they did of perspective.

*The Rev. Dr. Opimian*
Their system of painting did not require perspective. Their

---

* Trelawny's *Recollections*.
* ἥμισυ μὲν πίσσης κωνίτιδος, ἥμισυ δ' οἴνου,
   'Αρχῖν', ἀτρεκέως ἥδε λάγυνος ἔχει·
   λεπτοτέρης δ' οὐκ οἶδ' ἐρίφου κρέας· πλὴν ὅ γε πέμψας
   αἰνεῖσθαι πάντων ἄξιος Ἱπποκράτης.

*Anthologia Palatina, Appendix,* 72.

main subject was on one foreground. Buildings, rocks, trees, served simply to indicate, not to delineate, the scene.

*Mr. Falconer*
I must demur to their having only the minor key. The natural ascent of the voice is in the major key, and with their exquisite sensibility to sound they could not have missed the obvious expression of cheerfulness. With their three scales, diatonic, chromatic, and enharmonic, they must have exhausted every possible expression of feeling. Their scales were in true intervals; they had really major and minor tones; we have neither, but a confusion of both. They had both sharps and flats: we have neither, but a mere set of semitones, which serve for both. In their enharmonic scale the fineness of their ear perceived distinctions which are lost on the coarseness of ours.

*Mr. Minim*
With all that they never got beyond melody. They had no harmony, in our sense. They sang only in unisons and octaves.

*Mr. Falconer*
It is not clear that they did not sing in fifths. As to harmony in one sense, I will not go so far as to say with Ritson that the only use of the harmony is to spoil the melody; but I will say, that to my taste a simple accompaniment, in strict subordination to the melody, is far more agreeable than that Niagara of sound under which it is now the fashion to bury it.

*Mr. Minim*
In that case, you would prefer a song with a simple piano-forte accompaniment to the same song on the Italian stage.

*Mr. Falconer*
A song sung with feeling and expression is good, however accompanied. Otherwise, the pianoforte is not much to my mind. All its intervals are false, and temperament is a poor substitute for natural intonation. Then its incapability of sustaining a note has led, as the only means of producing effect, to those infinitesimal subdivisions of sound, in which

all sentiment and expression are twittered and frittered into
nothingness.

*The Rev. Dr. Opimian*
I quite agree with you. The other day a band passed my gate
playing 'The Campbells are coming'; but instead of the fine
old Scotch lilt, and the emphasis on 'Oho! oho!' what they
actually played was, 'The Ca-a-a-a-ampbells are co-o-o-o-
oming, Oh-o-ho-o-o! Oh-o-ho-o-o'; I thought to myself,
There is the essence and quintessence of modern music. I like
the old organ-music such as it was, when there were no keys
but C and F, and every note responded to a syllable. The effect
of the prolonged and sustained sound must have been truly
magnificent:

> 'Where, through the long-drawn aisle and fretted vault,
>  The pealing anthem swelled the note of praise.'

Who cares to hear sacred music on a piano?

*Mr. Minim*
Yet I must say that there is a great charm in that brilliancy of
execution which is an exclusively modern and very modern
accomplishment.

*Mr. Falconer*
To those who perceive it. All things are as they are perceived.
To me music has not charm without expression.

*Lord Curryfin (who, having observed* Mr. MacBorrowdale's
*determination not to be drawn into an argument, amused himself with
asking his opinion on all subjects).*

What is your opinion, Mr. Macborrowdale?

*Mr. MacBorrowdale*
I hold to the opinion I have already expressed, that this is as
good a glass of port as ever I tasted.

*Lord Curryfin*
I mean your opinion of modern music and musical instruments.

*Mr. MacBorrowdale*
The organ is very good for psalms, which I never sing, and the pianoforte for jigs, which I never dance. And if I were not to hear either of them from January to December, I should not complain of the privation.

*Lord Curryfin*
You are an utilitarian, Mr. MacBorrowdale. You are all for utility – public utility – and you see none in music.

*Mr. MacBorrowdale*
Nay, not exactly so. If devotion is good, if cheerfulness is good, and if music promotes each of them in proper time and place, music is useful. If I am as devout without the organ, and as cheerful without the piano, as I ever should be with them, that may be the defect of my head or my ear. I am not for forcing my tastes or no-tastes on other people. Let every man enjoy himself in his own way, while he does not annoy others. I would not deprive you of your enjoyment of a brilliant symphony, and I hope you would not deprive me of my enjoyment of a glass of old wine.

*The Rev. Dr. Opimian*

'Tres mihi convivæ prope dissentire videntur,
Poscentes vario multum diversa palato.'*

*Mr. Falconer*
Nor our reverend friend of the pleasure of a classical quotation.

*The Rev. Dr. Opimian*
And the utility, too, sir: for I think I am indebted to one for the pleasure of your acquaintance.

*Mr. Falconer*
When you did me the honour to compare my house to the Palace of Circe. The gain was mine.

* Three guests dissent most widely in their wishes:
  With different taste they call for different dishes.

*Mr. Pallet*
You admit, sir, that the Greeks had no knowledge of perspective.

*The Rev. Dr. Opimian*
Observing that they had no need of it. Their subject was a foreground like a relievo. Their background was a symbol, not a representation. 'No knowledge' is perhaps too strong. They had it where it was essential. They drew a peristyle, as it appeared to the eye, as accurately as we can do. In short, they gave to each distinct object its own proper perspective, but to separate objects they did not give their relative perspective, for the reason I have given, that they did not need it.

*Mr. Falconer*
There is to me one great charm in their painting, as we may judge from the specimens in Pompeii, which, though not their greatest works, indicate their school. They never crowded their canvas with figures. They presented one, two, three, four, or at most five persons, preferring one and rarely exceeding three. These persons were never lost in the profusion of scenery, dress, and decoration. They had clearly defined outlines, and were agreeable objects from any part of the room in which they were placed.

*Mr. Pallet*
They must have lost much in beauty of detail.

*The Rev. Dr. Opimian*
Therein is the essential difference of ancient and modern taste. Simple beauty – of idea in poetry, of sound in music, of figure in painting – was their great characteristic. Ours is detail in all these matters, overwhelming detail. We have not grand outlines for the imagination of the spectator or hearer to fill up: his imagination has no play of its own: it is overloaded with *minutiæ* and kaleidoscopical colours.

*Lord Curryfin*
Detail has its own beauty. I have admired a Dutch picture of a butcher's shop, where all the charm was in detail.

*The Rev. Dr. Opimian*
I cannot admire anything of the kind. I must take pleasure in the thing represented before I can derive any from the representation.

*Mr. Pallet*
I am afraid, sir, as our favourite studies all lead us to extreme opinions you think the Greek painting was the better for not having perspective, and the Greek music for not having harmony.

*The Rev. Dr. Opimian*
I think they had as much perspective and as much harmony as was consistent with that simplicity which characterised their painting and music as much as their poetry.

*Lord Curryfin*
What is your opinion, Mr. MacBorrowdale?

*Mr. MacBorrowdale*
I think you may just buz that bottle before you.

*Lord Curryfin*
I mean your opinion of Greek perspective?

*Mr. MacBorrowdale*
Troth, I am of opinion that a bottle looks smaller at a distance than when it is close by, and I prefer it as a full-sized object in foreground.

*Lord Curryfin*
I have often wondered that a gentleman so well qualified as you are to discuss all subjects should so carefully avoid discussing any.

*Mr. MacBorrowdale*
After dinner, my lord, after dinner. I work hard all the morning at serious things, sometimes till I get a headache, which, however, does not often trouble me. After dinner I like to crack my bottle and chirp and talk nonsense, and fit myself for the company of Jack of Dover.

*Lord Curryfin*
Jack of Dover! Who was he?

*Mr. MacBorrowdale*
He was a man who travelled in search of a greater fool than
himself, and did not find him.*

*The Rev. Dr. Opimian*
He must have lived in odd times. In our days he would not
have gone far without falling in with a teetotaller, or a decimal
coinage man, or a school-for-all man, or a competitive
examination man, who would not allow a drayman to lower a
barrel into a cellar unless he could expound the mathematical
principles by which he performed the operation.

*Mr. MacBorrowdale*
Nay, that is all pragmatical fooling. The fooling Jack looked
for was jovial fooling, fooling to the top of his bent, excellent
fooling, which, under the semblance of folly, was both merry
and wise. He did not look for mere unmixed folly, of which
there never was a deficiency. The fool he looked for was one
which it takes a wise man to make – a Shakespearian fool.*

*The Rev. Dr. Opimian*
In that sense he might travel far, and return, as he did in his
own day, without having found the fool he looked for.

*Mr. MacBorrowdale*
A teetotaller! Well! He is the true Heautontimorumenos, the
self-punisher, with a jug of toast-and-water for his Christmas
wassail. So far his folly is merely pitiable, but his intolerance
makes it offensive. He cannot enjoy his own tipple unless he
can deprive me of mine. A fox that has lost his tail. There is no

* *Jacke of Dover His Quest of Inquirie, or His Privy Search for the Veriest
Foole in England.* London, 1604. Reprinted for the Percy Society, 1842.
  * Œuvre, ma foi, où n'est facile atteindre:
    Pourtant qu'il faut parfaitement sage être,
    Pour le vrai fol bien naïvement feindre.

Eutrapel, p. 28.

tyrant like a thorough-paced reformer. I drink to his own reformation.

*Mr. Gryll*

He is like Bababec's faquir, who sat in a chair full of nails, *pour avoir de la considération*. But the faquir did not want others to do the same. He wanted all the consideration for himself, and kept all the nails for himself. If these meddlers would do the like by their toast-and-water, nobody would begrudge it them.

*The Rev. Dr. Opimian*

Now, sir, if the man who has fooled the greatest number of persons to the top of their bent were to be adjudged the fittest companion for Jack of Dover, you would find him in a distinguished meddler with everything, who has been for half-a-century the merry-andrew of a vast arena which he calls moral and political science, but which has in it a dash of everything that has ever occupied human thought.

*Lord Curryfin*

I know whom you mean; but he is a great man in his way, and has done much good.

*The Rev. Dr. Opimian*

He has helped to introduce much change; whether for good or for ill remains to be seen. I forgot he was your lordship's friend. I apologise, and drink to his health.

*Lord Curryfin*

Oh! pray, do not apologise to me. I would not have my friendships, tastes, pursuits, and predilections interfere in the slightest degree with the fullest liberty of speech on all persons and things. There are many who think with you that he is a moral and political Jack of Dover. So be it. Time will bring him to his level.

*Mr. MacBorrowdale*

I will only say of the distinguished personage, that Jack of Dover would not pair off with him. This is the true universal science, the oracle of *La Dive Bouteille*.

*Mr. Gryll*
It is not exactly Greek music, Mr. Minim, that you are giving us for our Aristophanic choruses.

*Mr. Minim*
No, sir; I have endeavoured to give you a good selection, as appropriate as I can make it.

*Mr. Pallet*
Neither am I giving you Greek painting for the scenery. I have taken the liberty to introduce perspective.

*The Rev. Dr. Opimian*
Very rightly both, for Aristophanes in London.

*Mr. Minim*
Besides, sir, we must have such music as your young ladies can sing.

*The Rev. Dr. Opimian*
Assuredly; and, so far as we have yet heard them rehearse, they sing it delightfully.

After a little more desultory conversation, they adjourned to the drawing-rooms.

# CHAPTER XV

## EXPRESSION IN MUSIC – THE DAPPLED PALFREY – LOVE AND AGE – COMPETITIVE EXAMINATION

τοῦτο βίος, τοῦτ' αὐτό· τρυφὴ βίος ἔρρετ' ἀνίαι·
ξωῆς ἀνθρώποις ὀλίγος χρόνος ἄρτι Δύαιος,
ἄρτι χοροί, στέφανοί τε φιλανθέες ἄρτι γυναῖκες.
σήμερον ἐσθλὰ πάθω, τὸ γὰρ αὔριον οὐδενὶ δῆλον.

*Anthologia Palatina*, v. 72.

This, this is life, when pleasure drives out care.
Short is the span of time we each may share.
To-day, while love, wine, song, the hours adorn,
To-day we live: none know the coming morn.

Lord Curryfin's assiduities to Miss Gryll had discomposed Mr. Falconer more than he chose to confess to himself. Lord Curryfin, on entering the drawing-rooms, went up immediately to the young lady of the house; and Mr. Falconer, to the amazement of the reverend doctor, sat down in the outer drawing-room on a sofa by the side of Miss Ilex, with whom he entered into conversation.

In the inner drawing-room some of the young ladies were engaged with music, and were entreated to continue their performance. Some of them were conversing, or looking over new publications.

After a brilliant symphony, performed by one of the young visitors, in which runs and crossings of demisemi-quavers in *tempo prestissimo* occupied the principal share, Mr. Falconer asked Miss Ilex how she liked it.

*Miss Ilex*
I admire it as a splendid piece of legerdemain; but it expresses nothing.

*Mr. Falconer*
It is well to know that such things can be done; and when we

have reached the extreme complications of art we may hope to return to Nature and simplicity.

*Miss Ilex*
Not that it is impossible to reconcile execution and expression. Rubini identified the redundancies of ornament with the overflowings of feeling, and the music of Donizetti furnished him most happily with the means of developing this power. I never felt so transported out of myself as when I heard him sing *Tu che al ciel spiegasti l'ali.*

*Mr. Falconer*
Do you place Donizetti above Mozart?

*Miss Ilex*
Oh, surely not. But for supplying expressive music to a singer like Rubini, I think Donizetti has no equal; at any rate no superior. For music that does not require, and does not even suit, such a singer, but which requires only to be correctly interpreted to be universally recognised as the absolute perfection of melody, harmony, and expresssion, I think Mozart has none. Beethoven perhaps: he composed only one opera, *Fidelio;* but what an opera that is! What an effect in the sudden change of the key, when Leonora throws herself between her husband and Pizarro: and again, in the change of the key with the change of the scene, when we pass from the prison to the hall of the palace! What pathos in the songs of affection, what grandeur in the songs of triumph, what wonderful combinations in the accompaniments, where a perpetual stream of counter-melody creeps along in the bass, yet in perfect harmony with the melody above!

*Mr. Falconer*
What say you to Haydn?

*Miss Ilex*
Haydn has not written operas, and my principal experience is derived from the Italian theatre. But his music is essentially dramatic. It is a full stream of perfect harmony in subjection to exquisite melody; and in simple ballad-strains, that go direct

to the heart, he is almost supreme and alone. Think of that air with which every one is familiar, 'My mother bids me bind my hair': the graceful flow of the first part, the touching effect of the semitones in the second: with true intonation and true expression, the less such an air is accompanied the better.

*Mr. Falconer*
There is a beauty and an appeal to the heart in ballads which will never lose its effect except on those with whom the pretence of fashion overpowers the feeling of Nature.*

*Miss Ilex*
It is strange, however, what influence that pretence has in overpowering all natural feelings, not in music alone.

'Is it not curious,' thought the doctor, 'that there is only one old woman in the room, and that my young friend should have selected her for the object of his especial attention?'

But a few simple notes struck on the ear of his young friend, who rose from the sofa and approached the singer. The doctor took his place to cut off his retreat.

Miss Gryll, who, though a proficient in all music, was particularly partial to ballads, had just begun to sing one.

### THE DAPPLED PALFREY*

'My traitorous uncle has wooed for himself:
Her father has sold her for land and for pelf:
My steed, for whose equal the world they might search,
In mockery they borrow to bear her to church.

Oh! there is one path through the forest so green,
Where thou and I only, my palfrey, have been:
We traversed it oft, when I rode to her bower
To tell my love tale through the rift of the tower.

* Braham said something like this to a Parliamentary Committee on Theatres in 1832.

* Founded on *Le Vair Palefroi:* among the *Fabliaux* published by Barbazan.

Thou know'st not my words, but thy instinct is good:
By the road to the church lies the path through the wood:
Thy instinct is good, and her love is as true:
Thou wilt see thy way homeward: dear palfrey, adieu.'

They feasted full late and full early they rose,
And churchward they rode more than half in a doze:
The steed in an instant broke off from the throng,
And pierced the green path, which he bounded along.

In vain was pursuit, though some followed pell-mell:
Through bramble and thicket they floundered and fell.
On the backs of their coursers some dozed as before,
And missed not the bride till they reached the church
door.

The knight from his keep on the forest-bound gazed:
The drawbridge was down, the portcullis was raised:
And true to his hope came the palfrey amain,
With his only loved lady, who checked not the rein.

The drawbridge went up: the portcullis went down:
The chaplain was ready with bell, book and gown:
The wreck of the bride-train arrived at the gate,
The bride showed the ring, and they muttered 'Too late!'

'Not too late for a feast, though too late for a fray;
What's done can't be undone: make peace while you
may:'
So spake the young knight, and the old ones complied;
And quaffed a deep health to the bridegroom and bride.

Mr. Falconer had listened to the ballad with evident pleasure. He turned to resume his place on the sofa, but finding it
preoccupied by the doctor, he put on a look of disappointment, which seemed to the doctor exceedingly comic.

'Surely,' thought the doctor, 'he is not in love with the old
maid,'

Miss Gryll gave up her place to a young lady, who in her
turn sang a ballad of a different character.

## LOVE AND AGE

I played with you 'mid cowslips blowing,
When I was six and you were four;
When garlands weaving, flower-balls throwing,
Were pleasures soon to please no more.
Through groves and meads, o'er grass and heather,
With little playmates, to and fro,
We wandered hand in hand together;
But that was sixty years ago.

You grew a lovely roseate maiden,
And still our early love was strong;
Still with no care our days were laden,
They glided joyously along;
And I did love you very dearly,
How dearly words want power to show;
I thought your heart was touched as nearly;
But that was fifty years ago.

The other lovers came around you,
Your beauty grew from year to year.
And many a splendid circle found you
The centre of its glittering sphere.
I saw you then, first vows forsaking,
On rank and wealth your hand bestow;
Oh, then I thought my heart was breaking. –
But that was forty years ago.

And I lived on to wed another;
No cause she gave me to repine;
And when I heard you were a mother,
I did not wish the children mine.
My own young flock, in fair progression
Made up a pleasant Christmas row:
My joy in them was past expression, –
But that was thirty years ago.

You grew a matron plump and comely,
You dwelt in fashion's brighter blaze;
My earthly lot was far more homely;
But I too had my festal days.
No merrier eyes have ever glistened
Around the hearthstone's wintry glow,
Than when my youngest child was christened, –
But that was twenty years ago.

Time passed. My eldest girl was married,
And I am now a grandsire grey;
One pet of four years old I've carried
Among the wild-flowered meads to play.
In our old fields of childish pleasure,
Where now, as then, the cowslips blow,
She fills her basket's ample measure, –
And that is not ten years ago.

But though first love's impassioned blindness
Has passed away in colder light,
I still have thought of you with kindness,
And shall do, till our last good-night.
The ever rolling silent hours
Will bring a time we shall not know,
When our young days of gathering flowers
Will be an hundred years ago.

*Miss Ilex*
That is a melancholy song. But of how many first loves is it
the true tale! And how many are far less happy!

*The Rev. Dr. Opimian*
It is simple, and well sung, with a distinctness of articulation
not often heard.

*Miss Ilex*
That young lady's voice is a perfect contralto. It is singularly
beautiful, and I applaud her for keeping within her natural
compass, and not destroying her voice by forcing it upwards,
as too many do.

*The Rev. Dr. Opimian*

Forcing, forcing, seems to be the rule of life. A young lady who forces her voice into *altissimo,* and a young gentleman who forces his mind into a receptacle for a chaos of crudities, are pretty much on a par. Both do ill, where, if they were contented with attainments within the limits of natural taste and natural capacity, they might both do well. As to the poor young men, many of them become mere crammed fowls, with the same result as Hermogenes, who, after astonishing the world with his attainments at seventeen came to a sudden end at the age of twenty-five, and spent the rest of a long life in hopeless imbecility.

*Miss Ilex*

The poor young men can scarcely help themselves. They are not held qualified for a profession unless they have overloaded their understanding with things of no use in it; incongruous things too, which could never be combined into the pursuits of natural taste.

*The Rev. Dr. Opimian*

Very true. Brindley would not have passed as a canal-maker, nor Edward Williams* as a bridge-builder. I saw the other day some examination papers which would have infallibly excluded Marlborough from the army and Nelson from the navy. I doubt if Haydn would have passed as a composer before a committee of lords like one of his pupils, who insisted on demonstrating to him that he was continually sinning against the rules of counterpoint; on which Haydn said to him, 'I thought I was to teach you, but it seems you are to teach me, and I do not want a preceptor,' and thereon he wished his lordship a good-morning. Fancy Watt being asked how much Joan of Naples got for Avignon when she sold it to Pope Clement the Sixth, and being held unfit for an engineer because he could not tell.

*Miss Ilex*

That is an odd question, doctor. But how much did she get for it?

* The builder of Pont-y-Pryd.

*The Rev. Dr. Opimian*
Nothing. He promised ninety thousand golden florins, but he did not pay one of them: and that, I suppose, is the profound sense of the question. It is true he paid her after a fashion, in his own peculiar coin. He absolved her of the murder of her first husband, and perhaps he thought that was worth the money. But how many of our legislators could answer the question? Is it not strange that candidates for seats in Parliament should not be subjected to competitive examination? Plato and Persius* would furnish good hints for it. I should like to see honourable gentlemen having to answer such questions as are deemed necessary tests for government clerks, before they would be held qualified candidates for seats in the legislature. That would be something like a reform in the Parliament. Oh that it were so, and I were the examiner! Ha, ha, ha, what a comedy!

The doctor's hearty laugh was contagious, and Miss Ilex joined in it. Mr. MacBorrowdale came up.

*Mr. MacBorrowdale*
You are as merry as if you had discovered the object of Jack of Dover's quest.

*The Rev. Dr. Opimian*
Something very like it. We have an honourable gentleman under competitive examination for a degree in legislative wisdom.

*Mr. MacBorrowdale*
Truly, that is fooling competition to the top of its bent.

*The Rev. Dr. Opimian*
Competitive examination for clerks, and none for legislators, is not this an anomaly? Ask the honourable member for Muckborough on what acquisitions in history and mental and moral philosophy he founds his claim of competence to make laws for the nation. He can only tell you that he has been

* Plato, *Alcibiades,* i; Persius, *Sat.* iv.

chosen as the most conspicuous Grub among the moneygrubs
of his borough to be the representative of all that is sordid,
selfish, hard-hearted, unintellectual, and antipatriotic, which
are the distinguishing qualities of the majority among them.
Ask a candidate for a clerkship what are his qualifications? He
may answer 'All that are requisite: reading, writing, and
arithmetic.' 'Nonsense,' says the questioner. 'Do you know
the number of miles in direct distance from Timbuctoo to the
top of Chimborazo?' 'I do not,' says the candidate. 'Then you
will not do for a clerk,' says the competitive examiner. Does
Moneygrub of Muckborough know? he does not; nor anything else. The clerk may be able to answer some of the
questions put to him. Moneygrub could not answer one of
them. But he is very fit for a legislator.

*Mr. MacBorrowdale*
Eh! but he is subjected to a pretty severe competitive examination of his own, by what they call a consituency, who just put
him to the test in the art of conjuring, to see if he can shift
money from his own pocket into theirs, without any inconve-
nient third party being aware of the transfer.

# CHAPTER XVI

## MISS NIPHET – THE THEATRE – THE LAKE – DIVIDED ATTRACTION – INFALLIBLE SAFETY

> Amiam: che non ha tregua
> Con gli anni umana vita, e si dilegua.
> Amiam: che il sol si muore, e poi rinasce;
> A noi sua breve luce
> S'asconde, e il sonno eterna notte adduce.
>
> TASSO, *Aminta.*

> Love, while youth knows its prime,
> For mortal life can make no truce with time.
> Love: for the sun goes down to rise as bright;
> To us his transient light
> Is veiled, and sleep comes on with everlasting night.

Lord Curryfin was too much a man of the world to devote his attentions in society exclusively to one, and make them the subject of special remark. He left the inner drawing-room, and came up to the doctor to ask him if he knew the young lady who had sung the last ballad. The doctor knew her well. She was Miss Niphet, the only daughter of a gentleman of fortune, residing a few miles distant.

*Lord Curryfin*
As I looked at her while she was singing, I thought of Southey's description of Laila's face in *Thalaba*

> A broad light floated o'er its marble paleness,
> As the wind waved the fountain fire.

Marble paleness suits her well. There is something statuesque in her whole appearance. I could not help thinking what an admirable Camilla she would make in Cimarosa's *Orazii*. Her features are singularly regular. They had not much play, but the expression of her voice was such as if she felt the full force of every sentiment she uttered.

*The Rev. Dr. Opimian*
I consider her to be a person of very deep feeling, which she
does not choose should appear on the surface. She is animated
in conversation when she is led into it. Otherwise, she is silent
and retiring, but obliging in the extreme; always ready to take
part in anything that is going forward. She never needs, for
example, being twice asked to sing. She is free from the vice
which Horace ascribes to all singers, of not complying when
asked, and never leaving off when they have once begun. If
this be a general rule, she is an exception to it.

*Lord Curryfin*
I rather wonder she does not tinge her cheeks with a slight
touch of artificial red, just as much as would give her a sort of
blush-rose complexion.

*Miss Ilex*
You will not wonder when you know her better. The
artificial, the false in any degree, however little, is impossible
to her. She does not show all she thinks and feels, but what she
does show is truth itself.

*Lord Curryfin*
And what part is she to take in the Aristophanic comedy?

*The Rev. Dr. Opimian*
She is the leader of the chorus.

*Lord Curryfin*
I have not seen her at the rehearsals.

*The Rev. Dr. Opimian*
So far her place has been supplied. You will see her at the next.

In the meantime, Mr. Falconer had gone into the inner
drawing-room, sat down by Miss Gryll, and entered into
conversation with her. The doctor observed them from a
distance, but with all the opportunity he had had for observation he was still undetermined in his opinion of the impression
they might have made on each other.

'It is well,' he said to himself, 'that Miss Ilex is an old maid. If she were as young as Morgana, I think she would win our young friend's heart. Her mind is evidently much to his mind. But so would Morgana's be, if she could speak it as freely. She does not; why not? To him at any rate. She seems under no restraint to Lord Curryfin. A good omen, perhaps, I never saw a couple so formed for each other. Heaven help me! I cannot help harping on that string. After all, the Vestals are the obstacle.'

Lord Curryfin, seeing Miss Niphet sitting alone at the side of the room, changed his place, sate down by her, and entered into conversation on the topics of the day, novels, operas, pictures, and various phenomena of London Life. She kept up the ball with him very smartly. She was every winter, May, and June, in London, mixed much in society, and saw everything that was to be seen. Lord Curryfin, with all his Protean accomplishments, could not start a subject on which she had not something to say. But she originated nothing. He spoke, and she answered. One thing he remarked as singular, that though she spoke with knowledge of many things, she did not speak as with taste or distaste of any. The world seemed to flow under her observation without even ruffling the surface of her interior thoughts. This perplexed his versatile lordship. He thought the young lady would be a subject worth studying: it was clear that she was a character. So far so well. He felt that he should not rest satisfied till he was able to define it.

The theatre made rapid progress. The walls were completed. The building was roofed in. The stage portion was so far finished as to allow Mr. Pallet to devote every morning to the scenery. the comedy was completed. The music was composed. The rehearsals went on with vigour, but for the present in the drawing-rooms.

Miss Niphet, returning one morning from a walk before breakfast, went into the theatre to see its progress, and found Lord Curryfin swinging over the stage on a seat suspended by long ropes from above the visible scene. He did not see her. He was looking upwards, not as one indulging in an idle pastime, but as one absorbed in serious meditation. All at once the seat was drawn up, and he disappeared in the blue canvas that represented the sky. She was not aware that gymnastics were to form part of the projected entertainment, and went away, associating the idea of his lordship, as many had done before, with something like a feeling of the ludicrous.

Miss Niphet was not much given to laughter, but whenever she looked at Lord Curryfin during breakfast she could not quite suppress a smile which hovered on her lips, and which was even the more forced on her by the contrast between his pantomimic disappearance and his quiet courtesy and remarkably good manners in company. The lines of Dryden –

> A man so various, that he seemed to be
> Not one, but all mankind's epitome,

– passed through her mind as she looked at him.

Lord Curryfin noticed the suppressed smile, but did not apprehend that it had any relation to himself. He thought some graceful facetiousness had presented itself to the mind of the young lady, and that she was amusing herself with her own fancy. It was, however, to him another touch of character, that lighted up her statuesque countenance with a new and peculiar beauty. By degrees her features resumed their accustomed undisturbed serenity. Lord Curryfin felt satisfied that in that aspect he had somewhere seen something like her, and after revolving a series of recollections, he remembered that it was a statue of Melpomene.

There was in the park a large lake, encircled with varieties of woodland, and by its side was a pavilion, to which Miss Niphet often resorted to read in an afternoon. And at no great distance from it was the boat-house, to which Lord Curryfin often resorted for a boat, to row or sail on the water. Passing the pavilion in the afternoon, he saw the young lady, and entering into conversation, ascertained what had so amused her in the morning. He told her he had been trying – severally by himself, and collectively with the workmen – the strength of the suspending lines for the descent of the Chorus of Clouds in the Aristophanic comedy. She said she had been very ungrateful to laugh at the result of his solicitude for the safety of herself and her young friends. He said that in having moved her to smile, even at his expense, he considered himself amply repaid.

From this time they often met in the pavilion, that is to say, he often found her reading there on his way to a boat, and stopped awhile to converse with her. They had always plenty to say, and it resulted that he was always sorry to leave her, and she was always sorry to part with him. By degrees the feeling of the ludicrous ceased to be the predominant sentiment which she associated with him. *L'amour vient sans qu'on y pense.*

The days shortened, and all things were sufficiently advanced to admit of rehearsals in the theatre. The hours from twelve to two – from noon to luncheon – were devoted to this pleasant pastime. At luncheon there was much merriment over the recollection of the morning's work, and after luncheon there was walking in the park, rowing or sailing on the lake, riding or driving in the adjacent country, archery in a spacious field; and in bad weather billiards, reading in the library, music in the drawing-rooms, battledore and shuttlecock in the hall; in short, all the methods of passing time agreeably which are available to good company, when there are ample means of space for their exercise; to say nothing of making love, which Lord Curryfin did with all delicacy and discretion – directly to Miss Gryll, as he had begun, and indirectly to Miss Niphet, for whom he felt an involuntary and almost unconscious admiration. He had begun to apprehend that with the former he had a dangerous rival in the Hermit of the Folly, and he thought the latter had sufficient charms to console even Orlando for the loss of Angelica. In short, Miss Gryll had first made him think of marriage, and whenever he thought his hopes were dim in that quarter, he found an antidote to despair in the contemplation of the statue-like damsel.

Mr. Falconer took more and more pleasure in Miss Gryll's society, but he did not declare himself. He was more than once on the point of doing so, but the images of the Seven Sisters rose before him, and he suspended the intention. On these occasions he always went home for a day or two to fortify his resolution against his heart. Thus he passed his time between the Grange and the Tower, 'Letting I dare not wait upon I would.'

Miss Gryll had listened to Lord Curryfin. She had neither

encouraged nor discouraged him. She thought him the most amusing person she had ever known. She liked his temper, his acquirements, and his manners. She could not divest herself of that feeling of the ludicrous which everybody seemed to associate with him; but she thought the chances of life presented little hope of a happier marriage than a woman who would fall in with his tastes and pursuits – which, notwithstanding their tincture of absurdity, were entertaining and even amiable – might hope for with him. Therefore she would not say No, though, when she thought of Mr. Falconer, she could not say Yes.

Lord Curryfin invented a new sail of infallible safety, which resulted, like most similar inventions in capsizing the inventor on the first trial. Miss Niphet, going one afternoon, later than usual, to her accustomed pavilion, found his lordship scrambling up the bank, and his boat, keel upwards, at some little distance in the lake. For a moment her usual self-command forsook her. She held out both hands to assist him up the bank, and as soon as he stood on dry land, dripping like a Triton in trousers, she exclaimed in such a tone as he had never before heard, 'Oh! my dear lord!' Then as if conscious of her momentary aberration, she blushed with a deeper blush than that of the artificial rose which he had once thought might improve her complexion. She attempted to withdraw her hands, but he squeezed them both ardently, and exclaimed in his turn, like a lover in a tragedy –

'Surely till now I never looked on beauty.'

She was on the point of saying, 'Surely, before now you have looked on Miss Gryll,' but she checked herself. She was content to receive the speech as a sudden ebullition of gratitude for sympathy, and, disengaging her hands, she insisted on his returning immediately to the house to change his 'dank and dripping weeds.'

As soon as he was out of sight she went to the boat-house to summon the men who had charge of it to the scene of the accident. Putting off in another boat they brought the capsized vessel to land, and hung up the sail to dry. She returned in the evening, and finding the sail dry, she set it on fire. Lord Curryfin, coming down to look after his tackle, found the young lady meditating over the tinder. She said to him –

'That sail will never put you under the water again.'

He was touched by this singular development of solicitude
for his preservation, but could not help saying something in
praise of his invention, giving a demonstration of the infalli-
bility of the principle, with several scientific causes of error in
working out the practice. He had no doubt it would be all
right on another experiment. Seeing that her looks expressed
unfeigned alarm at this announcement, he assured her that her
kind interest in his safety was sufficient to prevent his trying
his invention again. They walked back together to the house,
and in the course of conversation she said to him –

'The last time I saw the words Infallible Safety they were
painted on the back of a stage-coach which, in one of our
summer tours, we saw lying by the side of the road, with its
top in a ditch and its wheels in the air,'

The young lady was still a mystery to Lord Curryfin.

'Sometimes,' he said to himself, 'I could almost fancy
Melpomene in love with me. But I have seldom seen her
laugh, and when she has done so now and then, it has usually
been at me. That is not much like love. Her last remark was
anything but a compliment to my inventive genius.'

## CHAPTER XVII

### HORSE-TAMING – LOVE IN DILEMMA –
### INJUNCTIONS – SONOROUS VASES

> O gran contrasto in giovenil pensiero,
> Desir di laude, ed impeto d'amore!
>                                     ARIOSTO, c. 25.

> How great a strife in youthful minds can raise
> Impulse of love, and keen desire of praise.

Lord Curryfin, amongst his multifarious acquirements, had
taken lessons from the great horse-tamer, and thought himself
as well qualified as his master to subdue any animal of the

species, however vicious. It was therefore with great pleasure
he heard that there was a singularly refractory specimen in Mr.
Gryll's stables. The next morning after hearing this he rose
early, and took his troublesome charge in hand. After some
preliminary management he proceeded to gallop him round
and round a large open space in the park, which was visible
from the house. Miss Niphet, always an early riser, and
having just prepared for a walk, saw him from her chamber
window engaged in this perilous exercise, and though she
knew nothing of the peculiar character of his recalcitrant
disciple, she saw by its shakings, kickings, and plungings, that
it was exerting all its energies to get rid of its rider. At last it
made a sudden dash into the wood, and disappeared among
the trees.

It was to the young lady a matter of implicit certainty that
some disaster would ensue. She pictured to herself all the
contingencies of accident; being thrown to the ground and
kicked by the horse's hoofs, being dashed against a tree, or
suspended, like Absalom, by the hair. She hurried down and
hastened towards the wood, from which, just as she reached
it, the rider and horse emerged at full speed as before. But as
soon as Lord Curryfin saw Miss Niphet, he took a graceful
wheel round, and brought the horse to a stand by her side; for
by this time he had mastered the animal, and brought it to the
condition of Sir Walter's hunter in Wordsworth –

> Weak as a lamb the hour that it is yeaned
> And foaming like a mountain cataract.*

She did not attempt to dissemble that she had come to look
for him, but said –

'I expected to find you killed.'

He said, 'You see, all my experiments are not failures. I
have been more fortunate with the horse than the sail.'

At this moment one of the keepers appeared at a little
distance. Lord Curryfin beckoned to him, and asked him to
take the horse to the stables. The keeper looked with some
amazement, and exclaimed –

* Hartleap Well.

'Why this is the horse that nobody could manage!'

'You will manage him easily enough now,' said Lord Curryfin.

So it appeared; and the keeper took charge of him, not altogether without misgiving.

Miss Niphet's feelings had been over-excited, the more so from the severity with which she was accustomed to repress them. The energy which had thus far upheld her suddenly gave way. she sat down on a fallen tree and burst into tears. Lord Curryfin sat down by her and took her hand. She allowed him to retain it awhile; but all at once snatched it from him and sped towards the house over the grass, with the swiftness and lightness of Virgil's Camilla, leaving his lordship as much astonished at her movements as the Volscian crowd, *attonitis inhians animis,** had been at those of her prototype. He could not help thinking, 'Few women run gracefully; but she runs like another Atalanta.'

When the party met at breakfast, Miss Niphet was in her place, looking more like a statue than ever, with, if possible, more of marble paleness. Lord Curryfin's morning exploit of which the story had soon found its way from the stable to the hall, was the chief subject of conversation. He had received a large share of what he had always so much desired – applause and admiration; but now he thought he would willingly sacrifice all he had ever received in that line to see even the shadow of a smile, or the expression of a sentiment of any kind, on the impassive face of Melpomene. She left the room when she rose from the breakfast table, appeared at the rehearsal, and went through her part as usual; sat down at luncheon, and departed as soon as it was over. She answered, as she had always done, everything that was said to her, frankly, and to the purpose; and also, as usual, she originated nothing.

In the afternoon Lord Curryfin went down to the pavilion. She was not there. He wandered about the grounds in all directions, and returned several times to the pavilion, always in vain. At last he sat down in the pavilion, and fell into a meditation. He asked himself how it could be, that having

* Gaping with wondering minds.

begun by making love to Miss Gryll, having, indeed, gone too far to recede unless the young lady absolved him, he was now evidently in a transition state towards a more absorbing and violent passion for a person who, with all her frankness, was incomprehensible, and whose snowy exterior seemed to cover a volcanic fire, which she struggled to repress, and was angry with herself when she did not thoroughly succeed in so doing. If he were quite free he would do his part towards the solution of the mystery, by making a direct and formal proposal to her. As a preliminary to this, he might press Miss Gryll for an answer. All he had yet obtained from her was, 'Wait till we are better acquainted.' He was in a dilemma between Morgana and Melpomene. It had not entered into his thoughts that Morgana was in love with him; but he thought it nevertheless very probable that she was in a fair way to become so, and that even as it was she liked him well enough to accept him. On the other hand, he could not divest himself of the idea that Melpomene was in love with him, It was true, all the sympathy she had yet shown might have arisen from the excitement of strong feelings, at the real or supposed peril of a person with whom she was in the habit of daily intercourse. It might be so. Still, the sympathy was very impassioned; Though, but for his rashness in self-exposure to danger, he might never have known it. A few days ago he would not press Miss Gryll for an answer, because he feared it might be a negative. Now he would not, because he was at least not in haste for an affirmative. But supposing it were a negative, what certainty had he that a negative from Morgana would not be followed by a negative from Melpomene? Then his heart would be at sea without rudder or compass. We shall leave him awhile to the contemplation of his perplexities.

As his thoughts were divided, so were Morgana's if Mr. Falconer should propose to her, she felt she could accept him without hesitation. She saw clearly the tendency of his feelings towards her. She saw, at the same time, that he strove to the utmost against them in behalf of his old associations, though, with all his endeavours, he could not suppress them in her presence. So there was the lover who did not propose, and who would have been preferred; and there was the lover who had proposed, and who, if it had been clear that the former chance was hopeless, would not have been lightly given up.

If her heart had been as much interested in Lord Curryfin as it was in Mr. Falconer, she would quickly have detected a diminution in the ardour of his pursuit; but so far as she might have noticed any difference in his conduct, she ascribed it only to deference to her recommendation to 'wait till they were better acquainted.' The longer and the more quietly he waited, the better it seemed to please her. It was not on him, but on Mr. Falconer, that the eyes of her observance were fixed. She would have given Lord Curryfin his liberty instantly if she had thought he wished it.

Mr. Falconer also had his own dilemma, between his new love and his old affections. Whenever the first seemed likely to gain ascendency, the latter rose in their turn, like Antaeus from earth, with renovated strength. And he kept up their force by always revisiting the Tower when the contest seemed doubtful.

Thus, Lord Curryfin and Mr. Falconer were rivals, with a new phase of rivalry. In some of their variations of feeling, each wished the other success; the latter, because he struggled against a spell that grew more and more difficult to be resisted; the former, because he had been suddenly over-powered by the same king of light that had shone from the statue of Pygmalion. Thus their rivalry, such as it was, was entirely without animosity, and in no way disturbed the harmony of the Aristophanic party.

The only person concerned in these complications whose thoughts and feelings were undivided was Miss Niphet. She had begun by laughing at Lord Curryfin, and had ended by forming a decided partiality for him. She contended against the feeling; she was aware of his intentions towards Miss Gryll; and she would perhaps have achieved a conquest over herself if her sympathies had not been kept in a continual fever by the rashness with which he exposed himself to accidents by flood and field. At the same time, as she was more interested in observing Morgana than Morgana was in observing her, she readily perceived the latter's predilection for Mr. Falconer, and the gradual folding around him of the enchanted net. These observations, and the manifest progressive concentration of Lord Curryfin's affections on herself, showed her that she was not in the way of inflicting any very severe wound on her young friend's feeling, or encouraging a tendency to absolute hopelessness in her own.

Lord Curryfin was pursuing his meditation in the pavilion when the young lady, whom he had sought there in vain, presented herself before him in great agitation. He started up to meet her, and held out both his hands. She took them both, held them a moment, disengaged them, and sat down at a little distance, which he immediately reduced to nothing. He then expressed his disappointment at not having previously found her in the pavilion, and his delight at seeing her now. After a pause she said: 'I felt so much disturbed in the morning, that I should have devoted the whole day to recovering calmness of thought, but for something I have just heard. My maid tells me that you are going to try that horrid horse in harness, and in a newly invented high phaeton of your own, and that the grooms say they would not drive that horse in any carriage, nor any horse in that carriage, and that you have a double chance of breaking your neck. I have disregarded all other feelings to entreat you to give up your intention.'

Lord Curryfin assured her that he felt too confident in his power over horses, and in the safety of his new invention, to admit the possibility of danger: but that it was a very small sacrifice to her to restrict himself to tame horses and low carriages, or to abstinence from all horses and carriages, if she desired it.

'And from sailing boats,' she added.

'And from sailing-boats,' he answered.

'And from balloons,' she said.

'And from balloons,' he answered. 'But what made you think of balloons?'

'Because,' she said, 'they are dangerous, and you are inquiring and adventurous.'

'To tell you the truth,' he said, 'I have been up in a balloon. I thought it the most charming excursion I ever made. I have thought of going up again. I have invented a valve –'

'O heavens!' she exclaimed. 'But I have your promise touching horses, and carriages, and sails, and balloons.'

'You have,' he said. 'It shall be strictly adhered to.'

She rose to return to the house. But this time he would not

part with her, and they returned together.

Thus prohibited by an authority to which he yielded implicit obedience from trying further experiments at the risk of his neck, he restricted his inventive faculty to safer channels, and determined that the structure he was superintending should reproduce, as far as possible, all the peculiarities of the Athenian Theatre. Amongst other things, he studied attentively the subject of the *ēcheia,* or sonorous vases, which, in that vast theatre, propagated and clarified sound; and though in its smaller representative they were not needed, he thought it still possible that they might produce an agreeable effect. But with all the assistance of the Reverend Doctor Opimian, he found it difficult to arrive at a clear idea of their construction, or even of their principle; for the statement of Vitruvius, that they gave an accordant resonance in the fourth, the fifth, and the octave, seemed incompatible with the idea of changes of key, and not easily reconcilable with the doctrine of Harmonics. At last he made up his mind that they had no reference to key, but solely to pitch, modified by duly proportioned magnitude and distance: he therefore set to work assiduously, got a number of vases made, ascertained that they would give a resonance of some kind, and had them disposed at proper intervals round the audience part of the building. This being done, the party assembled, some as audience, some as performers, to judge of the effect. The first burst of choral music produced a resonance like the sound produced by sea-shells when placed against the ear, only many times multiplied, and growing like the sound of a gong: it was the exaggerated concentration of the symphony of a lime-grove full of cockchafers,* on a fine evening in the early summer. The experiment was then tried with single voices: the hum was less in itself, but greater in proportion. It was then tried with speaking: the result was the same: a powerful and perpetual hum, not resonant peculiarly to the diatessaron, the diapente, or the diapason, but making a new variety of continuous fundamental bass.

* The drone of the cockchafer, as he wheels by you in drowsy hum, sounds his *corno di bassetto* on F below the line. GARDINER'S *Music of Nature.*

'I am satisfied,' said Lord Curryfin, 'the art of making these vases is as hopelessly lost as that of making mummies. Miss Niphet encouraged him to persevere. She said:

'You have produced a decided resonance: the only thing is to subdue it, which you may perhaps effect by diminishing the number and enlarging the intervals of the vases.'

He determined to act on the suggestion, and she felt that, for some little time at least, she had kept him out of mischief. But whenever anything was said or sung in the threatre, it was necessary, for the time, to remove the *ēcheia*.


CHAPTER XVIII

LECTURES – THE POWER OF PUBLIC OPINION –
A NEW ORDER OF CHIVALRY


> si, Mimnermus uti censet, sine amore jocisque
> nil est jucundum, vivas in amore jocisque.
> > HOR. *Epist*. I. vi. 65, 66.
>
> If, as Mimnermus held, nought else can move
> Your soul to pleasure, live in sports and love.


The theatre was completed, and was found to be, without the *ēcheia*, a fine vehicle of sound. It was tried, not only in the morning rehearsals, but occasionally, and chiefly on afternoons of bad weather, by recitations, and even lectures; for though some of the party attached no value to that mode of dogmatic instruction, yet with the majority, and especially with the young ladies, it was decidedly in favour.

One rainy afternoon Lord Curryfin was entreated to deliver in the theatre his lecture on Fish; he readily complied, and succeeded in amusing his audience more, and instructing them as much, as any of his more pretentious brother lecturers could have done. We shall not report the lecture, but we refer to those who may be curious on the subject to the next meeting of the Pantopragmatic Society, under the presidency of Lord Facing-both-ways, and the vice-presidency of Lord Michin Malicho.

At intervals in similar afternoons of bad weather some others of the party were requested to favour the company with lectures or recitations in the theatre. Mr. Minim delivered a lecture on music, Mr. Pallet on painting; Mr. Falconer, though not used to lecturing, got up one on domestic life in the Homeric age. Even Mr. Gryll took his turn, and expounded the Epicurean philosophy. Mr. MacBorrowdale, who had no objection to lectures before dinner, delivered one on all the affairs of the world – foreign and domestic, moral, political, and literary. In the course of it he touched on Reform. 'The stone which Lord Michin Malicho – who was the Gracchus of the last Reform, and is the Sisyphus of the present – has been so laboriously pushing up hill, is for the present deposited at the bottom in the Limbo of Vanity. If it should ever surmount the summit and run down on the other side, it will infallibly roll over and annihilate the franchise of the educated classes; for it would not be worth their while to cross the road to exercise it against the rabble preponderance which would then have been created. Thirty years ago, Lord Michin Malicho had several cogent arguments in favour of Reform. One was, that the people were roaring for it, and that therefore they must have it. He has now in its favour the no less cogent argument, that the people do not care about it, and that the less it is asked for the greater will be the grace of the boon. On the former occasion the out-of-door logic was irresistible. Burning houses, throwing dead cats and cabbage-stumps into carriages, and other varieties of the same system of didactics, demonstrated the fitness of those who practised them to have representatives in Parliament. So they got their representatives, and many think Parliament would have been better without them. My father was a staunch Reformer. In his neighbourhood in London was the place of assembly of a Knowledge-is-Power Club. The members at the close of their meetings collected mending stones from the road, and broke the windows to the right and left of their line of march. They had a flag on which was inscribed, "The power of public opinion." Whenever the enlightened assembly met, my father closed his shutters, but, closing within, they did not protect

the glass. One morning he picked up, from where it had fallen
between the window and the shutter, a very large, and
consquently very demonstrative, specimen of dialectical granite. He preserved it carefully, and mounted it on a handsome
pedestal, inscribed with "The power of public opinion." He
placed it on the middle of his library mantelpiece, and the daily
contemplation of it cured him of his passion for Reform.
During the rest of his life he never talked, as he had used to do,
of "the people": he always said "the rabble," and delighted in
quoting every passage of *Hudibras* in which the rabble-rout is
treated as he had come to conclude it ought to be. He made
this piece of granite the nucleus of many political disquisitions.
It is still in my possession, and I look on it with veneration as
my principal tutor, for it had certainly a large share in the
elements of my education. If, which does not seem likely,
another reform lunacy should arise in my time, I shall take
care to close my shutters against "The power of public
opinion."'

The Reverend Doctor Opimian being called on to contribute his share to these diversions of rainy afternoons said –
'The sort of prose lecture which I am accustomed to deliver
would not be exactly appropriate to the present time and
place. I will therefore recite to you some verses, which I made
some time since, on what appeared to me a striking specimen
of absurdity on the part of the advisers of royalty here – the
bestowing the honours of knighthood, which is a purely
Christian institution, on Jews and Paynim; very worthy
persons in themselves, and entitled to any mark of respect
befitting their class, but not to one strictly and exclusively
Christian; money-lenders, too, of all callings the most antip-
athetic to that of a true knight. The contrast impressed itself
on me as I was reading a poem of the twelfth century, by Hues
de Tabaret – *L'Ordène de Chevalerie* – and I endeavoured to
express the contrast in the manner and form following:–

## A NEW ORDER OF CHIVALRY

### I

Sir Moses, Sir Aaron, Sir Jamramajee,
Two stock-jobbing Jews, and a shroffing Parsee,

Have girt on the armour of old Chivalrie,
And, instead of the Red Cross, have hoisted Balls Three.

Now fancy our Sovereign, so gracious and bland,
With the sword of Saint George in her royal right hand,
Instructing this trio of marvellous Knights
In the mystical meanings of Chivalry's rites.

'You have come from the bath, all in milk-white array,
To show you have washed worldly feelings away,
And, pure as your vestments from secular stain,
Renounce sordid passions and seekings for gain.

This scarf of deep red o'er your vestments I throw,
In token, that down them your life-blood shall flow,
Ere Chivalry's honour, or Christendom's faith,
Shall meet, through your failure, or peril or scaith.

These slippers of silk, of the colour of earth,
Are in sign of remembrance of whence you had birth;
That from earth you have sprung, and to earth you
return,
But stand for the faith, life immortal to earn.

This blow of the sword on your shoulder-blades true
Is the mandate of homage, where homage is due,
And the sign that your swords from the scabbard shall fly
When "St. George and the Right" is the rallying cry.

This belt of white silk, which no speck has defaced,
Is the sign of a bosom with purity graced,
And binds you to prove, whatsoever betides,
Of damsels distressed the friends, champions, and guides.

These spurs of pure gold are the symbols which say,
As your steeds obey them, you the Church shall obey,
And speed at her bidding, through country and town,
To strike, with your falchions, her enemies down.'

## II

Now fancy these Knights, when the speech they have
heard,
As they stand, scarfed, shoed, shoulder-dubbed, belted
and spurred,
With the cross-handled sword duly sheathed on the
thigh,
Thus simply and candidly making reply:

'By your Majesty's grace we have risen up Knights,
But we feel little relish for frays and for fights:
There are heroes enough, full of spirit and fire,
Always ready to shoot and be shot at for hire.

True, with bulls and with bears we have battled our
cause;
And the bulls have no horns, and the bears have no paws;
And the mightiest blow which we ever have struck
Has achieved but the glory of laming a duck.*

With two nations in arms, friends impartial to both,
To raise each a loan we shall be nothing loth;
We will lend them the pay, to fit men for the fray;
But shall keep ourselves carefully out of the way.

* In Stock Exchange slang, Bulls are speculators for a rise, Bears for
a fall. A lame duck is a man who cannot pay his differences, and is said
to waddle off. The patriotism of the money-market is well touched by
Ponsard, in his comedy *La Bourse*, Act iv. Scene 3 –

Alfred
Quand nous sommes vainqueurs, dire qu'on a baissé!
Si nous étions battus, on aurait donc haussé?

Delatour
On a craint qu'un succès, si brillant pour la France,
De la paix qu'on rêvait n'éloignât l'espérance.

Alfred
Cette Bourse, morbleu! n'a donc rien dans le cœur!
Ventre affamé n'a point d'oreilles . . . pour l'honneur!
Aussi je ne veux plus jouer – qu'après ma noce –
Et j'attends Waterloo pour me mettre à la hausse.

We have small taste for championing maids in distress;
For State we care little: for Church we care less:
To Premium and Bonus our homage we plight:
"Percentage!" we cry: and "A fig for the right!"

'Twixt Saint George and the Dragon we settle it thus:
Which has scrip above par is the Hero for us:
For a turn in the market, the Dragon's red gorge
Shall have our free welcome to swallow Saint George.'

Now, God save our Queen, and if aught should occur
To peril the crown or the safety of her,
God send that the leader, who faces the foe,
May have more of King Richard than Moses and Co.

# CHAPTER XIX

## A SYMPOSIUM – TRANSATLANTIC TENDENCIES – AFTER-DINNER LECTURES – EDUCATION

> Trincq est ung mot panomphée, célébré et entendu de toutes
> nations, et nous signifie, BEUUEZ. Et ici maintenons que non
> rire, ains boyre est le propre de l'homme. Je ne dy boyre
> simplement et absolument, car aussy bien boyvent les bestes; je
> dy boyre vin bon et fraiz.
>
> RABELAIS, 1. v. c. 45.

Some guests remained. Some departed and returned. Among
these was Mr. MacBorrowdale. One day after dinner on one
of his reappearances, Lord Curryfin said to him –

'Well, Mr. MacBorrowdale, in your recent observations,
have you found anything likely to satisfy Jack of Dover, if he
were prosecuting his inquiry among us?'

*Mr. MacBorrowdale*
Troth, no, my lord. I think, if he were among us, he would
give up the search as hopeless. He found it so in his own day,

and he would find it still more so now. Jack was both merry
and wise. We have less mirth in practice; and we have more
wisdom in pretension, which Jack would not have admitted.

### The Rev. Dr. Opimian
He would have found it like Juvenal's search for patriotic
virtue, when Catiline was everywhere, and Brutus and Cato
were nowhere.*

### Lord Curryfin
Well, among us, if Jack did not find his superior, or even his
equal, he would not have been at a loss for company to his
mind. There is enough mirth for those who choose to enjoy it,
and wisdom too, perhaps as much as he would have cared for.
We ought to have more wisdom, as we have clearly more
science.

### The Rev. Dr. Opimian
Science is one thing and wisdom is another. Science is an
edged tool with which men play like children and cut their
own fingers. If you look at the results which science has
brought in its train, you will find them to consist almost
wholly in elements of mischief. See how much belongs to the
word Explosion alone, of which the ancients knew nothing.
Explosion of powder-magazines; of coal-gas in mines and in
houses; of high-pressure engines in ships and boats and
factories. See the complications and refinements of modes of
destruction, in revolvers and rifles and shells and rockets and
cannon. See collisions and wrecks and every mode of disaster
by land and by sea, resulting chiefly from the insanity for
speed, in those who for the most part have nothing to do at the
end of the race, which they run as if they were so many
Mercuries speeding with messages from Jupiter. Look at our
scientific drainage which turns refuse into poison. Look at the
subsoil of London, whenever it is turned up to the air,

---

*                                    Et Catilinam
    quocumque in populo videas, quocumque sub axe:
    sed nec Brutus erit, Bruti nec avunculus usquam.
                                    JUV. Sat. xiv. 41–43.

converted by gas leakage into one mass of pestilent blackness, in which no vegetation can flourish, and above which, with the rapid growth of the ever-growing nuisance, no living thing will breathe with impunity. Look at our scientific machinery, which has destroyed domestic manufacture, which has substituted rottenness for strength in the thing made, and physical degradation in crowded towns for healthy and comfortable country life in the makers. The day would fail, if I should attempt to enumerate the evils which science has inflicted on mankind. I almost think it is the ultimate destiny of science to exterminate the human race.

*Lord Curryfin*
You have gone over a wide field, which we might exhaust a good bin of claret in fully discussing. But surely the facility of motion over the face of the earth and sea is both pleasant and profitable. We may now see the world with little expenditure of labour or time.

*The Rev. Dr. Opimian*
You may be whisked over it, but you do not see it. You go from one great town to another, where manners and customs are not even now essentially different, and with this facility of intercourse become progressively less and less so. The intermediate country – which you never see, unless there is a show mountain, or waterfall, or ruin, for which there is a station, and to which you go as you would to any other exhibition – the intermediate country contains all that is really worth seeing, to enable you to judge of the various characteristics of men and the diversified objects of Nature.

*Lord Curryfin*
You can suspend your journey if you please, and see the intermediate country, if you prefer it.

*The Rev. Dr. Opimian*
But who does prefer it? You travel round the world by a hand-book, as you do round an exhibition-room by a catalogue.

*Mr. MacBorrowdale*

Not to say that in the intermediate country you are punished
by bad inns and bad wine, of which I confess myself intoler-
ant. I knew an unfortunate French tourist who had made the
round of Switzerland, and had but one expression for every
stage of his journey: *Mauvaise auberge!*

*Lord Curryfin*

Well, then, what say you to the electric telegraph, by which
you converse at the distance of thousands of miles? Even
across the Atlantic, as no doubt we shall yet do,

*Mr. Gryll*

Some of us have already heard the doctor's opinion on that
subject.

*The Rev. Dr. Opimian*

I have no wish to expedite communication with the Americans. If we could apply the power of electrical repulsion to
preserve us from ever hearing anything more of them, I
should think that we had for once derived a benefit from
science.

*Mr. Gryll*

Your love for the Americans, doctor, seems something like
that of Cicero's friend Marius for the Greeks. He would not
take the nearest road to his villa, because it was called the
Greek Road.* Perhaps if your nearest way home were called
the American Road, you would make a circuit to avoid it.

*The Rev. Dr. Opimian*

I am happy to say I am not put to the test. Magnetism,
galvanism, electricity, are 'one form of many names.'* Without magnetism we should never have discovered America; to
which we are indebted for nothing but evil; diseases in the

---

* Non enim te puto Græcos ludos desiderare: præsertim quum
Græcos ita non ames, ut ne ad villam quidem tuam via Græca ire
soleas. CICERO, *Ep. ad Div.* vii. I.

* πολλῶν ὀνομάτων μορφὴ μία. ÆSCHYLUS, *Prometheus.*

worst forms that can afflict humanity, and slavery in the worst
form in which slavery can exist. The Old World had the
sugar-cane and the cotton-plant, though it did not so misuse
them. Then, what good have we got from America? What
good of any kind, from the whole continent and its islands,
from the Esquimaux to Patagonia?

*Mr. Gryll*
Newfoundland salt-fish, doctor.

*The Rev. Dr. Opimian*
That is something, but it does not turn the scale.

*Mr. Gryll*
If they have given us no good, we have given them none.

*The Rev. Dr. Opimian*
We have given them wine and classical literature; but I am
afraid Bacchus and Minerva have equally

>       Scattered their bounty upon barren ground.

On the other hand, we have given the red men rum, which has
been the chief instrument of their perdition. On the whole,
our intercourse with America has been little else than an
interchange of vices and diseases.

*Lord Curryfin*
Do you count it nothing to have substituted civilised for
savage men?

*The Rev. Dr. Opimian*
Civilised. The word requires definition. But looking into
futurity, it seems to me that the ultimate tendency of the
change is to substitute the worse for the better race; the Negro
for the Red Indian. The Red Indian will not work for a master.
No ill-usage will make him. Herein he is the noblest specimen
of humanity that ever walked the earth. Therefore, the white
man exterminates his race. But the time will come when by
mere force of numbers the black race will predominate and

exterminate the white. And thus the worse race will be substituted for the better, even as it is in St. Domingo, where the Negro has taken the place of the Caraib. The change is clearly for the worse.

*Lord Curryfin*

You imply that in the meantime the white race is better than the red.

*The Rev. Dr. Opimian*

I leave that as an open question. But I hold, as some have done before me, that the human mind degenerates in America, and that the superiority, such as it is, of the white race, is only kept up by intercourse with Europe. Look at the atrocities in their ships. Look at their Congress and their Courts of Justice; debaters in the first; suitors, even advocates, sometimes judges, in the second, settling their arguments with pistol and dagger. Look at their extensions of slavery, and their revivals of the slave-trade, now covertly, soon to be openly. If it were possible that the two worlds could be absolutely dissevered for a century, I think a new Columbus would find nothing in America but savages.

*Lord Curryfin*

You look at America, doctor, through your hatred of slavery. You must remember that we introduced it when they were our colonists. It is not so easily got rid of. Its abolition by France exterminated the white race in St. Domingo, as the white race had exterminated the red. Its abolition by England ruined our West Indian colonies.

*The Rev. Dr. Opimian*

Yes, in conjunction with the direct encouragement of foreign slave labour, given by our friends of liberty under the pretext of free trade. It is a mockery to keep up a squadron for suppressing the slave-trade on the one hand, while, on the other hand, we encourage it to an extent that counteracts in a tenfold degree the apparent power of suppression. It is a clear case of false pretension.

*Mr. Gryll*

You know, doctor, the Old World had slavery through-out its
entire extent; under the Patriachs, the Greeks, the Romans;
everywhere, in short. Cicero thought our island not likely to
produce anything worth having, excepting slaves;* and of
those none skilled, as some slaves were, in letters and music,
but all utterly destitute of both. And in the Old World the
slaves were of the same race with the masters. The Negroes
are an inferior race, not fit, I am afraid, for anything else.

*The Rev. Dr. Opimian*

Not fit, perhaps, for anything else belonging to what we call
civilised life. Very fit to live on little, and wear nothing, in
Africa; where it would have been a blessing to themselves and
the rest of the world if they had been left unmolested; if they
had had a Friar Bacon to surround their entire continent with a
wall of brass.

*Mr. Falconer*

I am not sure, doctor, that in many instances, even yet, the
white slavery of our factories is not worse than the black
slavery of America. We have done much to amend it, and shall
do more. Still, much remains to be done.

*The Rev. Dr. Opimian*

And will be done, I hope and believe. The Americans do
nothing to amend their system. On the contrary, they do all
they can to make bad worse. Whatever excuse there may be
for maintaining slavery where it exists, there can be none for
extending it into new territories; none for reviving the African
slave-trade. These are the crying sins of America. Our white
slavery, so far as it goes, is so far worse, that it is the

---

* Etiam illud jam cognitum est, neque argenti scripulum esse ullum
in illa insula, neque ullam spem prædæ, nisi ex mancipiis: ex quibus
nullos puto te literis aut musicis eruditos expectare. CICERO, *ad
Atticum,* iv. 16.

A hope is expressed by Pomponius Mela, 1. iii. *c.* 6 (he wrote under
Claudius), that, by the success of the Roman arms, the island and its
savage inhabitants would soon be better known. It is amusing enough
to peruse such passages in the midst of London. GIBBON, c. i.

degradation of a better race. But if it be not redressed, as I trust it will be, it will work out its own retribution. And so it is of all the oppressions that are done under the sun. Though all men but the red men will work for a master, they will not fight for an oppressor in the day of his need. Thus gigantic empires have crumbled into dust at the first touch of an invader's footstep. For petty, as for great oppressions, there is a day of retribution growing out of themselves. It is often long in coming. *Ut sit magna, tamen certe lenta ira, Deorum est.** But it comes.

> Raro antecedentem scelestum
> Deseruit pede Pœna claudo,*

*Lord Curryfin*
I will not say, doctor, 'I've seen, and sure I ought to know.' But I have been to America, and I have found there, what many others will testify, a very numerous class of persons who hold opinions very like your own: persons who altogether keep aloof from public life, because they consider it abandoned to the rabble; but who are as refined, as enlightened, as full of sympathy for all that tends to justice and liberty, as any whom you may most approve amongst ourselves.

*The Rev. Dr. Opimian*
Of that I have no doubt. But I look to public acts and public men.

*Lord Curryfin*
I should much like to know what Mr. MacBorrowdale thinks of all this.

*Mr. MacBorrowdale*
Troth, my lord, I think we have strayed far away from the good company we began with. We have lost sight of Jack of Dover. But the discussion had one bright feature. It did not

---

* The anger of the Gods, though great, is slow.
* The foot of Punishment, though lame
  O'ertakes at last preceding Wrong.

interfere with, it rather promoted, the circulation of the bottle: for every man who spoke pushed it on with as much energy as he spoke with, and those who were silent swallowed the wine and the opinion together, as if they relished them both.

*The Rev. Dr. Opimian*

So far, discussion may find favour. In my own experience I have found it very absorbent of claret. But I do not think it otherwise an incongruity after dinner, provided it be carried on, as our disquisitions have always been, with frankness and good humour. Consider how much instruction has been conveyed to us, in the form of conversations at banquet, by Plato and Xenophon and Plutarch. I read nothing with more pleasure than their *Symposia*: to say nothing of Athenæus, whose work is one long banquet.

*Mr. MacBorrowdale*

Nay, I do not object to conversation on any subject. I object to after-dinner lectures. I have had some unfortunate experiences. I have, on different occasions, met several men, who were in that respect all alike. Once started they never stopped. The rest of the good company, or rather the rest which without them would have been good company, was no company. No one could get in a word. They went on with one unvarying stream of monotonous desolating sound. This makes me tremble when a discussion begins. I sit in fear of a lecture.

*Lord Curryfin*

Well, you and I have lectured, but never after dinner. We do it when we have promised it, and when those who are present expect it. After dinner, I agree with you, it is the most doleful blight that can fall on human enjoyment.

*Mr. MacBorrowdale*

I will give you one or two examples of these postprandial inflictions. One was a great Indian reformer. He did not open his mouth till he had had about a bottle and a half of wine. Then he burst on us with a declamation on all that was wrong in India, and its remedy. He began in the Punjab, travelled to

Calcutta, went southward, got into the Temple of Juggernaut, went southward again, and after holding forth for more than an hour, paused for a moment. The man who sate next to him attempted to speak: but the orator clapped him on the arm, and said: 'Excuse me: now I come to Madras.' On which his neighbour jumped up and vanished. Another went on in the same way about currency. His first hour's talking carried him just through the Restriction Act of ninety-seven. As we had then more than half-a-century before us, I took my departure. But these were two whom topography and chronology would have brought to a close. The bore of all bores was the third. His subject had no beginning, middle, nor end. It was education. Never was such a journey through the desert of mind: the Great Sahara of intellect. The very recollection makes me thirsty.

*The Rev. Dr. Opimian*

If all the nonsense which, in the last quarter of a century, has been talked on all other subjects were thrown into one scale, and all that has been talked on the subject of education alone were thrown into the other, I think the latter would preponderate.

*Lord Curryfin*

We have had through the whole period some fine specimens of nonsense on other subjects: for instance, with a single exception, political economy.

*Mr. MacBorrowdale*

I understand your lordship's politeness as excepting the present company. You need not except me, I am 'free to confess,' as they say 'in another place,' that I have talked a great deal of nonsense on the subject myself.

*Lord Curryfin*

Then we have had latterly a mighty mass on the purification of the Thames.

*The Rev. Dr. Opimian*

Allowing full weight to the two last-named ingredients, they are not more than a counterpoise to Competitive Examination, which is also a recent exotic belonging to education.

*Lord Curryfin*
Patronage, it used to be alleged, considered only the fitness of the place for the man, not the fitness of the man for the place. It was desirable to reverse this.

*The Rev. Dr. Opimian*
True: but –

'dum vitant stulti vitium, in contraria currunt.'*

Questions which can only be answered by the parrotings of a memory crammed to disease with all sorts of heterogeneous diet can form no test of genius, taste, judgment, or natural capacity. Competitive Examination takes for its *norma:* 'It is better to learn many things ill than one thing well'; or rather: 'It is better to learn to gabble about everything than to understand anything.' this is not the way to discover the wood of which Mercuries are made. I have been told that this precious scheme has been borrowed from China: a pretty fountain-head for moral and political improvement: and if so, I may say, after Petronius: 'This windy and monstrous loquacity has lately found its way to us from Asia, and like a pestilential star has blighted the minds of youth otherwise rising to greatness.'*

*Lord Curryfin*
There is something to be said on behalf of applying the same tests, addressing the same questions, to everybody.

*The Rev. Dr. Opimian*
I shall be glad to hear what can be said on that behalf.

* When fools would from one vice take flight,
   They rush into its opposite.
                                        HOR. *Sat.* i. 2, 24.
   * Nuper ventosa isthæc et enormis loquacitas Athenas ex Asia commigravit, animosque juvenum, ad magna surgentes, veluti pestilenti quodam sidere afflavit.

*Lord Curryfin* (after a pause)
'Mass,' as the second grave-digger says in *Hamlet,* 'I cannot
tell.'


A chorus of laughter dissolved the sitting.




CHAPTER XX


ALGERNON AND MORGANA – OPPORTUNITY
AND REPENTANCE – THE FOREST IN WINTER


Les violences qu'on se fait pour s'empêcher d'aimer sont
souvent plus cruelles que les rigueurs de ce qu'on aime.
LA ROCHEFOUCAULD.


The winter set in early. December began with intense frost.
Mr. Falconer, one afternoon, entering the inner drawing-
room, found Miss Gryll alone. She was reading, and on the
entrance of her visitor laid down her book. He hoped he had
not interrupted her in an agreeable occupation. 'To observe
romantic method,' we shall give what passed between them
with the Christian names of the speakers.

*Morgana*
I am only reading what I have often read before, *Orlando
Innamorato*; and I was at the moment occupied with a passage
about the enchantress from whom my name was borrowed.
You are aware that enchantresses are in great favour here.

*Algernon*
Circe and Gryllus, and your name, sufficiently show that.
And not your name only, but – I should like to see the passage,
and should be still better pleased if you would read it to me.

*Morgana*
It is where Orlando, who had left Morgana sleeping by the

fountain, returns to seek the enchanted key, by which alone he
can liberate his friends.

Il Conte, che d'intrare havea gran voglia,
Subitamente al fonte ritornava:
Quivi trovò Morgana, che con gioglia
Danzava intorno, e danzando cantava.
Nè più leggier si move al vento foglia
Come ella sanza sosta si voltava,
Mirando hora a la terra ed hora al sole;
Ed al suo canto usava tal parole:

'Qualonque cerca al mondo haver thesoro,
Over diletto, o segue onore e stato,
Ponga la mano a questa chioma d'oro,
Ch' io porto in fronte, e quel farò beato.
Ma quando ha il destro a far cotal lavoro,
Non prenda indugio, che 'l tempo passato
Più non ritorna, e non si trova mai;
Ed io mi volto, e lui lascio con guai.'

Così cantava d' intorno girando
La bella Fata a quella fresca fonte;
Ma come gionto vide il Conte Orlando,
Subitamente rivoltò la fronte:
Il prato e la fontana abbandonando,
Prese il viaggio suo verso d' un monte,
Qual chiudea la valletta picciolina:
Quivi fuggendo Morgana cammina.*

---

* Bojardo, 1. ii. c. 8. *Ed. Vinegia,* 1544.

With earnest wish to pass the enchanted gate,
Orlando to the fount again advanced,
And found Morgana, all with joy elate,
Dancing around, and singing as she danced.
As lightly moved and twirled the lovely Fate
As to the breeze the lightest foliage glanced,
With looks alternate to the earth and sky,
She thus gave out her words of witchery:

*Algernon*

I remember the passage well. The beautiful *Fata,* dancing and singing by the fountain, presents a delightful picture.

*Morgana*

Then, you know, Orlando who had missed his opportunity of seizing the golden forelock while she was sleeping, pursues her a long while in vain through rocky deserts, *La Penitenza* following him with a scourge. The same idea was afterwards happily worked out by Machiavelli in his *Capitolo dell' Occasione.*

---

'Let him, who seeks unbounded wealth to hold,
Or joy, or honour, or terrestrial state,
Seize with his hand this lock of purest gold,
That crowns my brow, and blest shall be his fate.
But when time serves, behoves him to be bold,
Nor even a moment's pause interpolate:
The chance, once lost, he never finds again:
I turn, and leave him to lament in vain.'

Thus sang the lovely Fate in bowery shade
Circling in joy around the crystal fount;
But when within the solitary glade
Glittered the armour of the approaching Count,
She sprang upon her feet, as one dismayed,
And took her way towards a lofty mount
That rose the valley's narrow length to bound:
Thither Morgana sped along the ground.

I have translated *Fata,* Fate. It is usually translated Fairy. But the idea differs essentially from ours of a fairy. Amongst other things there is no *Fato,* no Oberon to the Titania. It does not, indeed, correspond with our usual idea of Fate, but it is more easily distinguished as a class; for our old acquaintances the Fates are an inseparable three. The Italian *Fata* is independent of her sisters: They are enchantresses in being immortal. They are beautiful, too, and their beauty is immortal: always in Bojardo. He would not have turned Alcina into an old woman, as Ariosto did; which I must always consider a dreadful blemish on the many charms of the *Orlando Furioso.*

*Algernon*

You are fond of Italian literature? You read the language beautifully. I observe you have read from the original poem, and not from Berni's *rifacciamento*

*Morgana*

I prefer the original. It is more simple, and more in earnest. Berni's playfulness is very pleasant, and his exordiums are charming; and in many instances he has improved the poetry. Still, I think he has less than the original of what are to me the great charms of poetry, truth and simplicity. Even the greater antiquity of style has its peculiar appropriateness to the subject. And Bojardo seems to have more faith in his narrative than Berni. I go on with him with ready credulity, where Berni's pleasantry interposes a doubt.

*Algernon*

You think that in narratives, however wild and romantic, the poet should write as if he fully believed in the truth of his own story.

*Morgana*

I do; and I think so in reference to all narratives, not to poetry only. What a dry skeleton is the history of the early ages of Rome, told by one who believes nothing that the Romans believed! Religion pervades every step of the early Roman history; and in a great degree down at least to the Empire; but, because their religion is not our religion, we pass over the supernatural part of the matter in silence, or advert to it in a spirit of contemptuous incredulity. We do not give it its proper place, nor present it in its proper colours, as a cause in the production of great effects. Therefore, I like to read Livy, and I do not like to read Niebuhr.

*Algernon*

May I ask if you read Latin?

*Morgana*

I do sufficiently to derive great pleasure from it. Perhaps, after this confession, you will not wonder that I am a spinster.

*Algernon*

So far, that I think it would tend to make you fastidious in
your choice. Not that you would be less sought by any who
would be worthy your attention. For I am told you have had
many suitors, and have rejected them all in succession. And
have you not still many, and among them one very devoted
lover, who would bring you title as well as fortune? A very
amiable person, too, though not without a comic side to his
character.

*Morgana*

I do not well know. He so far differs from all my preceding
suitors that in every one of them I found the presence of some
quality that displeased me, or the absence of some which
would have pleased me: the want, in the one way or the other,
of that entire congeniality in taste and feeling which I think
essential to happiness in marriage. He has so strong a desire of
pleasing, and such power of acquisition and assimilation, that I
think a woman truly attached to him might mould him to her
mind. Still, I can scarcely tell why, he does not complete my
idealities. They say, Love is his own avenger: and perhaps I
shall be punished by finding my idealities realised in one who
will not care for me.

*Algernon*

I take that to be impossible.

Morgana blushed, held down her head, and made no reply.
Algernon looked at her in silent admiration. A new light
seemed to break in on him. Though he had had so many
opportunities of forming a judgement on the point, it seemed
to strike him for the first time with irresistible conviction that
he had never before heard such a sweet voice, nor seen such an
expressive and intelligent countenance. And in this way they
continued like two figures in a *tableau vivant*, till the entrance
of other parties broke the spell which thus had fixed them in
their positions.

   A few minutes more, and their destinies might have been
irrevocably fixed. But the interruption gave Mr. Falconer the
opportunity of returning again to his Tower, to consider, in

the presence of the seven sisters, whether he should not be in the position of a Roman, who was reduced to the dilemma of migrating without his household deities, or suffering his local deities to migrate without him; and whether he could sit comfortably on either of the horns of this dilemma. He felt that he could not. On the other hand, could he bear to see the fascinating Morgana metamorphosed into Lady Curryfin? The time had been when he had half wished it, as the means of restoring him to liberty. He felt now that when in her society he could not bear the idea; but he still thought that in the midst of his domestic deities he might become reconciled to it.

He did not care for horses, nor keep any for his own use. But as time and weather were not always favourable to walking, he had provided for himself a comfortable travelling-chariot, without a box to intercept the view, in which, with post-horses after the fashion of the olden time, he performed occasional migrations. He found this vehicle of great use in moving to and fro between the Grange and the Tower; for then, with all his philosophy, Impatience was always his companion: Impatience on his way to the Grange, to pass into the full attraction of the powerful spell by which he was drawn like the fated ship to the magnetic rock in the *Arabian Nights:* Impatience on his way to the Tower, to find himself again in the 'Regions mild of pure and serene air,' in which the seven sisters seemed to dwell, like Milton's ethereal spirits, 'Before the starry threshold of Jove's court.' Here was everything to soothe, nothing to irritate or disturb him: nothing on the spot: but it was with him, as it is with many, perhaps with all: the two great enemies of tranquillity, Hope and Remembrance, would still intrude: not like a bubble and a spectre, as in the beautiful lines of Coleridge:* for the remembrance of Morga-

---

* Who late and lingering seeks thy shrine,
    On him but seldom, Power divine,
    Thy spirit rests. Satiety,
    And sloth, poor counterfeits of thee,
    Mock the tired worldling. Idle Hope,
    And dire Remembrance, interlope,
    And vex the feverish slumbers of the mind:
    The bubble floats before: the spectre stalks behind.
                        COLERIDGE'S *Ode to Tranquillity.*

na was not a spectre, and the hope of her love, which he cherished in spite of himself, was not a bubble: but their forces were not less disturbing, even in the presence of his earliest and most long and deeply cherished association.

He did not allow his impatience to require that the horses should be put to extraordinary speed. He found something tranquillising in the movement of a postillion in a smart jacket, vibrating on one horse upwards and downwards, with one invariable regulated motion like the cross-head of a side-lever steam-engine, and holding the whip quietly arched over the neck of the other. The mechanical monotony of the movement seemed less in contrast than in harmony with the profound stillness of the wintry forest: the leafless branches heavy with rime frost and glittering in the sun: the deep repose of nature, broken now and then by the traversing of deer, or the flight of wild birds: highest and loudest among them the long lines of rooks: but for the greater part of the way one long deep silence, undisturbed but by the rolling of the wheels and the iron tinkling of the hoofs on the frozen ground. By degrees he fell into a reverie, and meditated on his last dialogue with Morgana.

'It is a curious coincidence,' he thought, 'that she should have been dwelling on a passage in which her namesake enchantress inflicted punishment on Orlando for having lost his opportunity. Did she associate Morgana with herself and Orlando with me? Did she intend a graceful hint to me not to lose *my* opportunity? I seemed in a fair way to seize the golden forelock, if we had not been interrupted. Do I regret that I did not? That is just what I cannot determine. Yet it would be more fitting, that whatever I may do should be done calmly, deliberately, philosophically, than suddenly, passionately, impulsively. One thing is clear to me. It is now or never: this or none. The world does not contain a second Morgana, at least not of mortal race. Well: the opportunity will return. So far, I am not in the predicament in which we left Orlando. I may yet ward off the scourge of *La Penitenza*.'

But his arrival at home, and the sight of the seven sisters, who had all come to the hall-door to greet him, turned his thoughts for awhile into another channel.

He dined at his usual hour, and his two Hebes alternately

filled his glass with Madeira. After which the sisters played and sang to him in the drawing- room; and when he had retired to his chamber, had looked on the many portraitures of his Virgin Saint, and had thought by how many charms of life he was surrounded, he composed himself to rest with the reflection: 'I am here like Rasselas in the Happy Valley: and I can now fully appreciate the force of that beautiful chapter: *The wants of him who want nothing.*'

## CHAPTER XXI

### SKATING – PAS DE DEUX ON THE ICE – CONGENIALITY – FLINTS AMONG BONES

> Ubi lepos, joci, risus, ebrietas decent,
> Gratiæ, decor, hilaritas, atque delectatio,
> Qui quærit alia his, malum videtur quærere.
> PLATUS, *In Pseudolo.*

Where sport, mirth, wine, joy, grace, conspire to please,
He seeks but ill who seeks aught else than these.

The frost continued. The lake was covered over with solid ice. This became the chief scene of afternoon amusement, and Lord Curryfin carried off the honours of the skating. In the dead of the night there came across his memory a ridiculous stave:

> There's Mr. Tait, he cuts an eight,
> He cannot cut a nine:

and he determined on trying if he could not outdo Mr. Tait. He thought it would be best to try his experiment without witnesses: and having more than an hour's daylight before breakfast, he devoted that portion of the morning to his purpose. But cutting a nine by itself baffled his skill, and

treated him to two or three tumbles, which, however, did not
abate his ardour. At length he bethought him of cutting a nine
between two eights, and by shifting his feet rapidly at the
points of difficulty, striking in and out of the nine to and from
the eights on each side. In this he succeeded, and exhibiting his
achievement in the afternoon, adorned the surface of the ice
with successions of 898 till they amounted to as many
sextillions, with their homogeneous sequences. He then enclosed the line with an oval, and returned to the bank through
an admiring circle, who, if they had been as numerous as the
spectators to the Olympic games, would have greeted him
with as loud shouts of triumph as saluted Epharmostus of
Opus.*

Among the spectators on the bank were Miss Niphet and
Mr. MacBorrowdale, standing side by side. While Lord
Curryfin was cutting his sextillions, Mr. MacBorrowdale
said: 'There is a young gentleman who is capable of anything,
and who would shine in any pursuit, if he would keep to it. He
shines as it is, in almost everything he takes in hand in private
society: there is genius even in his failures, as in the case of the
theatrical vases; but the world is a field of strong competition,
and affords eminence to few in any sphere of exertion, and to
those few rarely but in one.'

*Miss Niphet*
Before I knew him, I never heard of him but as a lecturer on
Fish; and to that he seems to limit his public ambition. In
private life, his chief aim seems to be that of pleasing his
company. Of course, you do not attach much value to his
present pursuit. You see no utility in it.

*Mr. MacBorrowdale*
On the contrary I see great utility in it. I am for a healthy mind
in a healthy body: the first can scarcely be without the last, and
the last can scarcely be without good exercise in pure air. In
this way, there is nothing better than skating. I should be very
glad to cut eights and nines with his lordship: but the only

* διήρχετο κύκλον ὅσσα βοᾷ. PIND. *Olymp.* ix.
    With what a clamour he passed through the circle.

figure I should cut would be that of as many feet as would measure my own length on the ice.

Lord Curryfin, on his return to land, thought it his duty first to accost Miss Gryll, who was looking on by the side of Miss Ilex. He asked her if she ever skated. She answered in the negative. 'I have tried it,' she said, 'but unsuccessfully. I admire it extremely, and regret my inability to participate in it.' He then went up to Miss Niphet, and asked her the same question. She answered: 'I have skated often in our grounds at home.' 'Then why not now?' he asked. She answered: 'I have never done it before so many witnesses.' 'But what is the objection?' he asked. 'None that I know of,' she answered. 'Then,' he said, 'as I have done or left undone some things to please you, will you do this one thing to please me?' 'Certainly,' she replied: adding to herself: 'I will do anything in my power to please you.'

She equipped herself expeditiously, and started before he was well aware. She was half round the lake before he came up with her. She then took a second start, and completed the circle before he came up with her again. He saw she was an Atalanta on ice as on turf. He placed himself by her side, slipped her arm through his, and they started on a second round, which they completed arm-in-arm. By this time the blush-rose bloom which had so charmed him on a former occasion again mantled on her cheeks, though from a different cause, for it was now only the glow of healthful exercise; but he could not help exclaiming, 'I now see why and with what tints the Athenians coloured their statues.'

'Is it clear,' she asked, 'that they did so?'

'I have doubted it before,' he answered, 'but I am now certain that they did.'

In the meantime, Miss Gryll, Miss Ilex, and the Reverend Doctor Opimian had been watching their movements from the bank.

*Miss Ilex*

I have seen much graceful motion in dancing, in private society and on the Italian stage; and some in skating before to-day; but anything so graceful as that double-gliding over the ice by those two remarkably handsome young persons, I certainly never saw before.

## Miss Gryll
Lord Curryfin is unquestionably handsome, and Miss Niphet, especially with that glow on her cheeks, is as beautiful a young woman as imagination can paint. They moved as if impelled by a single will. It is impossible not to admire them both.

## The Rev. Dr. Opimian
They remind me of the mythological fiction that Jupiter made men and women in pairs, like the Siamese twins; but in this way they grew so powerful and presumptuous, that he cut them in two; and now the main business of each half is to look for the other; which is very rarely found, and hence so few marriages are happy. Here the two true halves seem to have met.

The doctor looked at Miss Gryll, to see what impression this remark might make on her. He concluded that, if she thought seriously of Lord Curryfin, she would show some symptom of jealousy of Miss Niphet; but she did not. She merely said – 'I quite agree with you, doctor. There is evidently great congeniality between them, even in their respective touches of eccentricity.'

But the doctor's remark had suggested to her what she herself had failed to observe; Lord Curryfin's subsidence from ardour into deference in his pursuit of herself. She had been so undividedly 'the cynosure of neighbouring eyes' that she could scarcely believe in the possibility of even temporary eclipse. Her first impulse was to resign him to her young friend. But then appearances might be deceitful. Her own indifference might have turned his attentions into another channel, without his heart being turned with them. She had seen nothing to show that Miss Niphet's feelings were deeply engaged in the question. She was not a coquette; but she would still feel it as a mortification that her hitherto unquestioned supremacy should be passing from her. She had felt all along that there was one cause which would lead her to a decided rejection of Lord Curryfin. But her Orlando had not

seized the golden forelock; perhaps he never would. After
having seemed on the point of doing so, he had disappeared
and not returned. He was now again within the links of the
sevenfold chain which had bound him from his earliest days.
She herself, too, had had, perhaps had still, the chance of the
golden forelock in another quarter. Might she not subject her
after-life to repentance, if her first hope should fail her when
the second had been irrevocably thrown away? The more she
contemplated the sacrifice, the greater it appeared. Possibly
doubt had given preponderance to her thoughts of Mr.
Falconer, and certainly had caused them to repose in the case
of Lord Curryfin; but when doubt was thrown into the latter
scale also, the balance became more even. She would still give
him his liberty, if she believed that he wished it; for then her
pride would settle the question; but she must have more
conclusive evidence on the point than the reverend doctor's
metaphorical deduction from a mythological fiction.

In the evening, while the party in the drawing-room were
amusing themselves in various ways, Mr. MacBorrowdale
laid a drawing on the table and said, 'Doctor, what should you
take that to represent?'

*The Rev. Dr. Opimian*
An unformed lump of I know not what.

*Mr. MacBorrowdale*
Not unformed. It is a flint formation of a very peculiar kind.

*The Rev. Dr. Opimian*
Very peculiar, certainly. Who on earth can have amused
himself with drawing a mis-shapen flint? There must be some
riddle in it; some enigma, as insoluble to me as *Aelia Laelia
Crispis.**

Lord Curryfin, and others of the party, were successively
asked their opinions. One of the young ladies guessed it to be

* This enigma has been the subject of many learned disquisitions.
The reader who is unacquainted with it may find it under the article
'Enigma' in the *Encyclopædia Britannica;* and probably in every other
encyclopædia.

the petrifaction of an antediluvian mussel. Lord Curryfin said petrifactions were often siliceous, but never pure silex, which this purported to be. It gave him the idea of an ass's head; which, however, could not by any process have been turned into flint.

Conjecture being exhausted, Mr. MacBorrowdale said, 'It is a thing they call a Celt. The ass's head is somewhat germane to the matter. The Artium Societatis Syndicus et Socii have determined that it is a weapon of war, evidently of human manufacture. It has been found, with many others like it, among bones of mammoths and other extinct animals, and is therefore held to prove that men and mammoths were contemporaries.'

*The Rev. Dr. Opimian*
A weapon of war? Had it a handle? Is there a hole for a handle?

*Mr. MacBorrowdale*
That does not appear.

*The Rev. Dr. Opimian*
These flints, and no other traces of men, among the bones of mammoths?

*Mr. MacBorrowdale*
None whatever.

*The Rev. Dr. Opimian*
What do the Artium Societatis Syndicus et Socii suppose to have become of the men who produced these demonstrations of high aboriginal art?

*Mr. MacBorrowdale*
They think these finished specimens of skill in the art of chipping prove that the human race is of greater antiquity than has been previously supposed; and the fact that there is no other relic to prove the position they consider of no moment whatever.

*The Rev. Dr. Opimian*

Ha! ha! ha! This beats the Elephant in the Moon,* which
turned out to be a mouse in a telescope. But I can help them to
an explanation of what became of these primeval men-of-
arms. They were an ethereal race, and evaporated.

## CHAPTER XXII

## THE SEVEN AGAINST THEBES – A SOLILOQUY
## ON CHRISTMAS

> Over the mountains,
>   And over the waves;
> Under the fountains,
>   And under the graves;
> Under floods that are deepest,
>   Which Neptune obey;
> Over rocks that are steepest,
>   Love will find out the way.
>       Old song in PERCY'S *Reliques.*

Harry Hedgerow had volunteered to be Mr. Falconer's Mer-
cury during his absences from the Tower, and to convey to
him letters and any communications which the sisters might
have to make. Riding at a good trot, on a horse more
distinguished for strength than grace, he found the shortest
days long enough for the purpose of going and returning,
with an ample interval for the refreshment of himself and his
horse. While discussing beef and ale in the servants' hall, he
heard a good deal of the family news, and many comments on
the visitors. From these he collected that there were several
young gentlemen especially remarkable for their attention to
the young lady of the mansion: that among them were two
who were more in her good graces than the others: that one of
these was the young gentleman who lived in the Duke's Folly,

* See Butler's poem, with that title, in his *Miscellaneous Works.*

and who was evidently the favourite: and that one of these was
the young lord, who was the life and soul of the company, but
who seemed to be very much taken with another young lady,
who had, at the risk of her own life, jumped into the water and
picked him out, when he was nearly being drowned. This
story had lost nothing in travelling. Harry, deducing from all
this the conclusion most favourable to his own wishes,
determined to take some steps for the advancement of his own
love-suit, especially as he had obtained some allies, who were
willing to march with him to conquest like the Seven against
Thebes.

The Reverend Doctor Opimian had finished his breakfast,
and had just sat down in his library, when he was informed
that some young men wished to see him. The doctor was
always accessible, and the visitors were introduced. He recognised his friend Harry Hedgerow, who was accompanied by
six others. After respectful salutations on their part, and
benevolent acceptance on his, Harry, as the only one previously known to the doctor, became spokesman for the deputa-
tion.

*Harry Hedgerow*
You see, sir, you gave me some comfort when I was breaking
my heart; and now we are told that the young gentleman at
the Folly is going to be married.

*The Rev. Dr. Opimian*
Indeed! you are better informed than I am.

*Harry Hedgerow*
Why, it's in everybody's mouth. He passes half his time at
Squire Gryll's, and they say it's all for the sake of the young
lady that's there: she that was some days at the Folly; that I
carried in, when she was hurt in the great storm. I am sure I
hope it be true. For you said, if he married, and suitable parties
proposed for her sisters, Miss Dorothy might listen to me. I
have lived in the hope of that ever since. And here are six
suitable parties to propose for her six sisters. That is the long
and the short of it.

*The Rev. Dr. Opimian*

The short of it, at any rate. You speak like a Spartan. You come to the point at once. But why do you come to me? I have no control over the fair damsels.

*Harry Hedgerow*

Why, no sir; but you are the greatest friend of the young gentleman. And if you could just say a word for us to him, you see, sir.

*The Rev. Dr. Opimian*

I see seven notes in the key of A minor, proposing to sound in harmony with the seven notes of the octave above; but I really do not see what I can do in the matter.

*Harry Hedgerow*

Indeed, sir, if you could only ask the young gentleman if he would object to our proposing to the young ladies.

*The Rev. Dr. Opimian*

Why not propose to them yourselves? You seem to be all creditable young men.

*Harry Hedgerow*

I have proposed to Miss Dorothy, you know, and she would not have me; and the rest are afraid. We are all something to do with the land and the wood; farmers, and foresters, and nurserymen, and all that. And we have all opened our hearts to one another. They don't pretend to look above us; but it seems somehow as if they did, and couldn't help it. They are so like young ladies. They daze us, like. Why, if they'd have us, they'd be all in reach of one another. Fancy what a family party there'd be at Christmas. We just want a good friend to put a good foot foremost for us; and if the young gentleman does marry, perhaps they may better themselves by doing likewise.

*The Rev. Dr. Opimian*

And so you seven young friends have each a different favourite among the seven sisters?

*Harry Hedgerow*
Why, that's the beauty of it.

*The Rev. Dr. Opimian*
The beauty of it? Perhaps it is. I suppose there is an agistor*
among you?

*Harry Hedgerow (after looking at his companions, who all shook
their heads)*
I am afraid not. Ought there to be? We don't know what it
means.

*The Rev. Dr. Opimian*
I thought that among so many foresters there might be an
agistor. But it is not indispensable. Well, if the young
gentleman is going to be married, he will tell me of it. And
when he does tell me, I will tell him of you. Have patience. It
may all come right.

*Harry Hedgerow*
Thank ye, sir. Thank ye, sir, kindly.

Which being echoed in chorus by the other six, they took their
departure, much marvelling what the reverend doctor could
mean by an agistor.

'Upon my word,' said the doctor to himself, 'a very
good-looking, respectable set of young men. I do not know
what the others may have to say for themselves. They
behaved like a Greek chorus. They left their share of the
dialogue to the coryphæus. He acquitted himself well, more
like a Spartan than an Athenian, but none the worse for that.
Brevity, in this case, is better than rhetoric. I really like that
youth. How his imagination dwells on the family party at
Christmas. When I first saw him, he was fancying how the

---

* An agistor was a forest officer who superintended the taking in of
strange cattle to board and lodge, and accounted for the profit to the
sovereign. I have read the word, but never heard it. I am inclined to
think that in modern times the duty was carried on under another
name, or merged in the duties of another office.

presence of Miss Dorothy would gladden his father's heart at that season. Now he enlarges the circle, but it is still the same predominant idea. He has lost his mother. She must have been a good woman, and his early home must have been a happy one. The Christmas hearth would not be so uppermost in his thoughts if it had been otherwise. This speaks well for him and his. I myself think much of Christmas and all its associations. I always dine at home on Christmas Day, and measure the steps of my children's heads on the wall, and see how much higher each of them has risen since the same time last year, in the scale of physical life. There are many poetical charms in the heraldings of Christmas. The halcyon builds its nest on the tranquil sea. "The bird of dawning singeth all night long." I have never verified either of these poetical facts. I am willing to take them for granted. I like the idea of the Yule-log, the enormous block of wood carefully selected long before, and preserved where it would be thoroughly dry, which burned on the old-fashioned hearth. It would not suit the stoves of our modern saloons. We could not burn it in our kitchens, where a small fire in the midst of a mass of black iron, roasts, and bakes, and boils, and steams, and broils, and fries, by a complicated apparatus which, whatever may be its other virtues, leaves no space for a Christmas fire. I like the festoons of holly on the walls and windows; the dance under the mistletoe; the gigantic sausage; the baron of beef; the vast globe of plum-pudding, the true image of the earth, flattened at the poles; the tapping of the old October; the inexhaustible bowl of punch; the life and joy of the old hall, when the squire and his household and his neighbourhood were as one. I like the idea of what has gone, and I can still enjoy the reality of what remains. I have no doubt Harry's father burns the Yule-log, and taps the old October. Perhaps, instead of the beef, he produces a fat pig roasted whole, like Eumæus, the divine swineherd in the *Odyssey*. How Harry will burn the Yule-log if he can realise this day-dream of himself and his six friends with the seven sisters! I shall make myself acquainted with the position and characters of these young suitors. To be sure, it is not my business, and I ought to recollect the words of Cicero; "Est enim difficilis cura rerum alienarum: quamquam Terentianus ille Chremes humani nihil a se alienum putat."* I hold with Chremes too. I am not without hope, from some symptoms I have lately seen, that rumour, in the present case, is in a fair way of being right; and if, with the accordance of the young gentleman as a keynote, these two heptachords should harmonise into a double octave, I do not see why I may not take my part as fundamental bass.'

## CHAPTER XXIII

## THE TWO QUADRILLES – POPE'S OMBRE – POETICAL TRUTH TO NATURE – CLEOPATRA

ἔγνωκα δ' οὖν . . .
τοὺς ζῶντας ὥσπερ εἰς πανήγυρίν τινα
ἀφειμένους ἐκ τοῦ θανάτου καὶ τοῦ σκότους
εἰς τὴν διατριβὴν εἰς τὸ φῶς τε τοῦθ' ὃ δὴ
ὁρῶμεν· ὃς δ' ἂν πλεῖστα γελάσῃ καὶ πίῃ,
καὶ τῆς Ἀφροδίτης ἀντιλάβηται τὸν χρόνον
τοῦτον ὃν ἀφεῖται, καὶ τύχῃ γ' ἐράνου τινὸς
πανηγυρίσας, ἥδιστ' ἀπῆλθεν οἴκαδε.

ALEXIS, *Tarantini.*

As men who leave their homes for public games,
We leave our native element of darkness
For life's brief light. And who has most of mirth,
And wine, and love, may, like a satisfied guest,
Return, contented, to the night he sprang from.

In the meantime Mr. Falconer, after staying somewhat longer than usual at home, had returned to the Grange. He found much the same party as he had left; but he observed, or imagined, that Lord Curryfin was much more than previously in favour with Miss Gryll; that she paid him more marked

---

* It is a hard matter to take active concern in the affairs of others; although the Chremes of Terence thinks nothing human alien to himself. *De Officiis,* 9.

attention, and watched his conduct to Miss Niphet with
something more than curiosity.

Amongst the winter evenings' amusements were two forms
of quadrille: the old-fashioned game of cards, and the more
recently fashionable dance. On these occasions it was of course
a carpet-dance. Now, dancing had never been in Mr. Falconer's line, and though modern dancing, especially in quadrilles,
is little more than walking, still in that 'little more' there is
ample room for grace and elegance of motion. Herein Lord
Curryfin outshone all the other young men in the circle. He
endeavoured to be as indiscriminating as possible in inviting
partners: but it was plain to curious observation, especially if a
spice of jealousy mingled with the curiosity, that his favourite
partner was Miss Niphet. When they occasionally danced a
polka, the reverend doctor's mythological theory came out in
full force. It seemed as if Nature had preordained that they
should be inseparable, and the interior conviction of both, that
so it ought to be, gave them an accordance of movement that
seemed to emanate from the innermost mind. Sometimes,
too, they danced the *Minuet de la Cour*. Having once done it,
they had been often unanimously requested to repeat it. In this
they had no competitors. Miss Gryll confined herself to
quadrilles, and Mr. Falconer did not even propose to walk
through one with her. When dancing brought into Miss
Niphet's cheeks the blush-rose bloom, which had more than
once before so charmed Lord Curryfin, it required little
penetration to see, through his external decorum, the passionate admiration with which he regarded her. Mr. Falconer
remarked it, and, looking round to Miss Gryll, thought he
saw the trace of a tear in her eye. It was a questionable
glistening: jealousy construed it into a tear. But why should it
be there? Was her mind turning to Lord Curryfin? and the
more readily because of a newly perceived obstacle? Had
mortified vanity any share in it? No: this was beneath
Morgana. Then why was it there? Was it anything like regret
that, in respect of the young lord, she too had lost her
opportunity? Was he himself blameless in the matter? He had
been on the point of declaration, and she had been apparently
on the point of acceptance: and instead of following up his
advantage, he had been absent longer than usual. This was ill;

but in the midst of the contending forces which severally acted
on him, how could he make it well? So he sate still, torment-
ing himself.

In the meantime, Mr. Gryll had got up at a card-table, in the
outer, which was the smaller drawing-room, a quadrille party
of his own, consisting of himself, Miss Ilex, the Reverend Dr.
Opimian, and Mr. MacBorrowdale.

*Mr. Gryll*

This is the only game of cards that ever pleased me. Once it
was the great evening charm of the whole nation. Now, when
cards are played at all, it has given place to whist, which, in
my younger days, was considered a dry, solemn, studious
game, played in moody silence, only interrupted by an
occasional outbreak of dogmatism and ill-humour. Quadrille
is not so absorbing but that we may talk and laugh over it, and
yet is quite as interesting as anything of the kind has need to
be.

*Miss Ilex*

I delight in quadrille. I am old enough to remember when, in
mixed society in the country, it was played every evening by
some of the party. But *Chaque âge a ses plaisirs, son esprit, et ses
mœurs.** It is one of the evils of growing old that we do not
easily habituate ourselves to changes of custom. The old, who
sit still while the young dance and sing, may be permitted to
regret the once always accessible cards, which, in their own
young days, delighted the old of the generation: and not the
old only.

*The Rev. Dr. Opimian*

There are many causes for the diminished attraction of cards in
evening society. Late dinners leave little evening. The old time
for cards was the interval between tea and supper. Now there
is no such interval, except here and there in out-of-the-way
places, where, perhaps, quadrille and supper may still flourish,
as in the days of Queen Anne. Nothing was more common in
country towns and villages, half a century ago, than parties

* Boileau.

meeting in succession at each other's houses for tea, supper, and quadrille. How popular this game had been you may judge from Gay's ballad, which represents all classes as absorbed in quadrille.* Then the facility of locomotion dissipates, annihilates neighbourhood. People are not now the fixtures they used to be in their respective localities, finding their amusements within their own limited circle. Half the inhabitants of a country place are here today and gone tomorrow. Even of those who are more what they call settled, the greater portion is less, probably, at home than whisking about the world. Then, again, where cards are played at all, whist is more consentaneous to modern solemnity: there is more wiseacre-ism about it: in the same manner that this other sort of quadrille, in which people walk to and from one another with faces of exemplary gravity, has taken the place of the old-fashioned country-dance. 'The merry dance, I dearly love' would never suggest the idea of a quadrille, any more than 'merry England' would call up any image not drawn from ancient ballads and the old English drama.

*Mr. Gryll*
Well, doctor, I intend to have a ball at Christmas, in which all modes of dancing shall have fair play, but country-dances shall have their full share.

* For example:

> When patients lie in piteous case,
>   In comes the apothecary,
> And to the doctor cries 'Alas!
>   *Non debes Quadrillare.'*
> The patient dies without a pill:
> For why? The doctor's at quadrille.

> Should France and Spain again grow loud,
>   The Muscovite grow louder,
> Britain, to curb her neighbours proud,
>   Would want both ball and powder;
> Must want both sword and gun to kill;
> For why? The general's at quadrille.

*The Rev. Dr. Opimian*

I rejoice in the prospect. I shall be glad to see the young dancing as if they were young.

*Miss Ilex*

The variety of the game called tredrille – the Ombre of Pope's *Rape of the Lock* – is a pleasant game for three. Pope had many opportunities of seeing it played, yet he has not described it correctly; and I do not know that this has been observed.

*The Rev. Dr. Opimian*

Indeed, I never observed it. I shall be glad to know how it is so.

*Miss Ilex*

Quadrille is played with forty cards: tredrille usually with thirty: sometimes, as in Pope's Ombre, with twenty-seven. In forty cards, the number of trumps is eleven in the black suits, twelve in the red:* in the thirty, nine in all suits alike.* In twenty-seven, they cannot be more than nine in one suit, and eight in the other three. In Pope's Ombre spades are trumps, and the number is eleven: the number which they would be if the cards were forty. If you follow his description carefully, you will find it to be so.

*Mr. MacBorrowdale*

Why, then, we can only say, as a great philosopher said on another occasion: The description is sufficient 'to impose on the degree of attention with which poetry is read.'

*Miss Ilex*

It is a pity it should be so. Truth to Nature is essential to poetry. Few may perceive an inaccuracy: but to those who do, it causes a great diminution, if not a total destruction, of pleasure in perusal. Shakespeare never makes a flower blossom

---

* Nine cards in the black, and ten in the red suits, in addition to the aces of spades and clubs, Spadille and Basto, which are trumps in all suits.

* Seven cards in each of the four suits in addition to Spadille and Basto.

out of season. Wordsworth, Coleridge, and Southey are true to Nature in this and in all other respects: even in their wildest imaginings.

*The Rev. Dr. Opimian*
Yet here is a combination, by one of our greatest poets, of flowers that never blossom in the same season –

> Bring the rathe primrose, that forsaken dies,
> The tufted crow-toe and pale jessamine,
> The white pink, and the pansie freakt with jet,
> The glowing violet,
> The musk-rose, and the well-attired woodbine,
> With cowslips wan, that hang the pensive head,
> And every flower that sad embroidery wears:
> Bid amaranthus all his beauty shed,
> And daffodillies fill their cups with tears,
> To deck the laureat hearse where Lycid lies.

And at the same time he plucks the berries of the myrtle and the ivy.

*Miss Ilex*
Very beautiful, if not true to English seasons: but Milton might have thought himself justified in making this combination in Arcadia. Generally, he is strictly accurate, to a degree that is in itself a beauty. For instance, in his address to the nightingale –

> Thee, chauntress, oft the woods among,
> I woo to hear thy even-song,
> And missing thee, I walk unseen,
> On the dry smooth-shaven green.

The song of the nightingale ceases about the time that the grass is mown.

*The Rev. Dr. Opimian*
The old Greek poetry is always true to Nature, and will bear any degree of critical analysis. I must say I take no pleasure in poetry that will not.

*Mr. MacBorrowdale*
No poet is truer to Nature than Burns, and no one less so than
Moore. His imagery is almost always false. Here is a highly
applauded stanza, and very taking at first sight –

> The night-dew of heaven, though in silence it weeps,
> Shall brighten with verdure the sod where he sleeps;
> And the tear that we shed, though in secret it rolls,
> Shall long keep his memory green in our souls.

But it will not bear analysis. The dew is the cause of the
verdure: but the tear is not the cause of the memory: the
memory is the cause of the tear.

*The Rev. Dr. Opimian*
There are inaccuracies more offensive to me than even false
imagery. Here is one, in a song which I have often heard with
displeasure. A young man goes up a mountain, and as he goes
higher and higher, he repeats *Excelsior:* but *excelsior* is only
taller in the comparison of things on a common basis, not
higher, as a detached object in the air. Jack's bean-stalk was
*excelsior* the higher it grew: but Jack himself was no more *celsus*
at the top than he had been at the bottom.

*Mr. MacBorrowdale*
I am afraid, doctor, if you look for profound knowledge in
popular poetry, you will often be disappointed.

*The Rev. Dr. Opimian*
I do not look for profound knowledge. But I do expect that
poets should understand what they talk of. Burns was not a
scholar, but he was always master of his subject. All the
scholarship of the world would not have produced *Tam o'
Shanter:* but in the whole of the poem there is not a false image
nor a misused word. What do you suppose these lines
represent?

> I turning saw, throned on a flowery rise,
>     One sitting on a crimson scarf unrolled:
> A queen, with swarthy cheeks and bold black eyes,
>     Brow-bound with burning gold.

*Mr. MacBorrowdale*
I should take it to be a description of the Queen of Bambo.

*The Rev. Dr. Opimian*
Yet thus one of our most popular poets describes Cleopatra:
and one of our most popular artists has illustrated the description by a portrait of a hideous grinning Æthiop. Moore led the
way to this perversion by demonstrating that the Egyptian
women must have been beautiful, because they were 'the
countrywomen of Cleopatra.'* Here we have a sort of coun-
ter-demonstration, that Cleopatra must have been a fright
because she was the countrywoman of the Egyptians. But
Cleopatra was a Greek, the daughter of Ptolemy Auletes, and
a lady of Pontus. The Ptolemies were Greeks, and whoever
will look at their genealogy, their coins, and their medals, will
see how carefully they kept their pure Greek blood uncon-
taminated by African intermixture. Think of this description
and this picture applied to one who Dio says – and all antiquity
confirms him – was 'the most superlatively beautiful of
women, splendid to see, and delightful to hear.'* For she was
eminently accomplished: she spoke many languages with
grace and facility. Her mind was as wonderful as her personal
beauty. There is not a shadow of intellectual expression in that
horrible portrait.

The conversation at the quadrille-table was carried on with
occasional pauses, and intermingled with the technicalities of
the game.
   Miss Gryll continued to alternate between joining in the
quadrille-dances and resuming her seat by the side of the
room, where she was the object of great attention from some
young gentlemen, who were glad to find her unattended by
either Lord Curryfin or Mr. Falconer. Mr. Falconer continued

---

* De Pauw, the great depreciator of everything Egyptian, has, on
the authority of a passage in Aelian, presumed to affix to the
countrywomen of Cleopatra the stigma of complete and unredeemed
ugliness. MOORE'S *Epicurean,* fifth note.

* περικαλλιστάτη γυναικῶν . . . . . . . . λαμπρά τε ἰδεῖν καὶ
ἀκουσθῆχαι οὖσα. DIO, xlii. 34.

to sit as if he had been fixed to his seat, like Theseus. The more he reflected on his conduct, in disappearing at that critical point of time and staying away so long, the more he felt that he had been guilty of an unjustifiable, and perhaps unpardonable, offence. He noticed with extreme discomposure the swarm of moths, as he called them to himself, who were fluttering in the light of her beauty: he would gladly have put them to flight; and this being out of the question, he would have been contented to take his place among them; but he dared not try the experiment.

Nevertheless, he would have been graciously received. The young lady was not cherishing any feeling of resentment against him. She understood, and made generous allowance for, his divided feelings. But his irresolution, if he were left to himself, was likely to be of long duration: and she meditated within herself the means of forcing him to a conclusion one way or the other.

## CHAPTER XXIV

### PROGRESS OF SYMPATHY – LOVE'S INJUNCTIONS – ORLANDO INNAMORATO

> δέρκεο τὴν νεᾶνιν, δέρκεο, κοῦρε·
> ἔγρεο, μή σε φύγῃ πέρδικος ἄγρα.
> ῥόδον ἀνθέων ἀνάσσει·
> ῥόδον ἐν κόραις Μυρίλλα.
>
> ANACREON.

See, youth, the nymph who charms your eyes;
Watch, lest you lose the willing prize.
As queen of flowers the rose you own,
And her of maids the rose alone.

While light, fire, mirth, and music were enlivening the party within the close-drawn curtains, without were moonless night and thickly falling snow; and the morning opened on one vast expanse of white, mantling alike the lawns and the trees, and weighing down the wide-spreading branches. Lord Curryfin, determined not to be baulked of his skating, sallied forth immediately after breakfast, collected a body of labourers, and swept clear an ample surface of ice, a path to it from the house, and a promenade on the bank. Here he and Miss Niphet amused themselves in the afternoon, in company with a small number of the party, and in the presence of about the usual number of spectators. Mr. Falconer was there, and contented himself with looking on.

Lord Curryfin proposed a reel, Miss Niphet acquiesced, but it was long before they found a third. At length one young gentleman, of the plump and rotund order, volunteered to supply the deficiency, and was soon deposited on the ice, where his partners in the ice-dance would have tumbled over him if they had not anticipated the result, and given him a wide berth. One or two others followed, exhibiting several varieties in the art of falling ungracefully. At last the lord and the lady skated away on as large a circuit as the cleared ice permitted, and as they went he said to her –

'If you were the prize of skating, as Atalanta was of running. I should have good hope to carry you off against all competitors but yourself.'

She answered, 'Do not disturb my thoughts, or I shall slip.'

He said no more, but the words left their impression. They gave him as much encouragement as, under their peculiar circumstances, he could dare to wish for, or she could venture to intimate.

Mr. Falconer admired their 'poetry of motion' as much as all the others had done. It suggested a remark which he would have liked to address to Miss Gryll, but he looked round for her in vain. He returned to the house in the hope that he might find her alone, and take the opportunity of making his peace.

He found her alone, but it seemed that he had no peace to make. She received him with a smile, and held out her hand to him, which he grasped fervently. He fancied that it trembled, but her features were composed. He then sat down at the table, on which the old edition of Bojardo was lying open as before. He said, 'You have not been down to the lake to see that wonderful skating.' She answered, 'I have seen it every day but this. The snow deters me today. But it is wonderful. Grace and skill can scarcely go beyond it.'

He wanted to apologise for the mode and duration of his departure and absence, but did not know how to begin. She gave him the occasion. She said, 'You have been longer absent than usual – from our rehearsals. But we are all tolerably perfect in our parts. But your absence was remarked – by some of the party. You seemed to be especially missed by Lord Curryfin. He asked the reverend doctor every morning if he thought you would return that day.'

*Algernon*
And what said the doctor?

*Morgana*
He usually said, 'I hope so.' But one morning he said something more specific.

*Algernon*
What was it?

*Morgana*
I do not know that I ought to tell you.

*Algernon*
Oh, pray do.

*Morgana*
He said, 'The chances are against it.' 'What are the odds?' said Lord Curryfin. 'Seven to one,' said the doctor. 'It ought not to be so,' said Lord Curryfin, 'for here is a whole Greek chorus against seven vestals.' The doctor said, 'I do not estimate the chances by the mere balance of numbers.'

*Algernon*
He might have said more as to the balance of numbers.

*Morgana*
He might have said more, that the seven outweighed the one.

*Algernon*
He could not have said that.

*Morgana*
It would be much for the one to say that the balance was even.

*Algernon*
But how if the absentee himself had been weighed against another in that one's own balance?

*Morgana*
One to one promises at least more even weight.

*Algernon*
I would not have it so. Pray, forgive me.

*Morgana*
Forgive you? For what?

*Algernon*
I wish to say, and I do not well know how, without seeming to assume what I have no right to assume, and then I must have double cause to ask your forgiveness.

*Morgana*
Shall I imagine what you wish to say, and say it for you?

*Algernon*
You would relieve me infinitely, if you imagine justly.

*Morgana*
You may begin by saying with Achilles –

> My mind is troubled, like a fountain stirred;
> And I myself see not the bottom of it.*

*Algernon*
I think I do see it more clearly.

* *Troilus and Cressida*, Act iii. Sc. 3.

*Morgana*
You may next say, I live an enchanted life. I have been in danger of breaking the spell; it has once more bound me with sevenfold force; I was in danger of yielding to another attraction; I went a step too far in all but declaring it; I do not know how to make a decent retreat.

*Algernon*
Oh! no, no, nothing like that.

*Morgana*
Then there is a third thing you may say; but before I say that for you, you must promise to make no reply, not even a monosyllable; and not to revert to the subject for four times seven days. You hesitate.

*Algernon*
It seems as if my fate were trembling in the balance.

*Morgana*
You must give me the promise I have asked for.

*Algernon*
I do give it.

*Morgana*
Repeat it then word for word.

*Algernon*
To listen to you in silence; not to say a syllable in reply; not to return to the subject for four times seven days.

*Morgana*
Then you may say, I have fallen in love; very irrationally – *(he was about to exclaim, but she placed her finger on her lips)* – very irrationally; but I cannot help it. I feel I must yield to my destiny. I will try to free myself from all obstacles; I will, if I can, offer my hand where I have given my heart. And this I will do, if I ever do, at the end of four times seven days: if not then, never.

She placed her finger on her lips again, and immediately left
the room, having first pointed to a passage in the open pages
of *Orlando Innamorato*. She was gone before he was aware that
she was going; but he turned to the book, and read the
indicated passage. It was a part of the continuation of Orlando's adventure in the enchanted garden, when, himself
pursued and scourged by *La Penitenza,* he was pursuing the
Fata Morgana over rugged rocks and through briery thickets.

> Cosi diceva. Con molta rovina
> Sempre seguia Morgana il cavalliero:
> Fiacca ogni bronco ed ogni mala spina,
> Lasciando dietro a se largo il sentiero:
> Ed a la Fata molto s'avicina
> E già d'averla presa è il suo pensiero:
> Ma quel pensiero è ben fallace e vano,
> Però che presa anchor scappa di mano.
>
> O quante volte gli dette di piglio,
> Hora ne' panni ed hor nella persona:
> Ma il vestimento, ch' è bianco e vermiglio,
> Ne la speranza presto l' abbandona:
> Pur una fiata rivoltando il ciglio,
> Come Dio volse e la ventura buona,
> Volgendo il viso quella Fata al Conte
> Ei ben la prese al zuffo ne la fronte.
>
> Allor cangiosse il tempo, e l'aria scura
> Divenne chiara, e il ciel tutto sereno,
> E l' aspro monte si fece pianura;
> E dove prima fu di spine pieno,
> Se coperse de fiori e de verdura:
> E 'l flagellar dell' altra venne meno;
> La qual, con miglior viso che non suole,
> Verso del Conte usava tal parole.
>
> Attenti, cavalliero, a quella chioma. . . .*

---

* Bojardo, *Orlando Innamorato*, 1. ii. c. 9. *Ed. di Vinegia,* 1544.

So spake Repentance. With the speed of fire
Orlando followed where the enchantress fled,

'She must have anticipated my coming,' said the young gentleman to himself. 'She had opened the book at this passage, and has left it to say to me for her – Choose between love and repentance. Four times seven days! That is to ensure calm for the Christmas holidays. The term will pass over

---

> Rending and scattering tree and bush and brier,
> And leaving wide the vestige of his tread.
> Nearer he drew, with feet that could not tire,
> And strong in hope to seize her as she sped.
> How vain the hope! Her form he seemed to clasp,
> But soon as seized, she vanished from his grasp.
>
> How many times he laid his eager hand
> On her bright form, or on her vesture fair;
> But her white robes, and their vermilion band,
> Deceived his touch, and passed away like air.
> But once, as with a half-turned glance she scanned
> Her foe – Heaven's will and happy chance were there –
> No breath for pausing might the time allow -
> He seized the golden forelock of her brow.
>
> Then passed the gloom and tempest from the sky;
> The air at once grew calm and all serene;
> And where rude thorns had clothed the mountain high,
> Was spread a plain, all flowers and vernal green.
> Repentance ceased her scourge. Still standing nigh,
> With placid looks, in her but rarely seen,
> She said: 'Beware how yet the prize you lose;
> The key of fortune few can wisely use.'

In the last stanza of the preceding translation, the seventh line is the essence of the stanza immediately following; the eighth is from a passage several stanzas forward, after Orlando has obtained the key, which was the object of his search:

> Che mal se trova alcun sotto la Luna,
> Ch' adopri ben la chiave di Fortuna.

The first two books of Bojardo's poem were published in 1486. The first complete edition was published in 1495.

The Venetian edition of 1544, from which I have cited this passage, and the preceding one in chapter XX, is the fifteenth and last complete Italian edition. The original work was superseded by the *Rifacciamenti* of Berni and Domenichi. Mr. Panizzi has rendered a great service

Twelfth Night. The lovers of old romance were subjected to a probation of seven years: —

> Seven long years I served thee, fair one,
> Seven long years my fee was scorn.

'But here, perhaps, the case is reversed. She may have feared a probation of seven years for herself; and not with-

---

to literature in reprinting the original. He collated all accessible editions. *Verum opere in longo fas est obrepere somnum.* He took for his standard, as I think unfortunately, the Milanese edition of 1539. With all the care he bestowed on his task, he overlooked one fearful perversion in the concluding stanza, which in all editions but the Milanese reads thus:

> Mentre ch' io canto, ahimè Dio redentore,
> Veggio l' Itàlia tutta a fiamma e a foco,
> Per questi Galli, che con gran furore
> Vengon per disertar non so che loco.
> Però vi lascio in questo vano amore
> Di Fiordespina ardente a poco a poco:
> Un' altra fiata, se mi fia concesso,
> Racconterovi il tutto per expresso.

> Even while I sing, ah me, redeeming Heaven!
> I see all Italy in fire and flame,
> Raised by these Gauls, who, by great fury driven,
> Come with destruction for their end and aim.
> The maiden's heart, by vainest passion riven,
> Not now the rudely broken song may claim;
> Some future day, if Fate auspicious prove,
> Shall end the tale of Fiordespina's love.

The Milanese edition of 1539 was a reprint of that of 1513, in which year the French, under Louis XII, had reconquered Milan. The Milanese editions read *valore* for *furore.*

It was no doubt in deference to the conquerors that the printer of 1513 made this substitution; but it utterly perverts the whole force of the passage. The French, under Charles VIII, invaded Italy in September, 1494, and the horror with which their devastations inspired Bojardo not only stopped the progress of his poem, but brought his life prematurely to a close. He died in December, 1494. The alteration of this single word changes almost into a compliment an expression of cordial detestation.

out reason. And what have I to expect if I let the four times
seven days pass by? Why, then, I can read in her looks – and
they are interpreted in the verses before me – I am assigned
to repentance, without the hope of a third opportunity.
She is not without a leaning towards Lord Curryfin. She
thinks he is passing from her, and on the twenty-ninth day, or
perhaps in the meantime, she will try to regain him. Of course
she will succeed. What rivalry could stand against her? If her
power over him is lessened, it is that she had not chosen to
exert it. She has but to will it, and he is again her slave.
Twenty-eight days! twenty-eight days of doubt and distrac-
tion.' And starting up, he walked out into the park, not
choosing the swept path, but wading knee-deep in snow
where it lay thickest in the glades. He was recalled to himself
by sinking up to his shoulders in a hollow. He emerged with
some difficulty, and retraced his steps to the house, thinking
that, even in the midst of love's most dire perplexities, dry
clothes and a good fire are better than a hole in the snow.


# CHAPTER XXV

## HARRY AND DOROTHY

μνηστῆρες δ' ὁμαδήσαν ἀνὰ μέγαρα σκιόεντα.
                              HOMERUS *in Odyssea.*

The youthful suitors, playing each his part,
Stirred pleasing tumult in each fair one's heart.
                              *Adapted – not translated.*


Harry Hedgerow had found means, on several occasions of
delivering farm and forest produce at the Tower, to introduce
his six friends to the sisters giving all the young men in turn to
understand that they must not think of Miss Dorothy; an
injunction which, in the ordinary perverse course of events,

might have led them all to think of no one else, and produced a complication very disagreeable for their introducer. It was not so, however. 'The beauty of it,' as Harry said to the reverend doctor, was that each had found a distinct favourite among the seven vestals. They had not, however, gone beyond giving pretty intelligible hints. They had not decidedly ventured to declare or propose. They left it to Harry to prosecute his suit to Miss Dorothy, purposing to step in on the rear of his success. They had severally the satisfaction of being assured by various handsome young gipsies, whose hands they had crossed with lucky shillings, that each of them was in love with a fair young woman, who was quite as much in love with him, and whom he would certainly marry before twelve months were over. And they went on their way rejoicing.

Now Harry was indefatigable in his suit, which he had unbounded liberty to plead; for Dorothy always listened to him complacently, though without departing from the answer she had originally given, that she and her sisters would not part with each other and their young master.

The sisters had not attached much importance to Mr. Falconer's absences; for on every occasion of his return the predominant feeling he had seemed to express was that of extreme delight at being once more at home.

One day, while Mr. Falconer was at the Grange, receiving admonition from *Orlando Innamorato*, Harry, having the pleasure to find Dorothy alone, pressed his suit as usual, was listened to as usual, and seemed likely to terminate without being more advanced than usual, except in so far as they both found a progressive pleasure, she in listening, and he in being listened to. There was to both a growing charm in thus 'dallying with the innocence of love,' and though she always said No with her lips, he began to read Yes in her eyes.

*Harry*
Well, but, Miss Dorothy, though you and your sisters will not leave your young master, suppose somebody should take him away from you, what would you say then?

*Dorothy*
What do you mean, Master Harry?

*Harry*

Why, suppose he should get married, Miss Dorothy?

*Dorothy*

Married!

*Harry*

How should you like to see a fine lady in the Tower, looking at you as much as to say, This is mine?

*Dorothy*

I will tell you very candidly, I should not like it at all. But what makes you think of such a thing?

*Harry*

You know where he is now?

*Dorothy*

At Squire Gryll's rehearsing a play for Christmas.

*Harry*

And Squire Gryll's niece is a great beauty, and a great fortune.

*Dorothy*

Squire Gryll's niece was here, and my sisters and myself saw a great deal of her. She is a very nice young lady; but he has seen great beauties and great fortunes before; he has always been indifferent to the beauties, and he does not care about fortune. I am sure he would not like to change his mode of life.

*Harry*

Ah, Miss Dorothy! you don't know what it is to fall in love. It tears a man up by the roots, like a gale of wind.

*Dorothy*

Is that your case, Master Harry?

*Harry*

Indeed it is, Miss Dorothy. If you didn't speak kindly to me, I do not know what would become of me. But you always speak kindly to me, though you won't have me.

*Dorothy*
I never said won't, Master Harry.

*Harry*
No, but you always say can't, and that's the same as won't, so long as you don't.

*Dorothy*
You are a very good young man, Master Harry. Everybody speaks well of you. And I am really pleased to think you are so partial to me. And if my young master and my sisters were married, and I were disposed to follow their example, I will tell you very truly, you are the only person I should think of, Master Harry.

Master Harry attempted to speak, but he felt choked in the attempt at utterance; and in default of words, he threw himself on his knees before his beloved, and clasped his hands together with a look of passionate imploring, which was rewarded by a benevolent smile. And they did not change their attitude till the entrance of one of the sisters startled them from their sympathetic reverie.

Harry, having thus made a successful impression on one of the Theban gates, encouraged his six allies to carry on the siege of the others; for which they had ample opportunity, as the absences of the young gentleman became longer, and the rumours of an attachment between him and Miss Gryll obtained more ready belief.

## CHAPTER XXVI

## DOUBTS AND QUESTIONS

οὐ χρὴ κακοῖσι θυμὸν ἐπιτρέπειν·
προκόψομεν γὰρ οὐδέν, ἀσάμενοι,
ὦ Βάκχι· φάρμακον δ' ἄριστον
οἶνον ἐνεικαμένοις μεθύσθαι.
                                        ALCÆUS.

Bacchus! 'Tis vain to brood on care,
    Since grief no remedy supplies;
Be ours the sparkling bowl to share,
    And drown our sorrows as they rise.

Mr. Falconer saw no more of Miss Gryll till the party
assembled in the drawing-rooms. She necessarily took the arm
of Lord Curryfin for dinner, and it fell to the lot of Mr.
Falconer to offer his to Miss Niphet, so that they sat at remote
ends of the table, each wishing himself in the other's place; but
Lord Curryfin paid all possible attention to his fair neighbour.
Mr. Falconer could see that Miss Gryll's conversation with
Lord Curryfin was very animated and joyous: too merry,
perhaps, for love: but cordial to a degree that alarmed him. It
was, however, clear by the general mirth at the head of the
table that nothing very confidential or sentimental was
passing. Still, a young lady who had placed the destiny of her
life on a point of brief suspense ought not to be so merry as
Miss Gryll evidently was. He said little to Miss Niphet; and
she, with her habit of originating nothing, sat in her normal
state of statue-like placidity, listening to the conversation near
her. She was on the left hand of Mr. Gryll. Miss Ilex was on
his right, and on her right was the Reverend Doctor Opimian.
These three kept up an animated dialogue. Mr. MacBorrowdale was in the middle of the table, and amused his two
immediate fair neighbours with remarks appertaining to the
matter immediately before them, the preparation and arrangement of a good dinner: remarks that would have done honour
to Francatelli.

After a while, Mr. Falconer bethought him that he would try to draw out Miss Niphet's opinion on the subject nearest his heart. He said to her: 'They are very merry at the head of the table.'

*Miss Niphet*
I suppose Lord Curryfin is in the vein for amusing his company, and he generally succeeds in his social purposes.

*Mr. Falconer*
You lay stress on social, as if you thought him not successful in all his purposes.

*Miss Niphet*
Not in all his inventions, for example. But in the promotion of social enjoyment he has few equals. Of course, it must be in congenial society. There is a power of being pleased, as well as a power of pleasing. With Miss Gryll and Lord Curryfin, both meet in both. No wonder that they amuse those around them.

*Mr. Falconer*
In whom there must also be a power of being pleased.

*Miss Niphet*
Most of the guests here have it. If they had not they would scarcely be here. I have seen some dismal persons, any one of whom would be a kill-joy to a whole company. There are none such in this party. I have also seen a whole company all willing to be pleased, but all mute from not knowing what to say to each other: not knowing how to begin. Lord Curryfin would be a blessing to such a party. He would be the steel to their flint.

*Mr. Falconer*
Have you known him long?

*Miss Niphet*
Only since I met him here.

*Mr. Falconer*
Have you heard that he is a suitor to Miss Gryll?

*Miss Niphet*
I have heard so.


*Mr. Falconer*
Should you include the probability of his being accepted in your estimate of his social successes?


*Miss Niphet*
Love affairs are under influences too capricious for the calculation of probabilities.


*Mr. Falconer*
Yet I should be very glad to hear your opinion. You know them both so well.


*Miss Niphet*
I am disposed to indulge you, because I think it is not mere curiosity that makes you ask the question. Otherwise I should not be inclined to answer it. I do not think he will ever be the affianced lover of Morgana. Perhaps he might have been if he had persevered as he began. But he has been used to smiling audiences. He did not find the exact reciprocity he looked for. He fancied that it was, or would be, for another. I believe he was right.


*Mr. Falconer*
Yet you think he might have succeeded if he had persevered.


*Miss Niphet*
I can scarcely think otherwise, seeing how much he has to recommend him.


*Mr. Falconer*
But he has not withdrawn.


*Miss Niphet*
No, and will not. But she is too high-minded to hold him to a proposal not followed up as it commenced; even if she had not turned her thoughts elsewhere.

*Mr. Falconer*

Do you not think she could recall him to his first ardour if she exerted all her fascinations for the purpose?

*Miss Niphet*

It may be so. I do not think she will try. *(She added, to herself:)* I do not think she would succeed.

Mr. Falconer did not feel sure she would not try: he thought he saw symptoms of her already doing so. In his opinion Morgana was, and must be, irresistible. But as he thought his fair neighbour somewhat interested in the subject, he wondered at the apparent impassiveness with which she replied to his questions.

In the meantime he found, as he had often done before, that the more his mind was troubled, the more Madeira he could drink without disordering his head.

## CHAPTER XXVII

### LOVE IN MEMORY

Il faut avoir aimè une fois en sa vie, non pour le moment où l'on aime, car on n'éprouve alors que des tourmens, des regrets, de la jalousie: mais peu à peu ces tourmens-là deviennent des souvenirs, qui charment notre arrière saison: . . . et quand vous verrez la vieillesse douce, facile et tolérante, vous pourrez dire comme Fontenelle: L'amour a passé par-là.

SCRIBE, *La Vieille*.

Miss Gryll carefully avoided being alone with Mr. Falconer, in order not to give him an opportunity of speaking on the forbidden subject. She was confident that she had taken the only course which promised to relieve her from a life of intolerable suspense; but she wished to subject her conduct to dispassionate opinion, and she thought she could not submit it to a more calmly judging person than her old spinster friend,

Miss Ilex, who had, moreover, the great advantage of being a woman of the world. She therefore took an early opportunity of telling her what had passed between herself and Mr. Falconer, and asking her judgment on the point.

*Miss Ilex*

Why, my dear, if I thought there had been the slightest chance of his ever knowing his own mind sufficiently to come to the desired conclusion himself, I should have advised your giving him a little longer time; but as it is clear to me that he never would have done so, and as you are decidedly partial to him, I think you have taken the best course which was open to you. He had all but declared to you more than once before; but this 'all but' would have continued and you would have sacrificed your life to him for nothing.

*Miss Gryll*

But do you think you would in my case have done as I did?

*Miss Ilex*

No, my dear, I certainly should not: for, in a case very similar, I did not. It does not follow that I was right. On the contrary, I think you are right, and I was wrong. You have shown true moral courage where it was most needed.

*Miss Gryll*

I hope I have not revived any displeasing recollections.

*Miss Ilex*

No, my dear, no; the recollections are not displeasing. The day dreams of youth, however fallacious, are a composite of pain and pleasure: for the sake of the latter the former is endured, nay, even cherished in memory.

*Miss Gryll*

Hearing what I hear you were, seeing what I see you are, observing your invariable cheerfulness, I should not have thought it possible that you could have been crossed in love, as your words seem to imply.

*Miss Ilex*

I was, my dear, and have been foolish enough to be constant
all my life to a simple idea; and yet I would not part with this
shadow for any attainable reality.

*Miss Gryll*

If it were not opening the fountain of an ancient sorrow, I
could wish to know the story, not from idle curiosity, but
from my interest in you.

*Miss Ilex*

Indeed, my dear Morgana, it is very little of a story: but such
as it is, I am willing to tell it you. I had the credit of being
handsome and accomplished. I had several lovers; but my
inner thoughts distinguished only one; and he, I think, had a
decided preference for me, but it was a preference of present
impression. If some Genius had commanded him to choose a
wife from any company of which I was one, he would, I feel
sure, have chosen me; but he was very much of an universal
lover, and was always overcome by the smiles of present
beauty. He was of a romantic turn of mind: he disliked and
avoided the ordinary pursuits of young men: he delighted in
the society of accomplished young women, and in that alone.
It was the single link between him and the world. He would
disappear for weeks at a time, wandering in forests, climbing
mountains, and descending into the dingles of mountain-
streams, with no other companion than a Newfoundland dog;
a large black dog, with a white breast, four white paws, and a
white tip to his tail: a beautiful, affectionate dog: I often patted
him on the head, and fed him with my hand. He knew me as
well as Bajardo* knew Angelica.

---

* Rinaldo's horse: he had escaped from his master, and had revelled
Sacripante with his heels:—
    Indi va mansueto alla donzella,
    Con umile sembiante e gesto umano:
    Come intorno al padrone il can saltella,
    Che sia due giorni o tre stato lontano.
    Bajardo ancora avea memoria d' ella,
    Che in Albracca il servia già di sua mano.
                         *Orlando Furioso*, c. i. s. 75.

Tears started into her eyes at the recollection of the dog. She paused for a moment.

*Miss Gryll*

I see the remembrance is painful. Do not proceed.

*Miss Ilex*

No, my dear. I would not, if I could, forget that dog. Well, my young gentleman, as I have said, was a sort of universal lover, and made a sort of half-declaration to half the young women he knew: sincerely for the moment to all: but with more permanent earnestness, more constant return, to me than to any other. If I had met him with equal earnestness, if I could have said or implied to him in any way, 'Take me while you may, or think of me no more,' I am persuaded I should not now write myself spinster. But I wrapped myself up in reserve. I thought it fitting that all advances should come from him: that I should at most show nothing more than willingness to hear, not even the semblance of anxiety to receive them. So nothing came of our love but remembrance and regret. Another girl, whom I am sure he loved less, but who understood him better, acted towards him as I ought to have done, and became his wife. Therefore, my dear, I applaud your moral courage, and regret that I had it not when the occasion required it.

*Miss Gryll*

My lover, if I may so call him, differs from yours in this: that he is not wandering in his habits, nor versatile in his affections.

*Miss Ilex*

The peculiar system of domestic affection in which he was brought up, and which his maturer years have confirmed, presents a greater obstacle to you than any which my lover's versatility presented to me, if I had known how to deal with it.

*Miss Gryll*

But how was it that, having so many admirers as you must have had, you still remained single?

*Miss Ilex*
Because I had fixed my heart on one who was not like any one
else. If he had been one of a class, such as most persons in this
world are, I might have replaced the first idea by another; but
'his soul was like a star, and dwelt apart.'

*Miss Gryll*
A very erratic star, apparently. A comet, rather.

*Miss Ilex*
No. For the qualities which he loved and admired in the object
of his temporary affection existed more in his imagination
than in her. She was only the framework of the picture of his
fancy. He was true to his idea, though not to the exterior
semblance on which he appended it, and to or from which he
so readily transferred it. Unhappily for myself, he was more
of a reality to me than I was to him.

*Miss Gryll*
His marriage could scarcely have been a happy one. Did you
ever meet him again.

*Miss Ilex*
Not of late years, but for a time occasionally in general
society, which he very sparingly entered. Our intercourse was
friendly; but he never knew, never imagined, how well I loved
him, nor even, perhaps, that I had loved him at all. I had kept
my secret only too well. He retained his wandering habits,
disappearing from time to time, but always returning home. I
believe he had no cause to complain of his wife. Yet I cannot
help thinking that I could have fixed him and kept him at
home. Your case is in many respects similar to mine; but the
rivalry to me was in a wandering fancy: to you it is in fixed
domestic affections. Still, you were in as much danger as I was
of being the victim of an idea and a punctilio: and you have
taken the only course to save you from it. I regret that I gave
in to the punctilio: but I would not part with the idea. I find a
charm in the recollection far preferable to

    The waveless calm, the slumber of the dead

which weighs on the minds of those who have never loved, or never earnestly.

# CHAPTER XXVIII

## ARISTOPHANES IN LONDON

Non duco contentionis funem, dum constet inter nos, quod fere totus mundus exerceat histrioniam.
　　　　　　　　　　　　PETRONIUS ARBITER.

I do not draw the rope of contention,* while it is agreed amongst us, that almost the whole world practises acting.

All the world's a stage. SHAKESPEARE.

En el teatro del mundo
Todos son representantes. CALDERON.

Tous les comédiens ne sont pas au théâtre. *French Proverb.*

Rain came, and thaw, followed by drying wind. The roads were in good order for the visitors to the Aristophanic comedy. The fifth day of Christmas was fixed for the performance. The theatre was brilliantly lighted, with spermaceti candles in glass chandeliers for the audience, and argand lamps for the stage. In addition to Mr. Gryll's own houseful of company, the beauty and fashion of the surrounding country, which comprised an extensive circle, adorned the semicircular seats; which, however, were not mere stone benches, but were

---

* A metaphor apparently taken from persons pulling in opposite directions at each end of a rope. I cannot see, as some have done, that it has anything in common with Horace's *Tortum digna sequi potius quam ducere funem:* 'More worthy to follow than to lead the tightened cord': which is a metaphor taken from a towing line, or any line acting in a similar manner, where one draws and another is drawn. Horace applies it to money, which he says should be the slave, and not the master of its possessor.

backed, armed, and padded into comfortable stalls. Lord
Curryfin was in his glory in the capacity of stage-manager.

The curtain rising, as there was no necessity for its being
made to fall,* discovered the scene, which was on the London
bank of the Thames, on the terrace of a mansion occupied by
the Spirit-rapping Society, with an archway in the centre of
the building, showing a street in the background. Gryllus was
lying asleep. Circe, standing over him, began the dialogue.

*Circe*
Wake, Gryllus, and arise in human form.

*Gryllus*
I have slept soundly, and had pleasant dreams.

*Circe*
I, too, have soundly slept. Divine how long.

*Gryllus*
Why, judging by the sun, some fourteen hours.

*Circe*
Three thousand years.

*Gryllus*
                That is a nap indeed.
But this is not your garden, nor your palace.
Where are we now?

*Circe*
                Three thousand years ago,
This land was forest, and a bright pure river
Ran through it to and from the Ocean stream.
Now, through a wilderness of human forms,
And human dwellings, a polluted flood

---

* The Athenian theatre was open to the sky, and if the curtain had
been made to fall it would have been folded up in mid-air, destroying
the effect of the scene. Being raised from below, it was invisible when
not in use.

Rolls up and down, charged with all earthly poisons,
Poisoning the air in turn.

*Gryllus*
      I see vast masses
Of strange unnatural things.

*Circe*
      Houses, and ships,
And boats, and chimneys vomiting black smoke,
Horses, and carriages of every form,
And restless bipeds, rushing here and there
For profit or for pleasure, as they phrase it.

*Gryllus*
Oh, Jupiter and Bacchus! what a crowd,
Flitting, like shadows without mind or purpose,
Such as Ulysses saw in Erebus.
But wherefore are we here?

*Circe*
      There have arisen
Some mighty masters of the invisible world,
And these have summoned us.

*Gryllus*
      With what design?

*Circe*
That they themselves must tell. Behold they come,
Carrying a mystic table, around which
they work their magic spells. Stand by, and mark.

Three spirit-rappers appeared, carrying a table, which they
placed on one side of the stage:—

  1. Carefully the table place
     Let our gifted brother trace
     A ring around the enchanted space.

2. Let him tow'rd the table point
   With his first forefinger joint,
   And with mesmerised beginning
   Set the sentient oak-slab spinning.
3. Now it spins around, around,
   Sending forth a murmuring sound,
   By the initiate understood
   As of spirits in the wood.
*All.* Once more Circe we invoke.

*Circe*
Here: not bound in ribs of oak,
Nor, from wooden disk revolving,
In strange sounds strange riddles solving,
But in native form appearing,
Plain to sight, as clear to hearing.

*The Three*
Thee with wonder we behold.
By thy hair of burning gold,
By thy face with radiance bright,
By thine eyes of beaming light,
We confess thee, mighty one,
For the daughter of the Sun
On thy form we gaze appalled.

*Circe*
Gryllus, too, your summons called.

*The Three*
Him of yore thy powerful spell
Doomed in swinish shape to dwell;
Yet such life he reckoned then
Happier than the life of men.
Now, when carefully he ponders
All our scientific wonders,
Steam-driven myriads, all in motion,
On the land and on the ocean,
Going, for the sake of going,
Wheresoever waves are flowing,

Wheresoever winds are blowing;
Converse through the sea transmitted,
Swift as ever thought has flitted;
All the glories of our time,
Past the praise of loftiest rhyme;
Will he, seeing these, indeed,
Still retain his ancient creed,
Ranking, in his mental plan,
Life of beast o'er life of man?

*Circe*
Speak, Gryllus.

*Gryllus*
        It is early yet to judge:
But all the novelties I yet have seen
Seem changes for the worse.

*The Three*
        If we could show him
Our triumphs in succession, one by one,
'Twould surely change his judgment: and herein
How might'st thou aid us, Circe!

*Circe*
        I will do so:
And calling down, like Socrates, of yore,
The clouds to aid us, they shall shadow forth,
In bright succession, all that they behold,
From air, on earth and sea. I wave my wand:
And lo! they come, even as they came in Athens,
Shining like virgins of ethereal life.

The Chorus of Clouds descended, and a dazzling array of
female beauty was revealed by degrees through folds of misty
gauze. They sang their first choral song: —

## CHORUS OF CLOUDS*

### I

Clouds ever-flowing, conspicuously soaring,
    From loud-rolling Ocean, whose stream* gave us birth
To heights, whence we look over torrents down-pouring
    To the deep quiet vales of the fruit-giving earth, –
As the broad eye of Æther, unwearied in brightness,
    Dissolves our mist-veil in glittering rays,
Our forms we reveal from its vapoury lightness,
    In semblance immortal, with far-seeing gaze.

### II

Shower-bearing Virgins, we seek not the regions
    Whence Pallas, the Muses, and Bacchus have fled,
But the city, where Commerce embodies her legions,
    And Mammon exalts his omnipotent head.
All joys of thought, feeling, and taste are before us,
    Wherever the beams of his favour are warm:
Though transient full oft as the veil of our chorus,
    Now golden with glory, now passing in storm.

Reformers, scientific, moral, educational, political, passed
in succession, each answering a question of Gryllus. Gryllus
observed, that so far from everything being better than it had
been, it seemed that everything was wrong and wanted
mending. The chorus sang its second song.

Seven competitive examiners entered with another table,
and sat down on the opposite side of the stage to the
spirit-rappers. They brought forward Hermogenes* as a
crammed fowl to argue with Gryllus. Gryllus had the best of

* The first stanza is pretty closely adapted from the strophe of
Aristophanes: ἀέναοι Νεφέλαι. The second is only a distant imitation
of the antistrophe: παρθένοι ὀμβροφόροι.

* In Homer, and all the older poets, the ocean is a river surrounding
the earth, and the seas are inlets from it.

* See Chapter XV.

the argument; but the examiners adjudged the victory to Hermogenes. The chorus sang its third song.

Circe, at the request of the spirit-rappers, whose power was limited to the production of sound, called up several visible spirits, all illustrious in their day, but all appearing as in the days of their early youth, 'before their renown was around them.' They were all subjected to competitive examination, and were severally pronounced disqualified for the pursuit in which they had shone. At last came one whom Circe recommended to the examiners as a particularly promising youth. He was a candidate for military life. Every question relative to his profession he answered to the purpose. To every question not so relevant he replied that he did not know and did not care. This drew on him a reprimand. He was pronounced disqualified, and ordered to join the rejected, who were ranged in a line along the back of the scene. A touch of Circe's wand changed them into their semblance of maturer years. Among them were Hannibal and Oliver Cromwell; and in the foreground was the last candidate, Richard Cœur-de-Lion. Richard flourished his battle-axe over the heads of the examiners, who jumped up in great trepidation, overturned their table, tumbled over one another, and escaped as best they might in haste and terror. The heroes vanished. The chorus sang its fourth song.

## CHORUS

### I

As before the pike will fly
Dace and roach and such small fry;
As the leaf before the gale,
As the chaff beneath the flail,
As before the wolf the flocks,
As before the hounds the fox;
As before the cat the mouse,
As the rat from falling house;
As the fiend before the spell
Of holy water, book, and bell, –
So has fled, in gaunt dismay,

This septemvirate of quacks
From the shadowy attacks
Of Cœur-de-Lion's battle-axe.

## II

Could he in corporeal might,
Plain to feeling as to sight,
Rise again to solar light,
How his arm would put to flight
All the forms of Stygian night
That round us rise in grim array,
Darkening the meridian day:
Bigotry, whose chief employ
Is embittering earthly joy;
Chaos, throned in pedant state,
Teaching echo how to prate;
And 'Ignorance with looks profound,'
Not 'with eye that loves the ground.'
But stalking wide, with lofty crest,
In science's pretentious vest.

## III

And now, great masters of the realms of shade,
   To end the task which called us down from air,
We shall present, in pictured show arrayed,
   Of this your modern world the triumphs rare,
That Gryllus's benighted spirit
May wake to your transcendent merit,
And, with profoundest admiration thrilled,
He may with willing mind assume his place
In your steam-nursed, steam-borne, steam-killed,
And gas-enlightened race.

*Circe*
Speak, Gryllus, what you see.

*Gryllus*
      I see the ocean,
And o'er its face ships passing wide and far;

Some with expanded sails before the breeze,
And some with neither sails nor oars, impelled
By some invisible power against the wind,
Scattering the spray before them. But of many
One is on fire, and one has struck on rocks
And melted in the waves like fallen snow.
Two crash together in the middle sea,
And go to pieces on the instant, leaving
No soul to tell the tale, and one is hurled
In fragments to the sky, strewing the deep
With death and wreck. I had rather live with Circe
Even as I was, than flit about the world
In those enchanted ships, which some Alastor
Must have devised as traps for mortal ruin.

*Circe*
Look yet again.

*Gryllus*
                Now the whole scene is changed.
I see long chains of strange machines on wheels,
With one in front of each, puffing white smoke
From a black hollow column. Fast and far
They speed, like yellow leaves before the gale,
When Autumn winds are strongest. Through their
windows
I judge them thronged with people; but distinctly
Their speed forbids my seeing.

*Spirit-Rapper*
                This is one
Of the great glories of our modern time,
'Men are become as birds,' and skim like swallows
The surface of the world.

*Gryllus*
                For what good end?

*Spirit-Rapper*
The end is in itself – the end of skimming
The surface of the world.

*Gryllus*
            If that be all,
I had rather sit in peace in my old home:
But while I look, two of them meet and clash,
And pile their way with ruin. One is rolled
Down a steep bank; one through a broken bridge
Is dashed into a flood. Dead, dying wounded,
Are there as in a battlefield. Are these
Your modern triumphs? Jove preserve me from them.

*Spirit-Rapper*
These ills are rare. Millions are borne in safety
Where one incurs mischance. Look yet again.

*Gryllus*
I see a mass of light brighter than that
Which burned in Circe's palace, and beneath it
A motley crew, dancing to joyous music,
But from that light explosion comes, and flame;
And forth the dancers rush in haste and fear
From their wide-blazing hall.

*Spirit-Rapper*
            Oh, Circe! Circe!
Thou show'st him all the evil of our arts
In more than just proportion to the good.
Good without evil is not given to man.
Jove, from his urns dispensing good and ill,
Gives all unmixed to some, and good and ill
Mingled to many – good unmixed to none.*
Our arts are good. The inevitable ill

* This is the true sense of the Homeric passage:—

δοιοὶ γάρ τε πίθοι κατακείαται ἐν Διὸς οὔδει
δώρων οἷα δίδωσι, κακῶν ἕτερος δέ τ’ ἑάων·
ᾧ μὲν καμμίξας δώῃ Ζεὺς τερπικέραυνος,
ἄλλοτε μέν τε κακῷ ὅ γε κύρεται, ἄλλοτε δ’ ἐσθλῷ·
ᾧ δέ κε τῶν λυγρῶν δώῃ λωβητὸν ἔθηκε,
καί ἑ κακὴ βούβρωστις ἐπὶ χθόνα δῖαν ἐλαύνει,
φοιτᾷ δ’ οὔτε θεοῖσι τετιμένος οὔτε βροτοῖσιν.

                          HOMER, Il. xxiv.

That mixes with them, as with all things human,
Is as a drop of water in a goblet
Full of old wine.

*Gryllus*
              More than one drop, I fear,
And those of bitter water.

*Circe*
              There is yet
An ample field of scientific triumph:
What shall we show him next?

*Spirit-Rapper*
              Pause we awhile.
He is not in the mood to feel conviction
Of our superior greatness. He is all
For rural comfort and domestic ease,
But our impulsive days are all for moving:
Sometimes with some ulterior end, but still
For moving, moving always. There is nothing
Common between us in our points of judgment.
He takes his stand upon tranquillity,
We ours upon excitement. There we place
The being, end, and aim of mortal life,
The many are with us: some few perhaps,
With him. We put the question to the vote
By universal suffrage. Aid us, Circe!

---

There are only two distributions: good and ill mixed, and unmixed
ill. None, as Heyne has observed, receive unmixed good. *Ex dolio
bonorum nemo meracius accipit: hoc memorare omisit.* This sense is implied,
not expressed. Pope missed it in his otherwise beautiful translation.

Two urns by Jove's high throne have ever stood,
The source of evil one, and one of good;
From thence the cup of mortal man he fills,
Blessings to these, to those distributes ills,
To most he mingles both: the wretch decreed
To taste the bad, unmixed, is curst indeed;
Pursued by wrongs, by meagre famine driven,
He wanders, outcast both of earth and heaven.   POPE

On talismanic wings your spells can waft
The question and reply. Are we not wiser,
Happier, and better, than the men of old,
Of Homer's days, of Athens, and of Rome!

*Voices Without*
  Ay. No. Ay, ay. No. Ay, ay ay, ay, ay,
We are the wisest race the earth has known,
The most advanced in all the arts of life,
In science and in morals.

*Spirit-Rapper*
        The ays have it.
What is that wondrous sound, that seems like thunder
Mixed with gigantic laughter?

*Circe*
        It is Jupiter,
Who laughs at your presumption; half in anger,
And half in mockery. Now, my worthy masters,
You must in turn experience in yourselves
The mighty magic thus far tried on others.

The table turned slowly, and by degrees went on spinning
with accelerated speed. The legs assumed motion, and it
danced off the stage. The arms of the chairs put forth hands,
and pinched the spirit-rappers, who sprang up and ran off,
pursued by their chairs. This piece of mechanical pantomime
was a triumph of Lord Curryfin's art, and afforded him ample
satisfaction for the failure of his resonant vases.

*Circe*
  Now, Gryllus, we may seek our ancient home
In my enchanted isle.

*Gryllus*
        Not yet, not yet
Good signs are toward of a joyous supper.
Therein the modern world may have its glory,
And I, like an impartial judge, am ready

To do it ample justice. But, perhaps,
As all we hitherto have seen are shadows,
So too may be the supper.

*Circe*
          Fear not Gryllus,
That you will find a sound reality,
To which the land and air, seas, lakes, and rivers,
Have sent their several tributes. Now, kind friends,
Who with your smiles have graciously rewarded
Our humble, but most earnest aims to please,
And with your presence at our festal board
Will charm the winter midnight, Music gives
The signal: Welcome and old wine await you.

*The Chorus*
Shadows tonight have offered portraits true
Of many follies which the world enthrall.
'Shadows we are, and shadows we pursue':
But, in the banquet's well-illumined hall,
Realities, delectable to all,
Invite you now our festal joy to share.
Could we our Attic prototype recall,
One compound word should give our bill of fare:*
But where our language fails, our hearts true welcome
bear.

Miss Gryll was replendent as Circe; and Miss Niphet, as
leader of the chorus, looked like Melpomene herself, slightly
unbending her tragic severity into that solemn smile which
characterised the chorus of the old comedy. The charm of the
first acted irresistibly on Mr. Falconer. The second would
have completed, if anything had been wanted to complete it,
the conquest of Lord Curryfin.

The supper passed off joyously, and it was a late hour of the
morning before the company dispersed.

---

* As at the end of *Ecclesiazusæ*.

## CHAPTER XXIX

## THE BALD VENUS – IÑEZ DE CASTRO – THE UNITY OF LOVE

> Within the temple of my purer mind
> One imaged form shall ever live enshrined.
> And hear the vows, to first affection due,
> Still breathed: for love that ceases ne'er was true.
> LEYDEN'S *Scenes of Infancy*.

An interval of a week was interposed between the comedy and the intended ball. Mr. Falconer having no fancy for balls, and disturbed beyond endurance by the interdict which Miss Gryll had laid on him against speaking for four times seven days on the subject nearest his heart, having discharged with becoming self-command his share in the Aristophanic comedy, determined to pass his remaining days of probation in the Tower, where he found, in the attentions of the seven sisters, not a perfect Nepenthe, but the only possible antidote to intense vexation of spirit. It is true, his two Hebes, pouring out his Madeira, approximated as nearly as anything could do to Helen's administration of the true Nepenthe. He might have sung of Madeira, as Redi's Bacchus sang of one of his favourite wines: –

> Egli è il vero oro potabile,
> Che mandar suole in esilio
> Ogni male inrimediabile:
> Egli è d' Elena il Nepente,
> Che fa stare il mondo allegro,
> Dai pensieri
> Foschi e neri
> Sempre sciolto, e sempre esente.*

Matters went on quietly at the Grange. One evening Mr. Gryll said quietly to the Reverend Doctor Opimian –

* Redi, *Bacco in Toscana*.

'I have heard you, doctor, more than once, very eulogistic
of hair as indispensable to beauty. What say you to the bald
Venus of the Romans – *Venus Calva?*'

*The Rev. Dr. Opimian*
Why, sir, if it were a question whether the Romans had any
such deity, I would unhesitatingly maintain the *negatur.* Where
do you find her?

*Mr. Gryll*
In the first place, I find her in several dictionaries.

*The Rev. Dr. Opimian*
A dictionary is nothing without an authority. You have no
authority but that of one or two very late writers, and two or
three old grammarians, who had found the word and guessed
at its meaning. You do not find her in any genuine classic. A
bald Venus. It is as manifest a contradiction in terms as hot ice,
or black snow.

*Lord Curryfin*
Yet I have certainly read, though I cannot at this moment say
where, that there was in Rome a temple to *Venus Calva,* and
that it was so dedicated in consequence of one of two
circumstances: the first being that through some divine anger
the hair of the Roman women fell off, and that Ancus Martius
set up a bald statue of his wife, which served as an expiation,
for all the women recovered their hair, and the worship of the
Bald Venus was instituted; the other being, that when Rome
was taken by the Gauls, and when they had occupied the city,
and were besieging the Capitol, the besieged having no
materials to make bowstrings, the women cut off their hair for
the purpose, and after the war a statue of the Bald Venus was
raised in honour of the women.

*The Rev. Dr. Opimian*
I have seen the last story transferred to the time of the younger
Maximin.* But when two or three explanations, of which

* Julius Capitolinus, *Max. Jun. c.* 7.

only one can possibly be true, are given of any real or supposed fact, we may safely conclude that all are false. These are ridiculous myths, founded on the misunderstanding of an obsolete word. Some hold that *Calva*, as applied to Venus, signifies pure; but I hold with others that it signifies alluring, with a sense of deceit. You will find the cognate verbs, *calvo* and *calvor*, active,*passive,* and deponent,* in Servius, Plautus, and Sallust. Nobody pretends that the Greeks had a bald Venus. The *Venus Calva* of the Romans was the *Aphrodite Dolie* of the Greeks.* Beauty cannot co-exist with baldness; but it may and does co-exist with deceit. Homer makes deceitful allurement an essential element in the girdle of Venus.* Sappho addresses her as craft-weaving Venus.* Why should I multiply examples, when poetry so abounds with complaints of deceitful love that I will be bound every one of this company could, without a moment's hesitation, find a quotation in point? – Miss Gryll, to begin with.

*Miss Gryll*
Oh, doctor, with every one who has a memory for poetry, it must be *l'embarras de richesses*. We could occupy the time till

---

* Est et Venus Calva ob hanc causam, quod cum Galli Capitolium obsiderent, et deessent funes Romanis ad tormenta facienda, prima Domitia crinem suum, post cæteræ matronæ, imitatæ eam, exsecuerunt, unde facta tormenta; et post bellum statua Veneri hoc nomine collacata est: licet alii Calvam Venerem quasi puram tradant: *alii Calvam, quod corda calviat, id est, fallat atque eludat.* Quidam dicunt, porrigine olim capillos cecidisse fœminis, et Ancum regem suæ uxori statuam Calvam posuisse, quod constitit piaculo; nam mox omnibus fœminis capilli renati sunt: unde institutum ut Calva Venus coleretur. – SERVIUS ad *Aen*. i. 720.

The substance of this passage is given in the text.

* Contra ille *calvi* ratus. SALLUST, *Hist*. iii.
Thinking himself to be deceitfully allured.

* Nam ubi domi sola sum, sopor manus *calvitur*.
                                        PLAUTUS *in Casina*.
For when I am at home alone, sleep alluringly deceives my hands.

* Ἀφροδίτη Δολίη.

* πάρφασις, ἥτ' ἔκλεψε νόον πύκα περ φρονεόντων. *Il*. xiv. 217.

* παῖ Διὸς δολοπλόκε.

midnight in going round and round on the subject. We should soon come to an end with instances of truth and constancy.

*The Rev. Dr. Opimian*
Not so soon, perhaps. If we were to go on accumulating examples, I think I could find you a Penelope for a Helen, a Fiordiligi for an Angelica, and Imogene for a Calista, a Sacripant for a Rinaldo, a Romeo for an Angelo, to nearly the end of the chapter. I will not say quite, for I am afraid at the end of the catalogue the numbers of the unfaithful would predominate.

*Miss Ilex*
Do you think, doctor, you would find many examples of love that is one for all; love never transferred from its first object to a second?

*The Rev. Dr. Opimian*
Plato holds that such is the essence of love, and poetry and romance present it in many instances.

*Miss Ilex*
And the contrary in many more.

*The Rev. Dr. Opimian*
If we look, indeed, into the realities of life, as they offer themselves to us in our own experience, in history, in biography, we shall find few instances of constancy to first love: but it would be possible to compile a volume of illustrious examples of love which, though it may have previously ranged, is at last fixed in single, unchanging constancy. Even Iñez de Castro was only the second love of Don Pedro of Portugal; yet what an instance is there of love enduring in the innermost heart, as if it had been engraved on marble.

*Miss Gryll*
What is that story, doctor? I know it but imperfectly.

*The Rev. Dr. Opimian*

Iñez de Castro was the daughter, singularly beautiful and accomplished, of a Castilian nobleman, attached to the court of Alphonso the Fourth of Portugal. When very young, she became the favourite and devoted friend of Constance, the wife of the young Prince Don Pedro. The princess died early, and the grief of Iñez touched the heart of Pedro, who found no consolation but in her society. Thence grew love, which resulted in secret marriage. Pedro and Iñez lived in seclusion at Coimbra, perfectly happy in each other, and in two children who were born to them, till three of Alphonso's courtiers, moved by I know not what demon of mischief – for I never could discover an adequate motive – induced the king to attempt the dissolution of the marriage, and, failing in this, to authorise them to murder Iñez during a brief absence of her husband. Pedro raised a rebellion, and desolated the estates of the assassins, who escaped, one into France, and two into Castile. Pedro laid down his arms on the entreaty of his mother, but would never again see his father, and lived with his two children in the strictest retirement in the scene of his ruined happiness. When Alphonso died, Pedro determined not to assume the crown till he had punished the assassins of his wife. The one who had taken refuge in France was dead; the others were given up by the King of Castile. They were put to death, their bodies were burned, and their ashes were scattered to the winds. He then proceeded to the ceremony of his coronation. The mortal form of Iñez, veiled and in royal robes, was enthroned by his side: he placed the queenly crown on her head, and commanded all present to do her homage. He raised in a monastery, side by side, two tombs of white marble, one for her, one for himself. He visited the spot daily, and remained inconsolable till he rejoined her in death. This is the true history, which has been sadly perverted by fiction.

*Miss Ilex*

There is, indeed, something grand in that long-enduring constancy: something terribly impressive in that veiled spectral image of robed and crowned majesty. You have given this, doctor, as an instance that the first love is not necessarily the strongest, and this, no doubt, is frequently true, Even

Romeo had loved Rosalind before he saw Juliet. But love which can be so superseded is scarcely love. It is acquiescence in a semblance: acquiescence, which may pass for love through the entire space of life, if the latent sympathy should never meet its perfect counterpart.

*The Rev. Dr. Opimian*
Which it very seldom does; but acquiescence in the semblance is rarely enduring, and hence there are few examples of lifelong constancy. But I hold with Plato that true love is single, indivisible, unalterable.

*Miss Ilex*
In this sense, then, true love is first love; for the love which endures to the end of life, though it may be the second in semblance, is the first in reality.

The next morning Lord Curryfin said to Miss Niphet: 'You took no part in the conversation last evening. You gave no opinion on the singleness and permanence of love.'

*Miss Niphet*
I mistrust the experience of others, and I have none of my own.

*Lord Curryfin*
Your experience, when it comes, cannot but confirm the theory. The love which once dwells on you can never turn to another.

*Miss Niphet*
I do not know that I ought to wish to inspire such an attachment.

*Lord Curryfin*
Because you could not respond to it?

*Miss Niphet*
On the contrary; because I think it possible I might respond to it too well.

She paused a moment, and then, afraid of trusting herself to carry on the dialogue, she said. 'Come into the hall, and play at battledore and shuttlecock.'

He obeyed the order; but in the exercise her every movement developed some new grace, that maintained at its highest degree the intensity of his passionate admiration.

## CHAPTER XXX

## A CAPTIVE KNIGHT – RICHARD AND ALICE

——dum fata sinunt, jungamus amores:
   mox veniet tenebris Mors adoperta caput:
jam subrepet iners ætas, nec amare decebit,
   dicree nec cano blanditias capite.

               TIBULLUS.

Let us, while Fate allows, in love combine,
   Ere our last night its shade around us throw,
Or Age, slow-creeping, quench the fire divine,
   And tender words befit not locks of snow.

The shuttlecock had been some time on the wing, struck to and fro with unerring aid, and to all appearances would never have touched the ground if Lord Curryfin had not seen, or fancied he saw, symptoms of fatigue on the part of his fair antagonist. He therefore, instead of returning the shuttlecock, struck it upward, caught it in his hand, and presented it to her, saying, 'I give in. The victory is yours.' She answered, 'The victory is yours, as it always is, in courtesy.'

She said this with a melancholy smile more fascinating to him than the most radiant expression from another. She withdrew to the drawing-room, motioning to him not to follow.

In the drawing-room she found Miss Gryll, who appeared to be reading; at any rate, a book was open before her.

*Miss Gryll*
You did not see me just now as I passed through the hall. You saw only two things: the shuttlecock and your partner in the game.

*Miss Niphet*
It is not possible to play and see anything but the shuttlecock.

*Miss Gryll*
And the hand that strikes it.

*Miss Niphet*
That comes unavoidably into sight.

*Miss Gryll*
My dear Alice, you are in love, and do not choose to confess it.

*Miss Niphet*
I have no right to be in love with your suitor.

*Miss Gryll*
He was my suitor, and has not renounced his pursuit; but he is your lover. I ought to have seen long ago that from the moment his eyes rested on you all else was nothing to him. With all that habit of the world which enables men to conceal their feelings in society, with all his exertion to diffuse his attentions as much as possible among all the young ladies in his company, it must have been manifest to a careful observer that when it came, as it seemed in ordinary course, to be your turn to be attended to, the expression of his features was changed from complacency and courtesy to delight and admiration. I could not have failed to see it if I had not been occupied with other thoughts. Tell me candidly, do you not think it is so?

*Miss Niphet*
Indeed, my dear Morgana, I did not designedly enter into rivalry with you; but I do think you conjecture rightly.

*Miss Gryll*
And if he were free to offer himself to you, and if he did so offer himself, you would accept him?

*Miss Niphet*
Assuredly I would.

*Miss Gryll*
Then when you next see him, he shall be free. I have set my happiness on another cast, and I will stand the hazard of the die.

*Miss Niphet*
You are very generous, Morgana: for I do not think you give up what you do not value.

*Miss Gryll*
No indeed. I value him highly. So much so, that I have hesitated, and might have finally inclined to him, if I had not perceived his invincible preference of you. I am sorry, for your sake and his, that I did not clearly perceive it sooner; but you see what it is to be spoiled by admirers. I did not think it possible that any one could be preferred to me. I ought to have thought it possible, but I had no experience in that direction. So now you see a striking specimen of mortified vanity.

*Miss Niphet*
You have admirers in abundance, Morgana: more than have often fallen to the lot of the most attractive young women. And love is such a capricious thing, that to be the subject of it is no proof of superior merit. There are inexplicable affinities of sympathy that make up an irresistible attraction, heaven knows how.

*Miss Gryll*
And these inexplicable affinities Lord Curryfin has found in you, and you in him.

*Miss Niphet*
He has never told me so.

*Miss Gryll*
Not in words: but looks and actions have spoken for him. You
have both struggled to conceal your feelings from others,
perhaps even from yourselves. But you are both too ing-
enuous to dissemble successfully. You suit each other thoroughly: and I have no doubt you will find in each other the
happiness I most cordially wish you.

Miss Gryll soon found an opportunity of conversing with
Lord Curryfin, and began with him somewhat sportively: 'I
have been thinking,' she said, 'of an old song which contains a
morsel of good advice –

> Be sure to be off with the old love,
> Before you are on with the new.

You begin by making passionate love to me, and all at once
you turn round to one of my young friends and say, "Zephyrs
whisper how I love you."'

*Lord Curryfin*
Oh no! no, indeed. I have not said that, nor anything to the
same effect.

*Miss Gryll*
Well, if you have not exactly said it, you have implied it. You
have looked it. You have felt it. You cannot conceal it. You
cannot deny it. I give you notice that, if I die for love of you, I
shall haunt you.

*Lord Curryfin*
Ah! Miss Gryll, if you do not die till you die for love of me,
you will be as immortal as Circe, whom you so divinely
represented.

*Miss Gryll*
You offered yourself to me, to have and to hold, for ever and
aye. Suppose I claim you. Do not look so frightened. You
deserve some punishment, but that would be too severe. But,
to a certain extent, you belong to me, and I claim the right to

transfer you. I shall make a present of you to Miss Niphet. So, according to the old rules of chivalry, I order you, as my captive by right, to present yourself before her, and tell her that you have come to receive her commands, and obey them to the letter. I expect she will keep you in chains for life. You do not look much alarmed at the prospect. Yet you must be aware that you are a great criminal; and you have not a word to say in your own justification.

*Lord Curryfin*
Who could be insensible to charms like yours, if hope could have mingled with the contemplation? But there were several causes by which hope seemed forbidden, and therefore –

*Miss Gryll*
And therefore when beauty, and hope, and sympathy shone under a more propitious star, you followed its guidance. You could not help yourself:

> What heart were his that could resist
>     That melancholy smile?

I shall flatter myself that I might have kept you if I had tried hard for it at first; but

> Il pentirsi da sesto nulla giova.

No doubt you might have said with the old song,

> I ne'er could any lustre see
> In eyes that would not look on me.

But you scarcely gave me time to look on you before you were gone. You see, however, like our own Mirror of Knighthood, I make the best of my evil fate, and

> Cheer myself up with ends of verse,
> And sayings of philosophers.

*Lord Curryfin*
I am glad to see you so merry; for even if your heart were more deeply touched by another than it ever could have been

by me, I think I may say of you, in your own manner,

> So light a heel
> Will never wear the everlasting flint.

I hope and I believe you will always trip joyously over the surface of the world. You are the personification of L'Allegro.

*Miss Gryll*
I do not know how that may be. But go now to the personification of La Penserosa. If you do not turn her into a brighter Allegro than I am, you may say I have no knowledge of woman's heart.

It was not long after this dialogue that Lord Curryfin found an opportunity of speaking to Miss Niphet alone. He said, 'I am charged with a duty, such as was sometimes imposed on knights in the old days of chivalry. A lady, who claims me as her captive by right, has ordered me to kneel at your feet, to obey your commands, and to wear your chains, if you please to impose them.'

*Miss Niphet*
To your kneeling I say, Rise; for your obedience, I have no commands; for chains, I have none to impose.

*Lord Curryfin*
You have imposed them. I wear them already, inextricably, indissolubly.

*Miss Niphet*
If I may say, with the witch in *Thalaba,*

> Only she,
> Who knit his bonds, can set him free.

I am prepared to unbind the bonds. Rise, my lord, rise.

*Lord Curryfin*
I will rise if you give me your hand to lift me up.

*Miss Niphet*
There it is. Now that it has helped you up, let it go.

*Lord Curryfin*
And do not call me my lord.

*Miss Niphet*
What shall I call you?

*Lord Curryfin*
Call me Richard, and let me call you Alice.

*Miss Niphet*
That is familiarity only sanctioned by longer intimacy than ours has been.

*Lord Curryfin*
Or closer?

*Miss Niphet*
We have been very familiar friends during the brief term of our acquaintance. But let go my hand.

*Lord Curryfin*
I have set my heart on being allowed to call you Alice, and on your calling me Richard.

*Miss Niphet*
It must not be so – at least, not yet.

*Lord Curryfin*
There is nothing I would not do to acquire the right.

*Miss Niphet*
Nothing?

*Lord Curryfin*
Nothing.

*Miss Niphet*
How thrives your suit with Miss Gryll?

*Lord Curryfin*
That is at an end. I have her permission – her command she
calls it – to throw myself at your feet, and on your mercy.

*Miss Niphet*
How did she take leave of you, crying or laughing?

*Lord Curryfin*
Why, if anything, laughing.

*Miss Niphet*
Do you not feel mortified?

*Lord Curryfin*
I have another and deeper feeling, which predominates over
any possible mortification.

*Miss Niphet*
And that is –

*Lord Curryfin*
Can you doubt what it is!

*Miss Niphet*
I will not pretend to doubt. I have for some time been well
aware of your partiality for me.

*Lord Curryfin*
Partiality! Say love, adoration, absorption of all feelings into
one.

*Miss Niphet*
Then you may call me Alice. But once more, let go my hand.

*Lord Curryfin*
My hand, is it not?

*Miss Niphet*
Yours, when you claim it.

*Lord Curryfin*
Then thus I seal my claim.

He kissed her hand as respectfully as was consistent with 'masterless passion'; and she said to him, 'I will not dissemble. If I have had one wish stronger than another – strong enough to exclude all others – it has been for the day when you might be free to say to me what you have now said. Am I too frank with you?'

*Lord Curryfin*
Oh heaven, no! I drink in your words as a stream from paradise.

He sealed his claim again, but this time it was on her lips. The rose again mantled on her cheek, but the blush was heightened to damask. She withdrew herself from his arms, saying, 'Once for all, till you have an indisputable right.'


# CHAPTER XXXI

## A TWELFTH-NIGHT BALL – PANTOPRAGMATIC COOKERY – MODERN VANDALISM – A BOWL OF PUNCH

sic erimus cuncti, postquam nos auferet Orcus:
  ergo vivamus, dum licet esse bene.

So must we be, when ends our mortal day:
  Then let us live, while yet live well we may.
                    *Trimalchio, with the silver skeleton: in*
                        PETRONIUS, c. 34.

Twelfth-night was the night of the ball. The folding-doors of the drawing-rooms, which occupied their entire breadth, were thrown wide open. The larger room was appropriated to grown dancers; the smaller to children, who came in some force, and were placed within the magnetic attraction of an enormous twelfth-cake, which stood in a decorated recess. The carpets had been taken up, and the floors were painted with forms in chalk* by skilful artists, under the superintendence of Mr. Pallet. The library, separated from all the apartments by ante-chambers with double doors, was assigned, with an arrangement of whist tables, to such of the elder portion of the party as might prefer that mode of amusement to being mere spectators of the dancing. Mr. Gryll, with Miss Ilex, Mr. MacBorrowdale, and the Reverend Dr. Opimian, established his own quadrille party in a corner of the smaller drawing-room, where they could at once play and talk, and enjoy the enjoyment of the young. Lord Curryfin was Master of the Ceremonies.

After two or three preliminary dances, to give time for the arrival of the whole of the company, the twelfth-cake was divided. The characters were drawn exclusively among the children and the little king and queen were duly crowned, placed on a theatrical throne, and paraded in state round both drawing-rooms, to their own great delight and that of their little associates. Then the ball was supposed to commence and was by general desire opened with a minuet by Miss Niphet and Lord Curryfin. Then came alternations of quadrilles and country-dances, interspersed with occasional waltzes and polkas. So the ball went merrily, with, as usual, abundant love-making in mute signs and in *sotto voce* parlance.

Lord Curryfin, having brought his own love-making to a satisfactory close, was in exuberant spirits, sometimes joining in the dance, sometimes – in his official capacity – taking the round of the rooms to see that everything was going on to everybody's satisfaction. He could not fail to observe that his proffered partnership in the dance, though always graciously, was not so ambitiously accepted as before he had disposed of

---

* These all wear out of me, like forms with chalk
    Painted on rich men's floors, for one feast-night:
says Wordsworth, of 'chance acquaintance,' in his neighbourhood.
*Miscellaneous Sonnets*, No. 39.

himself for life. A day had sufficed to ask and obtain the
consent of Miss Niphet's father, who now sate on the side of
the larger drawing-room, looking with pride and delight on
his daughter, and with cordial gratification on her choice; and
when it was once, as it was at once known, that Miss Niphet
was to be Lady Curryfin, his lordship passed into the class of
married men, and was no longer the object of that solicitous
attention which he had received as an undrawn prize in the
lottery of marriage while it was probable that somebody
would have him, and nobody knew who.

The absence of Mr. Falconer was remarked by several
young ladies, to whom it appeared that Miss Gryll had lost her
two most favoured lovers at once. However, as she had still
many others, it was not yet a decided case for sympathy. Of
course she had no lack of partners, and whatever might have
been her internal anxiety, she was not the least gay among the
joyous assembly.

Lord Curryfin, in his circuit of the apartments, paused at the
quadrille-table, and said, 'You have been absent two or three
days, Mr. MacBorrowdale – what news have you brought
from London?'

*Mr. MacBorrowdale*

Not much, my lord. Tables turn as usual, and the ghost-trade
appears to be thriving: for instead of being merely audible, the
ghosts are becoming tangible, and shake hands under the
tables with living wiseacres, who solemnly attest the fact.
Civilised men ill-use their wives; the wives revenge themselves in their own way, and the Divorce Court has business
enough on its hands to employ it twenty years at its present
rate of progression. Commercial bubbles burst, and high-
pressure boilers blow up, and mountebanks of all descriptions
flourish on public credulity. Everywhere there are wars and
rumours of wars. The Peace Society has wound up its affairs
in the Insolvent Court of Prophecy. A great tribulation is
coming on the earth, and Apollyon in person is to be perpetual
dictator of all the nations. There is, to be sure, one piece of
news in your line, but it will be no news to you. There is a
meeting of the Pantopragmatic Society, under the presidency
of Lord Facing-both-ways, who has opened it with a long

speech, philanthropically designed as an elaborate exercise in fallacies, for the benefit of young rhetoricians. The society has divided its work into departments, which are to meddle with everything, from the highest to the lowest – from a voice in legislation to a finger in Jack Horner's pie. I looked for a department of Fish, with your lordship's name at the head of it; but I did not find it. It would be a fine department. It would divide itself naturally into three classes – living fish, fossil fish, and fish in the frying-pan.

*Lord Curryfin*

I assure you, Mr. MacBorrowdale, all this seems as ridiculous now to me as it does to you. The third class of fish is all that I shall trouble myself with in future, and that only at the tables of myself and my friends.

*Mr. Gryll*

I wonder the Pantopragmatics have not a department of cookery; a female department, to teach young wives how to keep their husbands at home, by giving them as good dinners as they can get abroad, especially at club. Those anti-domestic institutions receive their chief encouragement from the total ignorance of cookery on the part of young wives: for in this, as in all other arts of life, it is not sufficient to order what shall be done: it is necessary to know how it ought to be done. This is a matter of more importance to social well-being than nine-tenths of the subjects the Pantopragmatics meddle with.

*The Rev. Dr. Opimian*

And therefore I rejoice that they do not meddle with it. A dinner prepared from a New Art of Cookery, concocted under their auspices, would be more comical and more uneatable than the Roman dinner in Peregrine Pickle. Let young ladies learn cookery by all means: but let them learn under any other tuition than that of the Pantopragmatic Society.

*Mr. Gryll*

As for the tribulation coming on the earth, I am afraid there is some ground to expect it, without looking for its foreshadowing exclusively to the Apocalypse. Niebuhr, who did not draw his opinion from prophecy, rejoiced that his career was coming to a close, for he thought we were on the eve of a darker age.

*The Rev. Dr. Opimian*
He had not before his eyes the astounding march of intellect, drumming and trumpeting science from city to city. But I am afraid that sort of obstreperous science only gives people the novel 'use of their eyes to see the way of blindness.*

> Truths which, from action's paths retired,
> My silent search in vain required,*

I am not likely to find in the successive gabblings of a dozen lecturers of Babel.

*Mr. Gryll*
If you could so find them, they would be of little avail against the new irruption of Goths and Vandals, which must have been in the apprehension of Niebuhr. There are Vandals on northern thrones, anxious for nothing so much as to extinguish truth and liberty wherever they show themselves — Vandals in the bosom of society everywhere even amongst ourselves, in multitudes, with precisely the same aim, only more disguised by knaves, and less understood by dupes.

*The Rev. Dr. Opimian*
And you may add, Vandals dominating over society throughout half America, who deal with free speech and even the

---

* *Gaoler.* For look you, sir: you know not which way you shall go.
  *Posthumus.* Yes, indeed do I, fellow.
  *Gaoler.* Your death has eyes in's head, then: I have not seen him so pictured. . . .
  *Posthumus.* I tell thee, fellow, there are none want eyes to direct them the way I am going, but such as wink, and will not use them.
  *Gaoler.* What an infinite mock is this, that a man should have the best use of eyes to see the way of blindness!
  *Cymbeline,* Act v. Scene 4.

* Collins, *Ode on the Manners.*

suspicion of free thought just as the Inquisition dealt with them, only substituting Lynch law and the gallows for a different mockery of justice, ending in fire and faggot.

*Mr. Gryll*

I confine my view to Europe. I dread northern monarchy, and southern anarchy; and rabble brutality amongst ourselves, smothered and repressed for the present, but always ready to break out into inextinguishable flame, like hidden fire under treacherous ashes.*

*Mr. MacBorrowdale*

In the meantime, we are all pretty comfortable: and sufficient for the day is the evil thereof; which in our case, so far as I can see, happens to be precisely none.

*Miss Ilex*

Lord Curryfin seems to be of that opinion, for he has flitted away from the discussion, and is going down a country dance with Miss Niphet.

*The Rev. Dr. Opimian*

He has chosen his time well. He takes care to be her last partner before supper, that he may hand her to the table. But do you observe how her tragic severity has passed away? She was always pleasant to look on, but it was often like contemplating ideal beauty in an animated statue. Now she is the image of perfect happiness, and irradiates all around her.

*Miss Ilex*

How can it be otherwise? The present and the future are all brightness to her. She cannot but reflect their radiance.

Now came the supper, which, as all present had dined early, was unaffectedly welcomed and enjoyed. Lord Curryfin looked carefully to the comfort of his idol, but was unremit-

---

*  —— incedis per ignes
    suppositos cineri doloso.

                    HOR. *Carm.* II. i.

ting in his attentions to her fair neighbours. After supper,
dancing was resumed, with an apparent resolution in the
greater portion of the company not to go home till morning.
Mr. Gryll, Mr. MacBorrowdale, the Reverend Doctor Opimian, and two or three elders of the party, not having had
their usual allowance of wine after their early dinner, remained
at the supper table over a bowl of punch, which had been
provided in ample quantity, and, in the intervals of dancing,
circulated, amongst other refreshments, round the sides of the
ball room, where it was gratefully accepted by the gentlemen,
and not absolutely disregarded even by the young ladies. This
may be conceded on occasion, without admitting Goldoni's
facetious position, that a woman, masked and silent, may be
known to be English by her acceptance of punch.*

* Lord Runebif, in Venice, meets Rosaura, who is masked, before a
*bottega di caffè.* She makes him a curtsey in the English fashion.
    *Milord.* Madama, molto compita, volete caffè?
    *Rosaura. (Fa cenno di no.)*
    *Milord.* Cioccolata?
    *Rosaura. (Fa cenno di no.)*
    *Milord.* Volete ponce?
    *Rosaura. (Fa cenno di sì.)*
    *Milord.* Oh! è Inglese.
                *La Vedova Scaltra,* A. iii. S. 10.

He does not offer her tea, which, as a more English drink than
either coffee or chocolate, might have entered into rivalry with punch:
especially if, as Goldoni represented in another comedy, the English
were in the habit of drinking it, not with milk, but with arrack. Lord
Arthur calls on his friend Lord Bonfil in the middle of the day, and
Lord Bonfil offers him tea, which is placed on the table with sugar and
arrack. While they are drinking it, Lord Coubrech enters.

    *Bonfil.* Favorite, bevete con noi.
    *Coubrech.* Il tè non si rifiuta.
    *Artur.* E bevanda salutifera.
    *Bonfil.* Volete rak?
    *Coubrech.* Sì, rak.
    *Bonfil.* Ecco, vi servo.
                *Pamela Fanciulla,* A. i.S. 15.

# CHAPTER XXXII

## HOPES AND FEARS – COMPENSATIONS IN LIFE – ATHENIAN COMEDY – MADEIRA AND MUSIC – CONFIDENCES

> ὑμεῖς δέ, πρέσβεις, χαίρετ', ἐν κακοῖς ὅμως
> ψυχῇ διδόντες ἡδονὴν καθ' ἡμέραν,
> ὡς τοῖς θανοῦσι πλοῦτος οὐδὲν ὠφελεῖ.
> — *The Ghost of Darius to the chorus, in
> the Persæ of* ÆSCHYLUS.

> Farewell, old friends: and even if ills surround you,
> Seize every joy the passing day can bring,
> For wealth affords no pleasure to the dead.

Dorothy had begun to hope that Harry's news might be true, but even Harry's sanguineness began to give way: the pertinacity with which the young master remained at home threw a damp on their expectations. But having once fairly started, in the way of making love on the one side and responding to it on the other, they could not but continue as they had begun, and she permitted him to go on building castles in the air, in which the Christmas of the ensuing year was arrayed in the brightest apparel of fire and festival.

Harry, walking home one afternoon, met the Reverend Doctor Opimian, who was on his way to the Tower, where he purposed to dine and pass the night. Mr. Falconer's absence from the ball had surprised him, especially as Lord Curryfin's rivalry had ceased, and he could imagine no good cause for his not returning to the Grange. The doctor held out his hand to Harry, who returned the grasp most cordially. The doctor asked him 'how he and his six young friends were prospering in their siege of the hearts of the seven sisters.

*Harry Hedgerow*

Why, sir, so far as the young ladies are concerned, we have no cause to complain. But we can't make out the young gentleman. He used to sit and read all the morning, at the top of the Tower. Now he goes up the stairs and after a little while he comes down again, and walks into the forest. Then he goes upstairs again, and down again, and out again. Something must be come to him, and the only thing we can think of is, that he is crossed in love. And he never gives me a letter or a message to the Grange. So, putting all that together, we haven't a merry Christmas, you see, sir.

*The Rev. Dr. Opimian*
I see, still harping on a merry Christmas. Let us hope that the next may make amends.

*Harry Hedgerow*
Have they a merry Christmas at the Grange, sir?

*The Rev. Dr. Opimian*
Very merry.

*Harry Hedgerow*
Then there's nobody crossed in love there, sir.

*The Rev. Dr. Opimian*
That is more than I can say. I cannot answer for others. I am not, and never was, if that is any comfort to you.

*Harry Hedgerow*
It is a comfort to me to see you, and hear the sound of your voice, sir. It always does me good.

*The Rev. Dr. Opimian*
Why then, my young friend, you are most heartily welcome to see and hear me whenever you please if you will come over to the Vicarage. And you will always find a piece of cold roast beef and a tankard of good ale; and just now a shield of brawn. There is some comfort in them.

*Harry Hedgerow*
Ah! thank ye, sir. They are comfortable things in their way. But it isn't for them I should come.

*The Rev. Dr. Opimian*

I believe you, my young friend. But a man fights best when he has a good basis of old English fare to stand on, against all opposing forces, whether of body or mind. Come and see me. And whatever happens in this world, never let it spoil your dinner.

*Harry Hedgerow*

That's father's advice, sir. But it won't always do. When he lost mother, that spoiled his dinner for many a day. He has never been the same man since, though he bears up as well as he can. But if I could take Miss Dorothy home to him, I'm sure that would all but make him young again. And if he had a little Harry to dandle next Christmas, wouldn't he give him the first spoonful out of the marrow-bone!

*The Rev. Dr. Opimian*

I doubt if that would be good food for little Harry, notwithstanding it was Hector's way of feeding Astyanax.* But we may postpone the discussion of his diet till he makes his appearance. In the meantime, live in hope; but live on beef and ale.

The doctor again shook him heartily by the hand, and Harry took his leave.

The doctor walked on, soliloquising as usual. 'This young man's father has lost a good wife, and has never been the same man since. If he had had a bad wife, he would have felt it as a happy release. This life has strange compensations. It helps to show the truth of Juvenal's remark, that the gods alone know what is good for us.* Now, here again is my friend at the Tower. If he had not, as I am sure he has, the love of Morgana, he would console himself with his Vestals. If he had not their sisterly affection, he would rejoice in the love of Morgana, but having both the love and affection, he is between two counter-attractions, either of which would make him happy, and both together make him miserable. Who can

* *Il.* xxii. vv. 500, 501.
* Juvenal, *Sat.* x. v. 346. *sqq.*

say which is best for him? or for them? or for Morgana
herself? I almost wish the light of her favour had shone on
Lord Curryfin. That chance has passed from her; and she will
not easily find such another. Perhaps she might have held him
in her bonds, if she had been so disposed. But Miss Niphet is a
glorious girl, and there is a great charm in such perfect
reciprocity. Jupiter himself, as I have before had occasion to
remark, must have prearranged their consentaneity. The
young lord went on some time, adhering, as he supposed, to
his first pursuit, and falling unconsciously and inextricably
into the second; and the young lady went on, devoting her
whole heart and soul to him, not clearly perhaps knowing it
herself, but certainly not suspecting that any one else could
dive into the heart of her mystery. And now they both seem
surprised that nobody seems surprised at their sudden appearance in the character of affianced lovers. His is another
example of strange compensation; for if Morgana had
accepted him on his first offer, Miss Niphet would not have
thought of him; but she found him a waif and stray, a flotsam
on the waters of love, and landed him at her feet without art or
stratagem. Artlessness and simplicity triumphed, where the
deepest design would have failed. I do not know if she had any
compensation to look for; but if she had, she has found it; for
never was a man with more qualities for domestic happiness,
and not Pedro of Portugal himself was more overwhelmingly
in love. When I first knew him, I saw only the comic side of
his character: he has a serious one too, and not the least
agreeable part of it: but the comic still shows itself. I cannot
well define whether his exuberant good humour is contagious, and makes me laugh by anticipation as soon as I fall into
his company, or whether it is impossible to think of him,
gravely lecturing on Fish, as a member of the Pantopragmatic
Society, without perceiving a ludicrous contrast between his
pleasant social face and the unpleasant social impertinence of
those would-be meddlers with everything. It is true, he has
renounced that folly; but it is not so easy to dissociate him
from the recollection. No matter: if I laugh, he laughs with
me: if he laughs, I laugh with him. 'Laugh when you can,' is a
good maxim: between well-disposed sympathies a very little
cause strikes out the fire of merriment –

As long liveth the merry man, they say,
As doth the sorry man, and longer by a day.

And a day so acquired is a day worth having. But then –

Another sayd sawe doth men advise,
That they be together both merry and wise.*

Very good doctrine, and fit to be kept in mind: but there is much good laughter without much wisdom, and yet with no harm in it.'

The doctor was approaching the Tower when he met Mr. Falconer, who had made one of his feverish exits from it, and was walking at double his usual speed. He turned back with the doctor, who having declined taking anything before dinner but a glass of wine and a biscuit, they went up together to the library.

They conversed only on literary subjects. The doctor, though Miss Gryll was uppermost in his mind, determined not to originate a word respecting her, and Mr. Falconer, though she was also his predominant idea, felt that it was only over a bottle of Madeira he could unbosom himself freely to the doctor.

The doctor asked, 'What he had been reading of late?' He said, 'I have tried many things, but I have always returned to *Orlando Innamorato*. There it is on the table, an old edition of the original poem.' The doctor said, 'I have seen an old edition, something like this, on the drawing-room table at the Grange.' He was about to say something touching sympathy in taste, but he checked himself in time. The two younger sisters brought in lights. 'I observe,' said the doctor, 'that your handmaids always move in pairs. My hot water for dressing is always brought by two inseparables, whom it seems profanation to call housemaids.'

*Mr. Falconer*
It is always so on my side of the house, that not a breath of scandal may touch their reputation. If you were to live here

* These two quotations are from the oldest comedy in the English language: *Ralph Roister Doister*, 1566. Republished by the Shakespeare Society, 1847.

from January to December, with a houseful of company, neither you nor I, nor any of my friends, would see one of them alone for a single minute.

*The Rev. Dr. Opimian*

I approve the rule. I would stake my life on the conviction that these sisters are

> Pure as the new-fall'n snow'
> When never yet the sullying sun
> Has seen its purity,
> Nor the warm zephyr touched and tainted it.*

But as the world is constituted, the most perfect virtue needs to be guarded from suspicion. I cannot, however, associate your habits with a houseful of company.

*Mr. Falconer*

There must be sympathies enough in the world to make up society for all tastes: more difficult to find in some cases than in others; but still always within the possibility of being found. I contemplated, when I arranged this house, the frequent presence of a select party. The Aristophanic comedy and its adjuncts brought me into pleasant company elsewhere. I have postponed the purpose, not abandoned it.

Several thoughts passed through the doctor's mind. He was almost tempted to speak them. 'How beautiful was Miss Gryll in Circe; how charmingly she acted. What was a select party without women? And how could a bachelor invite them?' But this would be touching a string which he had determined not to be the first to strike. So *à propos* of the Aristophanic comedy, he took down Aristophanes, and said, 'What a high idea of Athenian comedy is given by this single line, in which the poet opines 'the bringing out of comedy to be the most difficult of all arts.'* It would not seem to be difficult art

---

* Southey, *Thalaba.*

* κωμῳδοδιδασκαλίαν εἶναι χαλεπώτατον ἔργον ἁπάντων. *Equites.*

nowadays, seeing how much new comedy is nightly produced in London, and still more in Paris, which, whatever may be its literary value, amuses its audiences as much as Aristophanes amused the Athenians.

*Mr. Falconer*
There is this difference, that though both audiences may be equally amused, the Athenians felt they had something to be proud of in the poet, which our audiences can scarcely feel, as far as novelties are concerned. And as to the atrocious outrages on taste and feeling perpetrated under the name of burlesques, I should be astonished if even those who laugh at them could look back on their amusement with any other feeling than that of being most heartily ashamed of the author, the theatre, and themselves.

When the dinner was over, and a bottle of claret had been placed on the side of the doctor, and a bottle of Madeira by the side of his host, who had not been sparing during dinner of his favourite beverage, which had been to him for some days like ale to the Captain and his friends in Beaumont and Fletcher,* almost 'his eating and his drinking solely,' the doctor said, 'I am glad to perceive that you keep up your practice of having a good dinner; though I am at the same time sorry to see that you have not done your old justice to it.'

*Mr. Falconer*
A great philosopher had seven friends, one of whom dined with him in succession on each day of the week. He directed, amongst his last dispositions, that during six months after his death, the establishment of his house should be kept on the same footing, and that a dinner should be daily provided for himself and his single guest of the day, who was to be entreated to dine there in memory of him, with one of his executors (both philosophers) to represent him in doing the honours of the table alternately.

* Ale is their eating and their drinking solely.
                                        *Scornful Lady,* Act iv. Scene 2.

*The Rev. Dr. Opimian*
I am happy to see that the honours of your table are done by
yourself, and not by an executor, administrator, or assign.
The honours are done admirably, but the old justice on your
side is wanting. I do not, however, clearly see what the *feralis
cœna* of guest and executor has to do with the dinner of two
living men.

*Mr. Falconer*
Ah, doctor, you should say one living man and a ghost. I am
only the ghost of myself. I do the honours of my departed
conviviality.

*The Rev. Dr. Opimian*
I thought something was wrong; but whatever it may be, take
Horace's advice – 'Alleviate every ill with wine and song, the
sweet consolations of deforming anxiety.'*

*Mr. Falconer*
I do, doctor. Madeira, and the music of the Seven Sisters, are
my consolations, and great ones; but they do not go down to
the hidden care that gnaws at the deepest fibres of the heart,
like Ratatosk at the roots of the Ash of Ygdrasil.

*The Rev. Dr. Opimian*
In the Scandinavian mythology: one of the most poetical of all
mythologies. I have a great respect for Odin and Thor. Their
adventures have always delighted me; and the system was
admirably adapted to foster the high spirit of a military
people. Lucan has a fine passage on the subject.*

The doctor repeated the pasage of Lucan with great emphasis.
This was not what Mr. Falconer wanted. He had wished that
the doctor should inquire into the cause of his trouble; but
independently of the doctor's determination to ask no ques-

---

* Illic omne malum vino cantuque levato,
    deformis ægrimoniæ dulcibus alloquiis.

*Epod.* xiii.

* *Pharsalia*, i. 458–462.

tions, and to let his young friend originate his own disclosures, the unlucky metaphor had carried the doctor into one of his old fields, and if it had not been that he awaited the confidence, which he felt sure his host would spontaneously repose in him, the Scandinavian mythology would have formed his subject for the evening. He paused, therefore, and went on quietly sipping his claret.

Mr. Falconer could restrain himself no longer, and without preface or note of preparation he communicated to the doctor all that had passed between Miss Gryll and himself, not omitting a single word of the passages of Bojardo, which were indelibly impressed on his memory.

*The Rev. Dr. Opimian*
I cannot see what there is to afflict you in all this. You are in love with Miss Gryll. She is disposed to receive you favourably. What more would you wish in that quarter?

*Mr. Falconer*
No more in that quarter, but the Seven Sisters are as sisters to me. If I had seven real sisters, the relationship would subsist, and marriage would not interfere with it; but, be a woman as amiable, as liberal, as indulgent, as confiding as she may, she could not treat the unreal as she would the real tie.

*The Rev. Dr. Opimian*
I admit, it is not to be expected. Still there is one way out of the difficulty. And that is by seeing all the seven happily married.

*Mr. Falconer*
All the seven married? Surely that is impossible.

*The Rev. Dr. Opimian*
Not so impossible as you apprehend.

The doctor thought it a favourable opportunity to tell the story of the seven suitors, and was especially panegyrical on Harry Hedgerow, observing, that if the maxim *Noscitur a sociis* might be reversed, and a man's companions judged by himself, it would be a sufficient recommendation of the other six; whom, moreover, the result of his inquiries had given him ample reason to think well of. Mr. Falconer received with pleasure at Christmas a communication which at the Midsummer preceding would have given him infinite pain. It struck him all at once that, as he had dined so ill, he would have some partridges for supper, his larder being always well stocked with game. They were presented accordingly, after the usual music in the drawing-room, and the doctor, though he had dined well, considered himself bound in courtesy to assist in their disposal; when, recollecting how he had wound up the night of the ball, he volunteered to brew a bowl of punch, over which they sate till a late hour, discoursing of many things, but chiefly of Morgana.

## CHAPTER XXXIII

### THE CONQUEST OF THEBES

> ἦ σοφὸς ἦ σοφὸς ἦν,
> ὃς πρῶτος ἐν γνώμᾳ τόδ' ἐβάστασε,
> καὶ γλώσσᾳ διεμυθολόγησεν,
> ὡς τὸ κηδεῦσαι καθ' ἑαυτὸν ἀριστεύει μακρῷ·
> καὶ μήτε τῶν πλούτῳ διαθρυπτομένων,
> μήτε τῶν γέννᾳ μεγαλυνομένων,
> ὄντα χερνήταν ἐραστεῦσαι γάμων.
>
> ÆSCHYLUS. *Prometheus.*

> Oh! wise was he, the first who taught
> This lesson of observant thought,
> That equal fates alone may dress
> The bowers of nuptial happiness;
> That never, where ancestral pride
> Inflames, or affluence rolls its tide,
> Should love's ill-omened bonds entwine
> The offspring of an humbler line.

Mr. Falconer, the next morning, after the doctor had set out on his return walk, departed from his usual practice of not seeing one of the sisters alone, and requested that Dorothy would come to him in the drawing-room. She appeared before him, blushing and trembling.

'Sit down,' he said, 'dear Dorothy; I have something to say to you and your sisters; but I have reason for saying it first to you. It is probable, at any rate possible, that I shall very soon marry, and perhaps, in that case, you may be disposed to do the same. And I am told, that one of the best young men I have ever known is dying for love of you.'

'He is a good young man, that is certain,' said Dorothy; then becoming suddenly conscious of how much she had undesignedly admitted, she blushed deeper than before. And by way of mending the matter, she said, 'But I am not dying for love of him.'

'I dare say you are not,' said Mr. Falconer; 'you have no cause to be so, as you are sure of him, and only your consent is wanting.'

'And yours,' said Dorothy, 'and that of my sisters; especially my elder sisters; indeed, they ought to set the example.'

'I am sure of that,' said Mr. Falconer. 'So far, if I understand rightly, they have followed yours. It was your lover's indefatigable devotion that brought together suitors to them all. As to my consent, that you shall certainly have. So the next time you see Master Harry, send him to me.'

'He is here now,' said Dorothy.

'Then ask him to come in,' said Mr. Falconer.

And Dorothy retired in some confusion. But her lips could not contradict her heart. Harry appeared.

*Mr. Falconer*

So, Harry, you have been making love in my house, without asking my leave.

*Harry Hedgerow*

I couldn't help making love, sir; and I didn't ask your leave, because I thought I shouldn't get it.

*Mr. Falconer*

Candid, as usual, Harry. But do you think Dorothy would make a good farmer's wife?

*Harry Hedgerow*
I think, sir, she is so good, and so clever, and so ready and willing to turn her hand to anything, that she would be a fit wife for anybody, from a lord downwards. But it may be most for her own happiness to keep in the class in which she was born.

*Mr. Falconer*
She is not very pretty, you know.

*Harry Hedgerow*
Not pretty, sir! If she isn't a beauty, I don't know who is.

*Mr. Falconer*
Well, no doubt, she is a handsome girl.

*Harry Hedgerow*
Handsome is not the thing, sir. She's beautiful.

*Mr. Falconer*
Well, Harry, she is beautiful, if that will please you.

*Harry Hedgerow*
It does please me, sir. I ought to have known you were joking when you said she was not pretty.

*Mr. Falconer*
But, you know, she has no fortune.

*Harry Hedgerow*
I don't want fortune. I want her, and nothing else, and nobody else.

*Mr. Falconer*
But I cannot consent to her marrying without a fortune of her own.

*Harry Hedgerow*
Why then, I'll give her one beforehand. Father has saved some money, and she shall have that. We'll settle it on her, as the lawyers say.

*Mr. Falconer*

You are a thoroughly good fellow, Harry, and I really wish
Dorothy joy of her choice; but that is not what I meant. She
must bring you a fortune, not take one from you; and you
must not refuse it.

Harry repeated that he did not want fortune; and Mr. Falconer
repeated that, so far as depended on him, he should not have
Dorothy without one. It was not an arduous matter to bring
to an amicable settlement.

The affair of Harry and Dorothy being thus satisfactorily
arranged, the other six were adjusted with little difficulty; and
Mr. Falconer returned with a light heart to the Grange, where
he presented himself at dinner on the twenty-seventh day of
his probation.

He found much the same party as before; for though some
of them absented themselves for a while, they could not resist
Mr. Gryll's earnest entreaties to return. He was cordially
welcomed by all, and with a gracious smile from Morgana.


CHAPTER XXXIV


CHRISTMAS TALES – CLASSICAL TALES OF
WONDER – THE HOST'S GHOST – A TALE
OF A SHADOW – A TALE OF A BOGLE – THE
LEGEND OF ST. LAURA


> *Jane.* . . . We'll draw round
> The fire, and grandmamma perhaps will tell us
> One of her stories.
> *Harry.*        Ay, dear grandmamma!
> A pretty story! something dismal now!
> A bloody murder.
> *Jane.*        Or about a ghost.
>                 SOUTHEY, *The Grandmother's Tale.*

In the evening Mis Gryll said to the doctor,
  'We have passed Christmas without a ghost story. This is

not as it should be. One evening at least of Christmas ought to
be devoted to *merveilleuses histoires racontées autour du foyer;*
which Chateaubriand enumerates among the peculiar enjoy-
ments of those *qui n'ont pas quitté leur pays natal.* You must
have plenty of ghosts in Greek and Latin, doctor.

*The Rev. Dr. Opimian*

No doubt. All literature abounds with ghosts. But there are
not many classical ghosts that would make a Christmas tale
according to the received notion of a ghost story. The ghosts
of Patroclus in Homer, of Darius in Æschylus, of Polydorus in
Euripides, are fine poetical ghosts: but none of them would
make a ghost story. I can only call to mind one such story in
Greek: but even that, as it has been turned into ballads by
Goethe, in the *Bride of Corinth,* and by Lewis, in the *Gay Gold
Ring,\** would not be new to any one here. There are some
classical tales of wonder, not ghost stories, but suitable
Christmas tales. There are two in Petronius, which I once
amused myself by translating as closely as possible to the
originals, and, if you please, I will relate them as I remember
them. For I hold with Chaucer:

> Whoso shall telle a tale after a man,
> He most reherse, as nigh as ever he can,
> Everich word, if it be in his charge,

* Lewis says, in a note on the *Gay Gold Ring:* 'I once read in some
Grecian author, whose name I have forgotten, the story which
suggested to me the outline of the foregoing ballad. It was as follows:
A young man arriving at the house of a friend, to whose daughter he
was betrothed, was informed that some weeks had passed since death
had deprived him of his intended bride. Never having seen her, he
soon reconciled himself to her loss, especially as, during his stay at his
friend's house, a young lady was kind enough to visit him every night
in his chamber, whence she retired at day-break, always carrying with
her some valuable present from her lover. This intercourse continued
till accident showed the young man the picture of his deceased bride,
and he recognised, with horror, the features of his nocturnal visitor.
The young lady's tomb being opened, he found in it the various
presents which his liberality had bestowed on his unknown *innamor-
ata.'* – M.G. Lewis, *Tales of Wonder,* v. i. p. 99.

All speke he never so rudely and so large:
Or elles he moste tellen his tale untrewe,
Or feinen things, or finden wordes newe.*

This proposal being received with an unanimous 'By all
means, doctor,' the doctor went on: –

These stories are told at the feast of Trimalchio: the first by
Niceros, a freedman, one of the guests:

'While I was yet serving, we lived in a narrow street, where
now is the house of Gavilla. There, as it pleased the gods, I fell
in love with the wife of Terentius, the tavern-keeper – Melissa
Tarentiana – many of you knew her, a most beautiful kiss-
thrower.'

*Miss Gryll*
That is an odd term, doctor.

*The Rev. Dr. Opimian*
It relates, I imagine, to some graceful gesture of pantomimic
dancing: for beautiful hostesses were often accomplished
dancers. Virgil's Copa, which, by the way, is only half
panegyrical, gives us, nevertheless, a pleasant picture in this
kind. It seems to have been one of the great attractions of a
Roman tavern: and the host, in looking out for a wife, was
probably much influenced by her possession of this accomplishment. The dancing, probably, was of that kind which the
moderns call *demi-caractère,* and was performed in picturesque
costume –

The doctor would have gone off in a dissertation on dancing
hostesses, but Miss Gryll recalled him to the story, which he
continued, in the words of Niceros:

'But, by Hercules, mine was pure love; her manners
charmed me, and her friendliness. If I wanted money, if she
had earned an *as*, she gave me a *semis*. If I had money, I gave it
into her keeping. Never was woman more trustworthy. Her
husband died at a farm which they possessed in the country. I
left no means untried to visit her in her distress; for friends are

* *Canterbury Tales,* vv. 733–738.

shown in adversity. It so happened that my master had gone to Capua, to dispose of some cast-off finery. Seizing the opportunity, I persuaded a guest of ours to accompany me to the fifth milestone. He was a soldier, strong as Pluto. We set off before cockcrow; the moon shone like day; we passed through a line of tombs. My man began some ceremonies before the pillars. I sat down, singing, and counting the stars. Then, as I looked round to my comrade, he stripped himself, and laid his clothes by the wayside. My heart was in my nose: I could no more move than a dead man. But he walked three times round his clothes, and was suddenly changed into a wolf. Do not think I am jesting. No man's patrimony would tempt me to lie. But as I had begun to say, as soon as he was changed into a wolf, he set up a long howl, and fled into the woods. I remained a while, bewildered; then I approached to take up his clothes, but they were turned into stone. Who was dying of fear but I? But I drew my sword, and went on cutting shadows till I arrived at the farm. I entered the narrow way. The life was half boiled out of me; perspiration ran down me like a torrent: my eyes were dead. I could scarcely come to myself. My Melisa began to wonder, why I walked so late; 'and if you had come sooner, she said,' 'you might at least have helped us; for a wolf entered the farm and fell on the sheep, tearing them, and leaving them all bleeding. He escaped; but with cause to remember us; for our man drove a spear through his neck.' When I heard these things I could not think of sleep; but hurried homeward with the dawn; and when I came to the place where the clothes had been turned into stone, I found nothing but blood.

'When I reached home, my soldier was in bed, lying like an ox, and a surgeon was dressing his neck. I felt that he was a turnskin, and I could never after taste bread with him, not if you would have killed me. Let those who doubt of such things look into them. If I lie, may the wrath of all you Genii fall on me.'

This story being told, Trimalchio, the lord of the feast, after giving his implicit adhesion to it, and affirming the indisputable veracity of Niceros, relates another, as a fact of his own experience.

'While yet I wore long hair, for from a boy I led a Chian

life,* our little Iphis, the delight of the family, died; by
Hercules, a pearl: quick, beautiful, one of ten thousand.
While, therefore, his unhappy mother was weeping for him,
and we were plunged in sorrow, suddenly witches came in
pursuit of him, as dogs, you may suppose, of a hare. We had
then in the house a Cappadocian, tall, brave to audacity,
capable of lifting up an angry bull. He boldly, with a drawn
sword, rushed out through the gate, having his left hand
carefully wrapped up, and drove his sword through a
woman's bosom; here as it were; safe be what I touch! We
heard a groan; but, assuredly, I will not lie, we did not see the
women. But our stout fellow returning, threw himself into
bed, and all his body was livid, as if he had been beaten with
whips; for the evil hand had touched him. We closed the gate,
and resumed our watch over the dead; but when the mother
went to embrace the body of her son, she touched it, and
found it was only a figure, of which all the interior was straw,
no heart, nothing. The witches had stolen away the boy, and
left in his place a straw-stuffed image. I ask you – it is
impossible not – to believe, that there are women with more
than mortal knowledge, nocturnal women, who can make
that which is uppermost downmost. But our tall hero after
this was never again of his own colour; indeed, after a few
days, he died raving.'

'We wondered and believed,' says a guest who heard the
story, 'and kissing the table, we implored the nocturnals to
keep themselves to themselves, while we were returning from
supper.'

*Miss Gryll*
Those are pleasant stories, doctor; and the peculiar style of the
narrators testifies to their faith in their own marvels. Still, as
you say, they are not ghost stories.

*Lord Curryfin*
Shakespeare's are glorious ghosts, and would make good
stories, if they were not so familiarly known. There is a ghost

---

* Free boys wore long hair. A Chian life is a delicate and luxurious
life. Trimalchio implies that, though he began life as a slave, he was a
pet in the household, and was treated as if he had been free.

much to my mind in Beaumont and Fletcher's *Lover's Progress*.
Cleander has a beautiful wife, Calista, and a friend, Lisander.
Calista and Lisander love each other, *en tout bien, tout honneur*.
Lisander, in self-defence and in fair fight, kills a court
favourite, and is obliged to conceal himself in the country.
Cleander and Dorilaus, Calista's father, travel in search of
him. They pass the night at a country inn. The jovial host had
been long known to Cleander, who had extolled him to
Dorilaus; but on inquiring for him they find he has been dead
three weeks. They call for more wine dismiss their attendants,
and sit up alone, chatting of various things, and, among
others, of mine host, whose skill on the lute and in singing is
remembered and commended by Cleander. While they are
talking, a lute is struck within; followed by a song, beginning

>    'Tis late and cold, stir up the fire, –
>    Sit close, and draw the table nigher:
>    Be merry, and drink wine that's old.

And ending

>    Welcome, welcome, shall go round,
>    And I shall smile, though underground.

And when the song ceases, the host's ghost enters. They ask
him why he appears. He answers, to wait once more on
Cleander, and to entreat a courtesy –

>    —— to see my body buried
>    In holy ground: for now I lie unhallowed
>    By the clerk's fault: let my new grave be made
>    Amongst good fellows, that have died before me,
>    And merry hosts of my kind.

Cleander promises it shall be done; and Dorilaus, who is a
merry old gentleman throughout the play, adds –

>    And forty stoops of wine drank at thy funeral.

Cleander asks him –

> Is't in your power, some hours before my death,
> To give me warning?

The host replies –

>                     I cannot tell you truly:
> But if I can, so much on earth I loved you,
> I will appear again.

In a subsequent scene the ghost forewarns him, and he is soon after assassinated: not premeditatedly, but as an accident, in the working out, by subordinate characters, of a plot to bring into question the purity of Calista's love for Lisander.

*Miss Ilex*
In my young days ghosts were so popular that the first question asked about any new play was, Is there a ghost in it? The *Castle Spectre* had set this fashion. It was one of the first plays I saw, when I was a very little girl. The opening of the folding-doors disclosing the illuminated oratory; the extreme beauty of the actress who personated the ghost; the solemn music to which she moved slowly forward to give a silent blessing to her kneeling daughter; and the chorus of female voices chanting *Jubilate;* made an impression on me which no other scene of the kind has ever made. That is my ghost, but I have no ghost story worth telling.

*Mr. Falconer*
There are many stories in which the supernatural is only apparent, and is finally explained. But some of these, especially the novels of Brockden Brown, carry the principle of terror to its utmost limits. What can be more appalling than his *Wieland*? It is one of the few tales in which the final explanation of the apparently supernatural does not destroy or diminish the original effect.

*Miss Gryll*
Generally, I do not like that explaining away. I can accord a ready faith to the supernatural in all its forms, as I do the adventures of Ulysses and Orlando. I should be sorry to see the enchantments of Circe expounded into sleights of hand.

*The Rev. Dr. Opimian*
I agree with you, Miss Gryll. I do not like to find a ghost,
which has frightened me through two volumes, turned into a
Cock Lane ghost in the third.

*Miss Gryll*
We are talking about ghosts, but we have not a ghost story, I
want a ghost story.

*Miss Niphet*
I will try to tell you one, which I remember imperfectly. It
relates, as many such stories do, to a buried treasure. An old
miser had an only daughter; he denied himself everything, but
he educated her well, and treated her becomingly. He had
accumulated a treasure, which he designed for her, but could
not bear the thought of parting with it, and died without
disclosing the place of its concealment. The daughter had a
lover, not absolutely poor, nor much removed from it. He
farmed a little land of his own. When her father died, and she
was left destitute and friendless, he married her, and they
endeavoured by economy and industry to make up for the
deficiencies of fortune. The young husband had an aunt, with
whom they sometimes passed a day of festival, and Christmas
Day especially. They were returning home late at night on one
of these occasions; snow was on the ground; the moon was in
the first quarter, and nearly setting. Crossing a field, they
paused a moment to look on the beauty of the starry sky; and
when they again turned their eyes to the ground, they saw a
shadow on the snow; it was too long to have any distinct
outline; but no substantial form was there to throw it. The
young wife clung trembling to the arm of her husband. The
moon set, and the shadow disappeared. New Year's Day
came, and they passed it at the aunt's. On their return the
moon was full, and high in heaven. They crossed the same
field, not without hesitation and fear. In the same spot as
before they again saw the shadow; it was that of a man in a
large loose wrapper, and a high-peaked hat. They recognised
the outline of the old miser. The husband sustained his nearly
fainting wife; as their eyes were irresistibly fixed on it, it began
to move, but a cloud came over the moon, and they lost sight

of it. The next night was bright, and the wife had summoned all her courage to follow out the mystery; they returned to the spot at the same hour; the shadow again fell on the snow, and again it began to move, and glided away slowly over the surface of the snow. They followed it fearfully. At length it stopped on a small mound in another field of their own farm. They walked round and round it, but it moved no more. The husband entreated his wife to remain, while he sought a stick to mark the place. When she was alone, the shadow spread out its arms as in the act of benediction, and vanished. The husband found her extended on the snow; he raised her in his arms; she recovered and they walked home. He returned in the morning with a pickaxe and spade, cleared away the snow, broke into the ground, and found a pot of gold, which was unquestionably their own. And then, with the usual end of a nurse's tale, 'they lived happily all the rest of their lives.'

*Miss Ilex*

Your story, though differing in all other respects, reminds me of a ballad in which there is a shadow on the snow,

> Around it, and round, he had ventured to go,
> But no form that had life threw that stamp on the snow.*

*Mr. Gryll*

In these instances the shadow has an outline, without a visible form to throw it. I remember a striking instance of shadows without distinguished forms. A young chevalier was riding through a forest of pines, in which he had before met with fearful adventures, when a strange voice called on him to stop. He did not stop, and the stranger jumped up behind him. He tried to look back, but could not turn his head. They emerged into a glade, where he hoped to see in the moonlight the outline of the unwelcome form. But 'unaccountable shadows fell around, unstamped with delineations of themselves.'*

*Miss Gryll*

Well, Mr. MacBorrowdale, have you no ghost story for us?

---

* Miss Bannerman's *Tales of Superstition and Chivalry*.
* *The Three Brothers,* vol. iv. p. 193.

*Mr. MacBorrowdale*

In faith, Miss Gryll, ghosts are not much in my line: the main business of my life has been among the driest matters of fact; but I will tell you a tale of a bogle, which I remember from my boyish days.

There was a party of witches and warlocks assembled in the refectory of a ruined abbey, intending to have a merry supper, if they could get the materials. The had no money, and they had for servant a poor bogle, who had been lent to them by his Satanic majesty on condition that he should provide their supper if he could; but without buying or stealing. They had a roaring fire, with nothing to roast, and a large stone table, with nothing on it but broken dishes and empty mugs. So the firelight shone on an uncouth set of long hungry faces. Whether there was among them 'ae winsome wench and wawlie,'* is more than I can say; but most probably there was, or the bogle would scarcely have been so zealous in the cause. Still he was late on his quest. The friars of a still flourishing abbey were making preparations for a festal day, and had despatched a man with a cart to the nearest town, to bring them a supply of good things. He was driving back his cart well loaded with beef, and poultry, and ham; and a supply of choice rolls, for which a goodwife in the town was famous; and a new arrival of rare old wine, a special present to the Abbot from some great lord. The bogle having smelt out the prize, presented himself before the carter in the form of a sailor with a wooden leg, imploring charity. The carter said he had nothing for him, and the sailor seemed to go on his way. He reappeared in various forms, always soliciting charity, more and more importunately every time, and always receiving the same denial. At last he appeared as an old woman, leaning on a stick, who was more pertinacious in her entreaties than the preceding semblances; and the carter, after asseverating with an oath that a whole shipload of beggars must have been

---

* But Tam kend what was what fu' brawlie:
  There was ae winsome wench and wawlie,
  That night enlisted in the core,
  Lang after kend on Carrick shore.

                       *Tam o' Shanter.*

wrecked that night on the coast, reiterated that he had nothing for her. 'Only the smallest coin, master,' said the old woman. 'I have no coin,' said the carter. 'Just a wee bite and sup of something,' said the old woman; 'you are scarcely going about without something to eat and drink; something comfortable for yourself. Just look at the cart: I am sure you will find something good.' 'Something, something, something,' said the carter; 'if there is anything fit to eat or drink in the cart, I wish a bogle may fly away with it.' 'Thank you,' said the bogle, and changed himself into a shape which laid the carter on his back, with his heels in the air. The bogle made lawful prize of the contents of the cart. The refectory was soon fragrant with the odour of roast, and the old wine flowed briskly, to the great joy of the assembly, who passed the night in feasting, singing, and dancing, and toasting Old Nick.

*Miss Gryll*
And now, Mr. Falconer, you who live in an old tower, among old books, and are deep in the legends of saints, surely you must have a ghost story to tell us.

*Mr. Falconer*
Not exactly a ghost story, Miss Gryll, but there is a legend which took my fancy, and which I turned into a ballad. If you permit me, I will repeat it.

The permission being willingly granted. Mr. Falconer closed the series of fireside marvels by reciting –

## THE LEGEND OF SAINT LAURA

Saint Laura, in her sleep of death,
   Preserves beneath the tomb
– 'Tis willed where what is willed must be –*
In incorruptibility
   Her beauty and her bloom.

* Vuolsi così colà dove si puote
   Ciò che si vuole, e più non domandare.

DANTE.

So pure her maiden life had been,
    So free from earthly stain,
'Twas fixed in fate by Heaven's own Queen,
That till the earth's last closing scene
    She should unchanged remain.

Within a deep sarcophagus
    Of alabaster sheen,
With sculptured lid of roses white,
She slumbered in unbroken night,
    By mortal eyes unseen.

Above her marble couch was reared
    A monumental shrine,
Where cloistered sisters, gathering round,
Made night and morn the aisle resound
    With choristry divine.

The Abbess died: and in her pride
    Her parting mandate said,
They should her final rest provide
The alabaster couch beside,
    Where slept the sainted dead.

The abbess came of princely race:
    The nuns might not gainsay:
And sadly passed the timid band,
To execute the high command
    They dared not disobey.

The monument was opened then:
    It gave to general sight
The alabaster couch alone:
But all its lucid substance shone
    With preternatural light.

They laid the corpse within the shrine:
    They closed its doors again:
But nameless terror seemed to fall,
Throughout the livelong night, on all
    Who formed the funeral train.

Lo! on the morrow morn, still closed
   The monument was found:
But in its robes funereal drest,
The corpse they had consigned to rest
   Lay on the stony ground.

Fear and amazement seized on all:
   They called on Mary's aid:
And in the tomb, unclosed again,
With choral hymn and funeral train,
   The corpse again was laid.

But with the incorruptible
   Corruption might not rest:
The lonely chapel's stone-paved floor
Received the ejected corpse once more,
   In robes funereal drest.

So was it found when morning beamed:
   In solemn suppliant strain
The nuns implored all saints in heaven,
That rest might to the corpse be given,
   Which they entombed again.

On the third night a watch was kept
   By many a friar and nun:
Trembling, all knelt in fervent prayer,
Till on the dreary midnight air
   Rolled the deep bell-toll, 'One'!

The saint within the opening tomb
   Like marble statue stood:
All fell to earth in deep dismay:
And through their ranks she passed away,
   In calm unchanging mood.

No answering sound her footsteps raised
   Along the stony floor:
Silent as death, severe as fate,
She glided through the chapel gate,
   And none beheld her more.

The alabaster couch was gone:
  The tomb was void and bare:
For the last time, with hasty rite,
Even 'mid the terror of the night,
  They laid the abbess there.

'Tis said the abbess rests not well
  In that sepulchral pile:
But yearly, when the night comes round
As dies of 'One' the bell's deep sound
  She flits along the aisle.

But whither passed the virgin saint,
  To slumber far away,
Destined by Mary to endure,
Unaltered in her semblance pure,
  Until the judgement-day?

None knew, and none may ever know:
  Angels the secret keep:
Impenetrable ramparts bound,
Eternal silence dwells around
  The chamber of her sleep.

## CHAPTER XXXV

## REJECTED SUITORS – CONCLUSION

σοὶ δὲ θεοὶ τόσα δοῖεν ὅσα φρεσὶ σῇσι μενοινᾷς,
ἄνδρα τε καὶ οἶκον καὶ ὁμοφροσύνην ὀπάσειαν
ἐσθλήν· οὐ μὲν γὰρ τοῦ γε κρεῖσσον καὶ ἄρειον,
ἢ ὅθ' ὁμοφρονέοντε νοήμασιν οἶκον ἔχητον
ἀνὴρ ἠδὲ γυνή.

May the Gods grant what your best hopes pursue,
A husband, and a home, with concord true:
No greater boon from Jove's ethereal dome
Descends, than concord in the nuptial home.
             ULYSSES *to* NAUSICAA, *in the sixth book*
                                    *of the Odyssey.*

What passed between Algernon and Morgana when the
twenty-eighth morning brought his probation to a close, it is
unnecessary to relate. The gentleman being predetermined to
propose, and the lady to accept, there was little to be said, but
the little was conclusive.

Mr Gryll was delighted. His niece could not have made a
choice more thoroughly to his mind.

'My dear Morgana,' he said, 'all's well that ends well. Your
fastidiousness in choice has arrived at a happy termination.
And now you will perhaps tell me why you rejected so many
suitors, to whom you had in turn accorded a hearing. In the
first place, what was your objection to the Honourable Escor
A'Cass?* He was a fine, handsome, dashing fellow. He was
the first in the field, and you seemed to like him.'

*Miss Gryll*
He was too dashing, uncle: he gambled. I did like him, till I
discovered his evil propensity.

---

* ἐς κόρακας: *To-the-Crows:* the Athenian equivalent for our *o'-the
Devil:* a gambler's journey: not often a long one.

*Mr. Gryll*
And Sir Alley Capel?

*Miss Gryll*
He speculated; which is only another name for gambling. He never knew from day to day whether he was a rich man or a beggar. He lived in a perpetual fever, and I wish to live in tranquillity.

*Mr. Gryll*
To Mr. Ballot?

*Miss Gryll*
He thought of nothing but politics: he had no feeling of poetry. There was never a more complete negation of sympathy than between him and me.

*Mr. Gryll*
To Sir John Pachyderm?

*Miss Gryll*
He was a mere man of the world, with no feeling of any kind: tolerable in company, but tiresome beyond description in a tête-à-tête. I did not choose that he should bestow all his tediousness on me.

*Mr. Gryll*
To M. Enavant?

*Miss Gryll*
He was what is called a fast man, and was always talking of slow coaches. I had no fancy for living in an express train. I like to go quietly through life, and to see all that lies in my way.

Mr Gryll
To Mr. Geront?

*Miss Gryll*
He had only one fault, but that one was unpardonable. He was too old. To do him justice, he did not begin as a lover. Seeing

that I took pleasure in his society, he was led by degrees into
fancying that I might accept him as a husband. I liked his
temper, his acquirements, his conversation, his love of music
and poetry, his devotion to domestic life. But age and youth
cannot harmonise in marriage.

*Mr. Gryll*
Mr. Long Owen?

*Miss Gryll*
He was in debt, and kept it secret from me. I thought he only
wanted my fortune: but be that as it might, the concealment
destroyed my esteem.

*Mr. Gryll*
To Mr. Larvel?

*Miss Gryll*
He was too ugly. Expression may make plain features agree-
able, and I tried if daily intercourse would reconcile me to his.
But no. His ugliness was unredeemed.

*Mr. Gryll*
None of these objections applied to Lord Curryfin?

*Miss Gryll*
No, uncle; but he came too late. And besides, he soon found
what suited him better.

*Mr. Gryll*
There were others. Did any of the same objections apply to
them all?

*Miss Gryll*
Indeed, uncle, the most of them were nothing; or at best, mere
suits of good clothes; men made, as it were, to pattern by the
dozen; selfish, frivolous, without any earnest pursuit, or desire
to have one; ornamental drawing-room furniture, no more
distinguishable in memory than a set of chairs.

*Mr. Gryll*

Well, my dear Morgana, for mere negations there is not remedy; but for positive errors, even for gambling, it strikes me they are curable.

*Miss Gryll*

No, uncle. Even my limited observation has shown me that men are easily cured of unfashionable virtues, but never of fashionable vices.

Miss Gryll and Miss Niphet arranged that their respective marriages and those of the seven sisters should be celebrated at the same time and place. In the course of their castle-building before marriage, Miss Niphet said to her intended: 'When I am your wife, I shall release you from your promise of not trying experiments with horses, carriages, boats, and so forth; but with this proviso, that if ever you do try a dangerous experiment, it shall be in my company.'

'No, dear Alice,' he answered; 'you will make my life too dear to me to risk it in any experiment. You shall be my guiding star, and the only questions I shall ask respecting my conduct in life will be, Whether it pleases you?'

———————

Some natural tears they shed, but wiped them soon,

might have been applied to the sisters, when they stepped, on their bridal morning, into the carriages which were to convey them to the Grange.

It was the dissipation of a dream too much above mortal frailty, too much above the contingencies of chance and change, to be permanently realised. But the damsels had consented, and the suitors rejoiced; and if ever there was a man on earth with 'his saul abune the moon,' it was Harry Hedgerow, on the bright February morning that gave him the hand of his Dorothy.

There was a grand *déjeuner* at Gryll Grange. There were nine brides and the nine bridegrooms; a beautiful array of bridesmaids; a few friends of Mr. Gryll, Mr. Niphet, Lord

Curryfin, and Mr. Falconer; and a large party at the lower end
of the hall, composed of fathers, mothers, and sisters of the
bridegrooms of the seven Vestals. None of the bridegrooms
had brothers, and Harry had neither mother nor sister; but his
father was there in rustic portliness, looking, as Harry had
anticipated, as if he were all but made young again.

Among the most conspicuous of the party were the Reverend Doctor Opimian and his lady, who had on this
occasion stepped out of her domestic seclusion. In due course,
the reverend doctor stood up and made a speech, which may
be received as the epilogue of our comedy.

*The Rev. Dr. Opimian*

We are here to do honour to the nuptials; first, of the niece of
our excellent host, a young lady whom to name is to show her
title to the love and respect of all present; with a young
gentleman, of whom to say that he is in every way worthy of
her, is to say all that can be said of him in the highest order of
praise: secondly, of a young lord and lady, to whom those
who had the pleasure of being here last Christmas are indebted
for the large share of enjoyment which their rare and diversified accomplishments, and their readiness to contribute in
every way to social entertainment, bestowed on the assembled
party; and who, both in contrast and congeniality, – for both
these elements enter into perfect fitness of companionship –
may be considered to have been expressly formed for each
other: thirdly, of seven other young couples, on many
accounts most interesting to us all, who enter on the duties of
married life with as fair expectation of happiness as can
reasonably be entertained in this diurnal sphere. An old Greek
poet says: 'Four things are good for man in this world: first,
health; second, personal beauty; third, riches, not dishonour-
ably acquired; fourth, to pass life among friends.'* But
thereon says the comic poet Anaxandrides: 'Health is rightly

---

* ὑγιαίνειν μὲν ἄριστον ἀνδρὶ θνατῷ·
  δεύτερον δὲ φυὰν καλὸν γενέσθαι·
  τρίτον δὲ, πλουτεῖν ἀδόλως·
  καὶ τὸ τέταρτον, ἡβᾷν μετὰ τῶν φίλων.

                                        SIMONIDES.

placed first; but riches should have been second; for what is beauty ragged and starving?'* Be this as it may, we here see them all four: health in its brightest bloom; riches in two instances; more than complete in the other seven; beauty in the brides, good looks as far as young men need them, in the bridegrooms, and as bright a prospect of passing life among friends as ever shone on any. Most earnestly do I hope that the promise of their marriage morning may be fulfilled in its noon and in its sunset; and when I add, may they all be as happy in their partners as I have been, I say what all who know the excellent person beside me will feel to be the best good wish in my power to bestow. And now to the health of the brides and bridegrooms, in bumpers of champagne. Let all the attendants stand by, each with a fresh bottle, with only one uncut string. Let all the corks, when I give the signal, be discharged simultaneously; and we will receive it as a peal of Bacchic ordnance, in honour of the Power of Joyful Event,* whom we may assume to be presiding on this auspicious occasion.

## THE END

* Athenæus, 1. xv. p. 694.
* This was a Roman deity. *Invocato hilaro atque prospero Eventu.*
APULEIUS, *Metamorph.,* l. iv.

# W.N.P. BARBELLION

## THE JOURNAL OF A DISAPPOINTED MAN

While millions of young men were being slaughtered on the battlefields of Europe a young Englishman was dying of an incurable disease. He was Bruce Frederick Cummings ('W.N.P. Barbellion'), born in 1889, struck down with multiple sclerosis in early manhood and dead at thirty. Yet into those few short years he crammed a lifetime of passionate intensity. He breathed life into every sentence of the journal which he created to analyse his emotions and painful existence. His courage was boundless – he was in love with life and far from being a catalogue of misfortune, the journal is infused with a rage to live.

Started at the age of thirteen, the journal documents the rest of his life, including his remarkable studies in natural history. The result is an inspired and expressive masterpiece by a 'scientist with an artist's sensitivity'. There never was a half-dead man more alive.

# DANIEL DEFOE

# CAPTAIN SINGLETON

Defoe had that power to create the illusion of truth which is the very life force of fiction, and nowhere is this more evident than in his portrait of the piratical Captain Singleton.

Taken by a gypsy child-stealer, Singleton soon finds himself cast ashore on the island of Madagascar; how he crosses Africa with a party of marooned sailors from Mozambique to the Gold Coast is a book in itself. His years of piracy are still to come. The story moves to the West Indies where he falls in with William the Quaker, an unusual pirate with whom Singleton becomes a lifelong friend, sharing adventures from the Spanish Main to the Indian Ocean before, filled with remorse, he decides to end it all. . . .

# EDMUND GOSSE

## FATHER AND SON

Lord David Cecil considered this book to be one of the half-dozen English prose masterpieces of the twentieth century; a classic among autobiographies.

After a difficult birth, Edmund Gosse was left for dead, while all anxiety and attention were concentrated on his mother. An old woman turned her attention to the abandoned infant and succeeded in reviving him and so Gosse lived to write: 'For all the rapture of life, for all its turmoils, its anxious desires, its manifold pleasures, and even for its sorrow and suffering, I bless and praise that anonymous old lady from the bottom of my heart'.

*Father and Son* mingles merriment and humour with a discussion of the most solemn subjects . . . 'Most funny books try to be funny throughout while theology is scandalised if it awakens a single smile. But life is not constituted thus . . .' and if the proof lies anywhere, it lies here.

# THOMAS HARDY
# A CHANGED MAN

This collection contains, as well as the title story, *The Waiting Supper; Alicia's Diary; The Grave by the Handpost; Enter a Dragoon; A Tryst at an Ancient Earthwork; What the Shepherd Saw; A Committee-Man of 'The Terror'; Master John Horseleigh, Knight; The Duke's Reappearance;* and *The Romantic Adventures of a Milkmaid.*

Hardy's love of the eerie and the supernatural are brought out in full measure here. His skill at depicting topographical detail is also apparent, particularly in *A Changed Man* – set in Casterbridge and instantly recognisable to readers familiar with that town. The story is that of a young hussar captain who resigns his commission to preach in a poor parish and, by so doing, causes his wife to leave him for another soldier. It is a fine portrait in a vivid set of stories guaranteed to delight all Hardy devotees.

# CAPTAIN MARRYAT

## PETER SIMPLE

Simple, Peter may have been at the start. Early in
the story, there is a delightful scene where he finds
that his ship-mates have been using his account
with the bumboat woman to make their own
purchases and yet another when the young innocent wanders into the red light district and is
accosted by 'a young lady, very nicely dressed.
"Well, Reefer, how are you off for soap", she
said'. . .

But he does not stay simple for long; by the end of
this yarn Peter has become Viscount Privilege, a
husband and father. He is no longer the fool, but
the head of the family. The intervening chapters
are full of high adventure – the old sailing navy is
portrayed with the realism and attention to detail
at which Marryat excelled.

# HESTER
# LYNCH PIOZZI

## ANECDOTES OF
## SAMUEL JOHNSON

The young Mrs Thrale was the intimate friend and confidante of Samuel Johnson, the Great Cham of literature. When her odious husband, who had treated her 'like a kept mistress', finally died she announced her marriage to the 'Italian musick master', Piozzi, and Dr Johnson, brutally wounded, ended their friendship. But tirelessly, for nearly twenty years, her pen had recorded a colourful and lively picture of a lodger, hero and counsellor who was to become one of the giants of literary history.

'Impulsive and impressionable . . . her appetite for life was prodigious' – *Virginia Woolf*.

# R.S. SURTEES
## MR FACEY ROMFORD'S HOUNDS

'Our friend was called Charley at school, but his real name was Francis – hence, perhaps "Facey".' Thus is Mr Romford introduced to the reader and from the first page on, we are transported into the zany, comic, full-blooded world of the Victorian hunting scene as created by Surtees. Soapey Sponge crops up again as do many of the best and memorable characters from that previous novel, *Mr Sponge's Sporting Tour* (also available in this series) including Lucy Glitters who triumphs at last.

His inventions are absurd but marvellously sustained, his creations are comic and often silly but they are so real and their adventures, whilst larger than life, are nevertheless rooted in fact and real knowledge. The whole is perfectly complimented by the illustrations of John Leech.

# R.S. SURTEES

## MR SPONGE'S
## SPORTING TOUR

R.S. Surtees is *the* novelist of hunting with splendid characters and full-blooded dialogue, full of comedy and satire and a zest for living. Nowhere is this more apparent than in the creation of Soapey Sponge; 'A good, pushing, free-and-easy sort of man, wishing to be a gentleman without knowing how.' He is accompanied by a gallery of memorable characters including Benjamin Buckram, Jack Spraggon, Mr Jogglebury Crowdey, Facey Romford and the inimitable Lucy Glitters. All the riff-raff of the hunting field and the small watering place united in a love of out-of-doors activities and revealed in all their humour and idiosyncrasies.

No one portrayed the Victorian country and sporting scene better than Surtees and John Leech's illustrations are the perfect match.

# JONATHAN SWIFT
## JOURNAL TO STELLA

The *Journal to Stella* was addressed to Esther Johnson, whom Swift met as a girl when she was staying in Surrey. She afterwards settled in Ireland at his suggestion. The *Journal* was dispatched in fortnightly packets to Ireland and is a day by day record of Swift's life in London. The entries provide a close observation of London events and society in the early eighteenth century and, as such, are a valuable biographical and historical record. At the same time, in their expression, they show a tenderness and affection not found elsewhere in Swift's writings, revealing him at his most personal and intimate.

# FANNY TROLLOPE

## DOMESTIC MANNERS OF THE AMERICANS

Pursued by debt, Fanny Trollope, mother of the famous novelist, emigrated to Ohio. Here she was assisted by her husband – a poor provider – in a fancy goods bazaar, a venture which failed as surely as others before. But when, on her return to England, she published *Domestic Manners of the Americans* in 1832, she achieved profit and fame overnight, and was able to support her family ever after by her pen.

Her candid and sometimes critical observations were bitterly resented in the United States. Throughout Europe, however, the book was quickly admired as an authentic account of a novel society where momentous change and expansion had already begun. The New World, with its contrasts powerfully described, already seemed foreign to the Old. . . .